ALSO BY ELIE WIESEL

Night

Dawn

The Accident

The Town Beyond the Wall

The Gates of the Forest

The Jews of Silence

Legends of Our Time

A Beggar in Jerusalem

One Generation After

Souls on Fire

The Oath

Ani Maamin (cantata)

Zalmen, or The Madness of God (play)

Messengers of God

A Jew Today

Four Hasidic Masters

The Trial of God (play)

The Testament

Five Biblical Portraits

Somewhere a Master

The Golem (illustrated by Mark Podwal)

The Fifth Son

Against Silence (edited by Irving Abrahamson)

The Oslo Address

Twilight

The Six Days of Destruction (with Albert Friedlander)

A Journey into Faith (conversations with John Cardinal O'Connor)

A Song for Hope (cantata)

From the Kingdom of Memory

Sages and Dreamers

The Forgotten

A Passover Haggadah (illustrated by Mark Podwal)

All Rivers Run to the Sea

Memoir in Two Voices (with François Mitterand)

King Solomon and His Magic Ring (illustrated by Mark Podwal)

And the Sea Is Never Full

The Judges

Conversations with Elie Wiesel (with Richard D. Heffner)

Wise Men and Their Tales

THE TIME
OF THE
UPROOTED

THE TIME OF THE UPROOTED

A Novel

ELIE WIESEL

Translated by David Hapgood

ALFRED A. KNOPF   *New York*   2005

THIS IS A BORZOI BOOK
PUBLISHED BY ALFRED A. KNOPF

www.aaknopf.com

Originally published in France as *Le Temps des Déracinés* by Editions du
Seuil, Paris, in 2003. Copyright © 2003 by Elirion Associates, Inc.
Copyright © 2003 by Editions du Seuil.

Library of Congress Cataloging-in-Publication Data
Wiesel, Elie, [date]
[Temps des déracinés. English]
The time of the uprooted / Elie Wiesel ;
translated by David Hapgood.
p.   cm.
ISBN 1-4000-4172-4 (alk. paper)
1. Jewish children in the Holocaust—Fiction.
2. Jews—Europe—Fiction. [1. Holocaust, Jewish (1939–1945)—
Fiction.]   I. Hapgood, David.   II. Title.
PQ2683.I32T3613 2005
843'.914—dc22   2004048929

Manufactured in the United States of America
First American Edition

For Elisha and Lynn

Look, young friend and brother
Do your eyes see the young woman with the grave
    manner who is destined to you?
See how she leans her head to her left as if seeking
    your hand on her shoulder, see the dream of
    mystery and desire that hovers over her beautiful
    and melancholy face; that dream is yours.
Look, and you will know what it is to love.
But it will be too late.

Paritus the One-Eyed, Letter to the lost disciple

THE TIME
OF THE
UPROOTED

I'M FOUR YEARS OLD, OR MAYBE FIVE. IT'S A SAB-bath afternoon. Mother is lying down in the next room. I'd asked her to read to me from the book she had by her side, but she has one of her frequent headaches. So I ask my father to tell me a story, but just then there's a knock at the door. "Go see who it is," says my father, reluctantly glancing up from the journal he's keeping. A stranger is at the door.

"May I come in?" he asks. A big bearded man, broad across the shoulders, with sad eyes—there's something disturbing about him. His gaze seems heavy with secrets, and glows with a pale and holy fire.

"Who's there?" my father asks, and I reply, "I don't know."

"Call me a wanderer," the stranger says, "a wandering man who's worn-out and hungry."

"Who do you want to see?" I ask, and he says to me, "You."

"Who is it, a beggar?" my father asks. "Tell him to come

THE TIME OF THE UPROOTED

in." No matter what the hour, my father would never deny his home to a stranger seeking a meal or a night's shelter, and certainly not on the Sabbath.

The stranger comes in at a slow but unhesitating pace. Father stands to greet him and leads him to the kitchen. He shows the stranger where to wash his hands before reciting the usual prayer, offers him a seat, and sets before him a plate of *cholent* and *hallah*. But the stranger doesn't touch it. "You're not hungry?" my father says.

"Oh yes, I'm hungry, and I'm thirsty, but not for food."

"Then what is it you want?"

"I want words and I want faces," says the stranger. "I travel the world looking for people's stories." I'm enchanted by the stranger's voice. It is the voice of a storyteller: It envelops my soul. He continues: "I came here today to put you to the test, to measure your hospitality. And I can tell you that what I've seen pleases me." With that, he gets to his feet and strides to the door.

"Don't tell me you are the prophet Elijah," says my father.

"No, I'm no prophet." The stranger smiles down at me. "I told you, I'm just a wanderer. A crazy wanderer."

Ever since that encounter, I've loved vagabonds with their sacks full of tales of princes who became what they are for love of freedom and solitude. I delight in madmen. I love to see their crazed, melancholy faces and to hear their bewitching voices, which arouse in me forbidden images and desires. Or rather, it's not the madness itself I love, but those it possesses, those whose souls it claims, as if to show them the limits of their possibilities—and then makes them determined to go further, to push themselves beyond those limits. It's second nature with me. Some collect paintings; others love horses. Me, I'm attracted to madmen. Some fear them, and so put them away where no one can hear them cry out. I find some madmen entertaining, but others do indeed frighten me, as if they know that a man is just the restless and mysterious shadow of a dream, and that dream may be God's. I have to confess that I enjoy their company, I want to see through their eyes the world die each night, only to be reborn with dawn, to pursue their thoughts as if they were wild horses, to hear them laugh and make others laugh, to intoxicate myself without wine, and to dream with my eyes open.

Is today Monday? Maybe it's Tuesday, but no, it's Thursday. As if it matters. The wanderer can't seem to wake up, which is unlike him, and so it was with Isaac and Job when they were *full of years,* as Scripture tells us. In his dream, he has just seen his father. He stands solemnly for a long moment, and then father and son embrace. He awakes with a start, then falls back into heavy, oppressive slumber. No more father. Talk to him, he doesn't answer. Stretch out a hand, he turns away. With an effort, he opens his eyes. He knows he's alone, that he should get up, that he has a long and trying day ahead, but he can't seem to place the day in his exile's life: Does it belong to his future, to his past? His soul is lost in the fog and is taking him to some terrifying place of the damned. Somewhere an old woman ravaged in body and memory is watching for him, perhaps to punish him for misdeeds long forgotten, for promises carelessly tossed aside. Who is she? A beauty he dreamed of as a boy but could not hold on to? One of his daughters, stricken in her mind and lost in the depths of time? He searches his memory; their dark faces circle around him and seem about to close in and suffocate him. He knows that he is destined for a fateful encounter with a mysterious woman. A turning point? The end of a stage of his life? If so, isn't it time for some kind of *heshbon hanefesh*—an accounting of his soul— in which he would review the fires he's been through and the many lives he's led?

He shakes himself awake, gets up, goes to the washbasin, and examines his reflection in the mirror. He sees his yellow- ish gray pallor, his sagging features, his dull gaze. He doesn't recognize the man staring back at him. All he's done is to change nightmares.

MY NAME IS GAMALIEL. YES, GAMALIEL, AND I'LL thank you not to ask me why. It's just another name, right? You're given a name, you carry it around, and if it's too much of a burden, you get rid of it. As for you, dear reader, do I ask you how come you're named William, or Maurice, or Sig- mund, or Serge, or Sergei? Yes, Gamaliel isn't an everyday name, and let me tell you, it has its own story, and it's not one you hear every day, either. That's true of everybody, you'll say—and so what? If they want, they can tell me the story of their lives; I'll hear them out. Let me add that I'm also named Péter. Péter was my childhood. For you, childhood means playing with a ball, rolling a hoop, pony rides in the park, birthdays and holidays, vacations at the shore or in the moun- tains. My childhood was in a nightclub. It has a story, too.

I'll get around to that.

Just bear with me.

· · ·

FOR NOW, LET'S STICK TO GAMALIEL. ODD KIND of name, I know. You don't see it very often. Sounds Sephardic. So how did I get it? You really want to know? I inherited it. Yes, some people inherit houses, or businesses, stamp collections, bank accounts. I inherited my name. My paternal grandfather left it to me. Did I know him? Of course not; he died before I was born, or else I'd have been given another name. But then how did his parents happen to choose so unusual a name, one that seems better suited to a tired old man than to a newborn baby? Did they find it in the traditions of their Sephardic ancestors, those who were expelled from Spain, or perhaps those who stayed on, the Marranos, who pretended to convert but secretly retained their Jewish identity? You can find the first Gamaliel in the Bible: Gamaliel, son of Phadassur, chief of the tribe of Manasseh; and in the *Larousse Encyclopedia,* where he is described as "a Jew and a great luminary." And of course in the Talmud, where he's frequently quoted. His grandfather was Hillel the Elder. He lived and taught somewhere in Palestine during the first century, well before the destruction of the Second Temple. Yes, I bear the name of a great leader, known for his wisdom and moderation, universally respected in Israel. He was president of the Sanhedrin and of a well-known academy. Nothing was decided without his consent. I would have liked to have known him. Actually, that can be done. All I have to do is look in the records of discussions in which he took part. I've been doing that every chance I've gotten since I came to America, which by now is quite a while ago. I like to study, and I love to read. I never tire of reading. I have a lot to catch up on.

Besides, you could say it's what I do for a living.

I write so I can learn to read and read and read.

9

From the *Book of Secrets*

The air-raid alarm is silent, making it a quiet night,
but even so, the Archbishop of Székesváros has a
nightmare. The Archbishop, Monsignor János
Báranyi, dreams he is in the Vatican, waiting for an
audience with the Pope. Feverishly, he is searching for
the first word he'll speak, the one crucial word that
will convince the Pope of his humility and his
obedience. He cannot find that word. All he can think
of are garbled phrases that might as well be false
prayers dictated to him by some evil spirit. What shall
I do? Lord in heaven, what shall I do? Without that
first word, nothing else he says will matter; the Lord's
Creation will be damned. The Archbishop is in a
panic. Time is running out: In a few minutes, the door
will open and he will be kneeling before the successor
to Saint Peter. The Pope will tell him to rise and speak
about his mission, but he, a poor sinner from a distant
province, will still be seeking that first word. Help me,
Lord, help me! Suddenly, his mother is there holding
him by the shoulders. She is long dead. The
Archbishop knows that even in his dream—but then
what is she doing here, in the Pope's waiting room?
How has she come into his dream? He is about to ask
her, when the door opens, opens so softly that it does
not disturb a fly perched on its golden doorknob. Now
the Archbishop cries out in horror. . . . It's the Angel
of Death, who tells him to come forward. . . .

Gamaliel rereads the passage. Now he finds he dislikes the
last lines, so he crosses them out and writes instead:

... When the door opens, the Archbishop sees a
beautiful stately young Jew, who, with a graceful
gesture of his arm, invites the Archbishop to enter
and be seated. But he cannot move: The Archbishop is
like a man paralyzed. Who is the Jew? By what right is
he in the Pope's innermost sanctum? Now his mother
comes to his rescue, saying, "All these years, you didn't
know that Christ was Jewish, too. It's my fault, my
son; I should have taught you that when you were a
child. And now . . ." "And now what, Mama?" "And
now you know," she says.

Strangely enough, it is not the first time this dream
has troubled the Archbishop's sleep.

Of this much, Gamaliel is certain: Georges Lebrun may
be a good Christian, but he doesn't know much about religion, so he won't make head or tail of this novel he has so
long been anticipating. But Lebrun wants it. He needs it as an
ailing lover needs the drug that keeps him alive. Gamaliel
was still living in Paris when he showed Lebrun the first
pages, written in French. He had begun to learn the language
in Budapest, from an Agence France-Presse correspondent
who was a "friend"—a customer?—of Ilonka. Gamaliel had
gone on to master French so well, he had aroused the envy of
the writer Georges Lebrun thought he was. Years had gone
by, and now Gamaliel was living in New York, but Lebrun
was still after him for his manuscript. He wanted it with all
his heart; he dreamed of it. That was what he kept saying to
Gamaliel, by letter, by telephone, and in person when their
paths happened to cross: "That book belongs to me. If you
don't give it to me, I'll kill you. I'll do worse: I'll make you
wish you'd never been born." Not this time. Gamaliel knew

he had made a mistake in letting his silent partner read the manuscript he had barely begun. But to hell with him: Let him find himself another ghostwriter. Here, in this story, Gamaliel speaks for himself. It's time.

GAMALIEL IS WALKING THROUGH A DARK AND depressing section of Brooklyn. He is no longer young. He walks hunched over, the eternal stranger protecting his secret, as he heads toward a silent building for forgotten people. He has no idea what awaits him, but he senses that somehow he is going to meet his fate there. Can he exorcize that fate, or at least come to terms with it?

Running through his head are the silly narratives he used to dream up for amateur writers who wanted to be thought professional. That was how he paid the rent. Love stories for shop girls, Kiplingesque adventures in exotic settings, financial conspiracies, gritty detective stories: scribbling, not writing. None of them had the substance or the range of the story he's been wanting to write for these many years. But that's an all-absorbing task, one that requires researching in depth such questions as the origins of Christianity, its metamorphoses, its doctrines, which ban any kind of doubt or any reference to human sexuality. The Apostles and their Gospels. The Church fathers and their screeds against the Jews: how to explain their hatred for the children of Israel? The connection between the Bible of the Jews and the Christian New Testament. The many ways they had of putting the Son foremost, relegating the Father to the background. The Vatican and its hierarchy, its culture and its rules, its power and the limits of that power. The silence of Pope Pius XII about the persecution and annihilation of the Jews, the open spirit of John XXIII. What is the theological meaning of the celibacy the Church imposes on its priests and nuns? What's an archbishop, and how do you get to be one? And if you're a mystic, how do you find it out? What must you accomplish to be admitted to the secret knowledge of the Teachers, with their exceptional and terrifying gifts? Gamaliel must be thoroughly informed in his account of the strange events that brought together a dignitary of the Catholic Church and a rabbi versed in the Kabbalah. Several times he has thought he was on the right track—the story rang true—but when he reread it the next day, he saw that the scene demanded a different outcome from the one he'd conceived for it. But where does the story want to go? He can't tell now. He'll get it right next time. Next time? That's the mantra of refugees and wanderers, thinks Gamaliel, always the outsider. When is next time? Tomorrow? Later on? In another life? In another person? You'll have to come back, with other papers, with other affidavits. Go to the next window.

Let's note here that Gamaliel, the stranger in this story, isn't really a stranger. Like everyone else, he has an identity: He has an address, friends, connections, habits, and, yes, he has his quirks and his whims. But the refugee in him is always on the alert, ready to speak the word that will upset all he's taken for granted about the way he lives. It is said that a man never recovers from torture, that a woman never recovers from rape. The same is true of those who have been uprooted: once a refugee, always a refugee. He escapes from one place of exile, only to find himself in another: Nowhere is he at home. He never forgets the place he came from; his life is always provisional. Happiness for him is a moment's rest. Love that is supposedly eternal? A blink of the eye. For a man in his situation, at every step, the end seems near.

Is the bell about to toll for him?

For some time now, Gamaliel has felt himself growing old; *never* has become the key word: the many adventures he will never undertake, the girls he will never kiss, the children he will never have, the faraway places he will never discover, the cello he will never learn to play, the ecstasy he will never again feel next to a body that is vibrant with life—without fearing he will fail. The passing years grow heavy; their weight drags him down. Gamaliel tires more easily. He is often out of breath; his mind wanders. His need to sleep becomes urgent. He's lived a lot of years. How many does he have left? He's wasted an appalling number of them. Did he bungle his youth? Alexander the Great died at thirty-three, Spinoza at forty-four; the Baal Shem-Tov was sixty. Mozart, Pushkin, Rilke, Herzl: They enriched the world in the course of their short, frenzied lives. And how about Gamaliel himself? Who will carry on his name? What will he leave behind? Just words, and not even the ones he would want to have endure. Vanity of vanities: It's all absurd. Music is what he has always regretted: He wishes he had gone to the conservatory. Paritus the One-Eyed used to say, "When the words start singing, I start dancing." But not Gamaliel. Everyone else is dancing. He has never learned how.

The exile's days are growing few, as are those of the season, and the century is drawing to its close. How many times has he stood at the cliff's edge and wanted to withdraw—but to where? "From one abyss to another," murmured a great Hasidic teacher, but he did not say whether he was describing the adventure of our passage through this life or, rather, our search for peace and the ultimate answer. Despair is the refugee's everyday companion, even when he is enjoying himself or entertaining others. He despairs of his work, in which he supplies his clients with shoddy writing that will make no difference to anyone. Despairs of a life divorced from reality, and from his two daughters, cut off from him by a hatred he has never been able to understand and accept. His heart sinks at the thought of them. Where are they now? What's become of them? So many years since they rejected him, utterly, convicted him with no right of appeal. Was it his fault, or was it the fault of his wife, Colette, who had killed herself to make his punishment more complete? After her mother's suicide, Katya, who liked to call herself the elder of the twins, had also tried to take her own life. The younger twin, Sophie, had gone off to an ashram in India, where she changed her name and made herself a new existence, in which she had no connection with her father. All Gamaliel's efforts to find his daughters had been in vain: gone, no forwarding address, vanished without a trace. Unhappy offspring of an unhappy marriage, in a time without a gleam of light or an oasis to relieve its melancholy, a marriage entered into unwillingly in a Paris that was itself discouraging and deceitful. Why had he never remarried? Was he afraid? Afraid of stirring up the remorse that threatens to kill off any chance he has of redeeming himself, of fulfilling any promise there is in him?

As he walks along the Brooklyn street, hands stuffed in the pockets of his raincoat, Gamaliel is trying to shake off his memories, let them go haunt someone else under some other sky. His gloomy thoughts turn to the events that are threatening the world at the end of the century. In the name of the fatherland, supposedly civilized countries send to death young people who would rather be dancing the frenzied dance of desire. Under the noble pretext of advancing science, man becomes a slave to machines. There is a risk that those who claim to be honoring their people's past in fact may do it discredit. They talk themselves into saying nothing. The gods of hate hide behind slogans of brotherhood; they fool everybody, including themselves.

In his melancholy mood, Gamaliel wishes he could be in the company of his four friends: Bolek with his secret, Diego with his stories of the Spanish Civil War, Yasha with his cat, Gad with his adventures. All so different and yet so close to one another. He would like to be listening to their voices, proving himself worthy of their confidence but never judging them, adding his exile's testimony to theirs. He might never see them again. He has no idea why that thought comes to his mind, but he knows it is not the first time; it's as if he expects each of their meetings to end in disaster. Usually, he dismisses the notion with a smile: you and your crazy forebodings. But today he doesn't smile it away. He feels as if his friends are slipping out of his sight, out of his life. As if they pitied him. Is he ill? Those who are ill feel sorry for those they love. Is this true for refugees as well?

Adam and Eve: the first to be uprooted, the first exiles, the first stateless ones, driven out of the first family home, where life was beautiful even when it wasn't. Like them, their descendants today wander the earth, fleeing the serpent with its deadly poison. Others decide their fate. They are no longer free to act, to believe, to choose their places, nor even to renounce freedom. As in ancient Greece, where they were called *apolis,* they are considered harmful, or dangerous, and so they are kept aside from humanity.

"All of us are like Adam," said a Sage in antiquity. Not I, Gamaliel says to himself. I'm not Adam; Eve is my mother, not my wife. And I want to protect the children, my own and all the others, from the world of my madness. Where are they growing up, in what accursed land beset by what enemies? Why so much hatred? And what about himself, Gamaliel, the exile? He has done no harm, has taken nothing from others. Hasn't seduced their women or led their children astray. Hasn't taken their place in the sun. And yet. Why is he so unloved? Why do people he has never met shun this solitary intruder who carries his past like a load on his shoulders? It's strange: The word *refugee* has lost its biblical meaning. The Bible provides for cities of refuge, where those who kill someone by accident can take shelter from avengers. Of course, the refugees are not entirely free of guilt, so, Scripture specifies, they must remain in these cities of asylum until their sin is expiated by the death of the High Priest. And that is why, adds the Talmud, the refugees are so often visited by the mother of the High Priest, who brings them clothing and sweets and fruits in the hope that if their lives are pleasant enough, they will not pray for her son's death. In our time, it's the innocent who need refuge.

Gamaliel shakes his head: What is the point of collecting all this information from so many sacred and secular texts, when their authors all end up in the potter's field of history? Yes, it's true I learned about King David's turbulent life of love and war, and his son and successor Solomon's pearls of wisdom, but also the treason of his other sons, Absalom and Adonijah. But what use is that to me today? I know that the first translation of the Bible was ordered by Ptolemy, who had seventy scholars locked in cells, each in solitary confinement, and that Diogenes lived like a dog, so he was nicknamed "the cynic." That the Talmud is compared to an ocean deep beyond measure. That Maimonides wrote some of his works in Arabic, and Spinoza wrote in Latin. That Erasmus dedicated his *Praise of Folly* to Thomas More, who

17

coined the word *utopia,* the place that never was. That Höl-
derlin went mad and closed himself off from the world thirty-
six years before he died. That Goethe hated the Bible, which
he considered a trash heap of "Egypto-Babylonian sodomy."
I made a study of the laws governing the right of asylum in
antiquity, and asceticism in the Middle Ages. So? Just where
did all that get me? There are so many who know more than I
do, who understand the world better than I do. I would be
truly learned, a great scholar, if only I could retain everything I've learned from those I have known. But then would I
still be me? And isn't all that only words? Words grow old,
too; they change their meaning and their usage. They get
sick just as we do; they die of their wounds and then they are
relegated to the dust of dictionaries.

And where am I in all this?

GAMALIEL GLANCES ABSENTLY AT HIS WATCH. IT'S
still early. Go to Manhattan and drop in unannounced on one
of his friends? No, not enough time for that. He goes to a
diner that is a hangout for students from a nearby campus.
Some of them are standing around, talking sports and poli-
tics. He takes the only seat left at a small round table. A bored
waiter comes by to take his order: a bottle of mineral water.
"That's it? How about some coffee to wake you up?" All
right, coffee. He picks up snatches of conversation around
the table: "Politicians, none of them are any good," a man
who needs a shave is saying; "they're all crooks. . . . Have you
heard the latest? I tell you, if it were up to me . . ." The man
sitting next to him, an angry young anarchist, by his looks,
interrupts: "You'd do what? Don't try to tell me you'd have
the courage to go out and waste them. So you'd better shut

up, right?" Echoes of the sixties, with their student rebel-
lions. If he were in a better mood, Gamaliel would join in the
conversation, and take notes that might come in handy
someday. . . . It's important to listen, to collect such information. A writer is a recording machine, so he tells himself at
times. He picks up the sounds of the world, arranges them in
order, labels them with symbols only he can understand. So,
who is that young anarchist? Does he know the man he's
just insulted? Suppose it's his own father? For a moment,
Gamaliel imagines the two men in some other setting, at
home perhaps, still quarreling; and he sees a woman, the
young man's mother, who is begging them to stop. But then
the two men turn on her. "It's all your fault," shouts her
unshaven husband. "You spoiled him." "That's true, I did
spoil him," the woman says. "I wanted to make a prince of
him. You, too—I spoiled you also. I saw you as a king. I loved
you once, you know." "I swear you're crazy. Kings and
princes! In storybooks, they're handsome and happy, but not
in real life. In real life, there're just poor ordinary guys like
me, or garbage like that good-for-nothing son of yours. Or
fools like you . . ." Gamaliel closes his eyes. I'll have to
remember that. I can use it in chapter two, when the man
realizes he is fed up and decides to get even with the whole
world. . . .

NOT ONE TREE GRACES THE STREET Eastern
Europeans call Forest Avenue, in ironic recognition of the
fruitlessness of human endeavor: No trees line the ways of
our lives. As he walks down the street, Gamaliel is trying to
get his mind off the book he is writing. Its purported author,
the famous Georges Lebrun, has already announced it in

more than one television interview. "Well, Monsieur Lebrun, when may we expect your next novel?" an attractive journalist asked him recently, with only a momentary pretense of interest. "Oh, you know," the author replied, giving that lazy shrug that was part of his image, "when a writer is so engaged with the work he is creating, the process is so complex, so enigmatic, that to say how long it will take . . ." Gamaliel stifles a snicker: The impostor has learned his lines well. If, after all the novels to which Georges Lebrun has signed his name over the years, without having written a single readable page, he still has no idea when he will deliver his next manuscript, it is for the excellent reason that his ghostwriter, Gamaliel, doesn't know, either. "At least tell us what it's about. . . ." "Oh no," the author protests, sounding frightened now. "One must never talk of the baby before it is born. . . ." Yes, Georges Lebrun is playing his role perfectly. And how about me? Gamaliel wonders. What is my role here?

Once, the celebrated author had seen his ghost at a big party given by a major publishing house. Lebrun was surrounded by admiring women who knew his photo better than his books. He tried to avoid Gamaliel, but Bolek, Gamaliel's fellow refugee, who knew them both, mischievously brought the two together. "You've read his latest novel, haven't you?" he asked Gamaliel, deadpan. And Gamaliel replied as he was shaking Lebrun's hand, "Of course I have—and how about you?" Lebrun, red-faced, muttered a threat, which Gamaliel pretended not to hear.

Gamaliel was a reluctant ghost at the beginning, in Paris. He hated those "authors" who bought title to his work. Even the first one? No, not Georges Lebrun. His name was Bernard Murat. A charming man, a professor, with a head of undisciplined hair, enormous horn-rimmed glasses, awkward in movement. He appealed to Gamaliel: "I've begun a book on a medieval heretic—a well-born Spanish monk—but I'm in poor health and I don't have the strength to finish it. Help me out and I'll make it worth your while." How did he know Gamaliel could be of use to him? It was guesswork. They had met one evening at Bolek's place. Gamaliel's friend Bolek was a Polish Jew, who, on the infrequent occasions when he'd had too much to drink, would imagine he was a character in a Dostoyevsky novel. A dozen or so guests were sipping lukewarm tea, smoking up the room, and telling dirty jokes. Everyone was laughing, except Gamaliel. As he was leaving, the professor asked if he might walk a few blocks with him. As they were walking, the professor offered in a tremulous voice to hire Gamaliel as his ghostwriter. "I don't know you," he said. "I don't know who you are; our friend Bolek has told me nothing about you. Still, I'm certain you're a writer." "But I haven't published anything!" Gamaliel exclaimed. "One can be a writer without publishing," said the professor. "And I haven't written anything yet!" "One can be a writer without writing," the professor replied, imperturbable. Gamaliel stole a glance at the professor, and could not help teasing him: "And can you be a teacher without teaching?" The professor gave him a serious answer: "A writer can write without having readers, but to teach, you must have students around you. And unless I finish my book, I'm likely to lose my classes." And so Gamaliel accepted the bargain. He felt sorry for the professor, who really believed that his reputation and career depended on the publication of his work. And his honor, too. In a word, his life. "But I'm not a historian," Gamaliel protested, and immediately regretted his words. It little mattered whether he was a historian; Bernard Murat was, and that was all that counted.

Thanks to Murat, Gamaliel would read and reread the essential works on intellectual and spiritual life in the Middle Ages. He began with Europe, and then he focused his attention on Rome and Barcelona. Crescas and Pico della Mirandola, Averroes and Ibn Ezra. Maimonides, and, of course, Paritus the One-Eyed, that scholar whose imagination knew no bounds. How could one hear the voices of heaven, what was the true faith, and how could one recognize it? In those days, it was all too easy to fall into heresy. It was enough if you merely hesitated, or stood out in the crowd of the faithful, or refused to give the usual answers. Or if you said no: no to absolute power, no to the pitiless authority of the Church, and no, a hundred times no, to its dogmas. No to anything that denied freedom, even if you had to die for it, or with it. So it was that Giordano Bruno appeared as a hero in Bernard Murat's book. Was Giordano at fault when he declared that without Creation there could be no Creator? Before they tore out his tongue, Giordano had a bitterly honest debate with his inquisitor, who for a moment almost gave in to pity, before he got hold of himself. Fertile imagination? Gamaliel went so far as to give his Giordano a companion in misfortune, a brother in his faith, a partner in his bold quest for the truth that is human, as opposed to the truth that claims to be divine. Gamaliel named this man Manuel de Toledo, and gave him the story of his life. One fine day, Manuel said goodbye to the three sons and a daughter he would never see again: He was arrested by monks at the command of the Grand Inquisitor. He would never leave the stifling, filthy cell, where the guard was Christ: a nod to Dostoyevsky's Karamazov, of course. Despite his torturers, Manuel's mind stayed clear and he kept his dignity as a free man. And meanwhile, Gamaliel's wallet was fattening. But then in a moment of candor, the professor handed him back the manuscript, saying, "Fiction is a lethal trap for a historian like me. I'm better off doing without it."

Gamaliel's second contract was signed under more down-to-earth circumstances. It was Bolek again—Bolek knew everything about everybody—who said to him one day, "You're broke, and don't try to deny it. I can see it just looking at you. Well, I'm broke also, so that makes two of us. But I have an idea for you." He burst out laughing. "You remember the story of the loyal wife who goes in tears to the rabbi because, she says, her husband doesn't know how to play cards? 'So what's the problem?' the rabbi asks, and she says, 'The problem is, he doesn't know how to play, but he keeps on playing.' " Gamaliel laughed, then said, "I don't see the connection." Now Bolek was serious: "I know a playboy who's got it in his head that he wants to be a famous writer." "So? Does he have a problem?" asked Gamaliel. "He doesn't have a publisher?" "No, it's not that he needs a publisher. What he needs is talent."

Gamaliel was still single, as was his friend, and they were both penniless. Bolek was right: Why not try to earn a little money? Gamaliel was introduced to Georges Lebrun the next day at a Left Bank café popular with young artists and intellectuals; the two men took an immediate dislike to each other. Svelte and well built, Lebrun looked like a model or a ballroom dancer. He was vain and he smelled of money.

"It's very simple," Lebrun said, gulping his scotch. "I need recognition and you need money. Number one: I'm the author. Number two: If I don't like a particular page or a particular character, either you change it to suit me or you get rid of it. And then, and never forget this: silence from now on. If you breathe a word of this to anyone, you'll be back on the street before you know it. Understand?"

Gamaliel started to get up and leave without bothering to answer, but Bolek stopped him, then whispered in his ear, "Pay no attention; he's always like that."

"How does he dare talk to me as if I were his servant?"

"He's trying to impress you."

"I'll never write for someone who's such an imbecile, and a bad-mannered one besides."

"He'll pay you well, and that's all that matters. Just do your writing and you'll never have to see him again. Give me the manuscript and I'll deliver it. So for a few months at least, we won't have to worry about paying the rent."

Bolek was always the practical one. You had to admire that in him. And he was right. But now he put forward a different argument: "Suppose by accident you were to write a good book. You don't know anyone in Paris, so you wouldn't be able to find a publisher. Then either no one reads your masterpiece, in which case it doesn't exist, or else it's published, not under your name, but it exists."

"Suppose it's not good enough as literature?"

"In that case, you should be glad your name's not on it. That said, I know you well enough to be sure you can't help putting some good work into it. Would it be right to deprive readers of that?"

With nothing to lose but his self-respect, Gamaliel wrote a draft, taking his time about it, and handed it to Bolek. In Gamaliel's opinion, his manuscript lacked everything that a good novel requires. It was kitsch. A tearjerker. You want cheap emotions, here they are. What was worse, he had made errors in syntax and spelling that made him blush. After all, his first teacher, Ilonka's friend or customer in Budapest, was no magician: He would have needed more time to help Gamaliel master French. Don't worry, Bolek reassured him; he knew a teacher at the lycée who was proud of his grammar. He would ask the teacher to correct the manuscript in return for a share of the money. Six months later, Lebrun was being hailed by *le tout* Paris as the most promising writer of the postwar years. Women adored him; their husbands despised him but did not dare show it. Gamaliel was amused by this hubbub in society, one that would surely echo in literary circles. He waited patiently for Lebrun, once he had calmed down, to seek him out and demand another masterpiece.

He did not have long to wait.

Thus, writing became a job for Gamaliel: a way to live better and to pay for comfortable lodgings. As a trade, it was fairly interesting, and it paid pretty well. No sooner had he finished an assignment than he would forget it: The sorry collections of clichés that he ground out as a writer for hire were of no further interest to him. He would return to his one true passion, the *Book of Secrets,* which made him forget all his frustrations. In it he would put everything he could draw from his memory and from his soul. In the characters he created, was he not unconsciously putting himself in the story? The Jewish painter Chaim Soutine used to say, according to a close friend of his, that for some paintings he did not have to call on memory, and yet those paintings portrayed nothing but his memories. Gamaliel sometimes wondered if the same was true of words. Words could be a writer's best friend, but they could also be formidable opponents. He suffered like a sick man when the words would not submit, would not let themselves be tamed. But when his imagination was on fire and the words allowed themselves to flow, he would bless his happiness and all Creation. At times, his words would take root in a reddening sky; at others, they would sink into a cemetery haunted by malevolent shadows, as in the brain of a madman. Why did Gogol, back from Jerusalem, weep when he had finished *Dead Souls*? Piotr Rawicz tasted ashes as he was writing "The End" on the last page of his novel *Blood from the Sky*. Does a writer love the words he writes, or does he reject them when they part company? Gamaliel believes, most of the time, that a word has a shadow that accompanies and stretches out from it; and the pain he suffers is inflicted by that shadow. But if he separates the word from its shadow, he will expose it in all its nakedness, and that is dangerous: Once on display, it will attract too many ears, too many knowing looks.

ONE DAY, BOLEK INTRODUCED GAMALIEL TO A sturdy old shopkeeper from Brooklyn. The man kept looking around suspiciously, as if he thought every passerby might be an informer. He was more straightforward than Lebrun:

"They tell me you know how to write. I don't. Matter of fact, I hardly know how to read. Not surprising. My school was the ghetto, the war, the camp. I was a partisan in Russia. In the forest. Saw a lot, did a lot. Fighting the Germans, of course. Also their collaborators. I had my reasons, twelve of them. Twelve members of my family butchered in one morning. Right in front of our home. So write my story as best you can, if you can; write it your way and, of course, put your name on it. I'll pay you well."

A tempting offer. But though peace can be told in words, war cannot. Words can incite the murderous hatred that is war, but words cannot describe it. In principle, one should not be able to put it into words, this horror that is war, this blasphemy that is war, this grotesque agony, this licensed slaughter, this glorified butchery that is war. James Joyce knew that, as did Franz Kafka; neither wrote about the First World War. War kills the dream along with the dreamer: It blinds the mind's eye so it cannot see the horizon.

Thus it was that although Gamaliel was moved to write the man's story, he had to tear it up. He told him by letter:

"I do not know how to write your story. I do not know how to revive those haunted faces, those silent voices who, through you, would summon us to hear them tell of their deaths and perhaps our own. All I can do is tell you that I can't do it—and shake your hand."

A few years later, he sent the Brooklyn shopkeeper this quotation from a book by Maurice Blanchot he had just read: "And how can we agree not to know? We read the books about Auschwitz. The last wish of those who were there, their last charge to us, was: know what happened here, never forget, and yet know that you will never know."

HE THOUGHT OF CALLING DIEGO. HE STILL HAD time before his appointment at the hospital.

Diego, with his jutting chin and black forelock over eyes that opened wide, as if he were forever hearing an unexpected sound. There was an air of challenge about the short, stocky Jew from Lithuania who claimed he was Spanish. Right now, he was probably guzzling his lemonade the way he did his wine ration under the African sun, while recalling his adventures in the Foreign Legion in Morocco and the Djebel of Algeria, or the time he spent locked up in Franco's prisons and France's internment camps. At times, he would pretend to be drunk and shout, "I am a free man!" And then, as if sobered by his own frenzy, he would add, "I'll lay down my life but never my freedom." He loved to tell about his skirmishes with French bureaucracy. One such tale, punctuated as always with laughter:

Paris, 1958. On a lovely, tranquil day, Diego went to the Bureau of Missing Persons at police headquarters. One place he didn't have to wait in line. "Yes?" the clerk said irritably, without looking up, while putting aside his pen and inkwell. Diego waited for the clerk to look up. He wanted to see the man's eyes. He hated to talk to someone who would not meet his eyes, who would conceal his expression. "So?" the clerk asked. "You want something?"

"Yes," said Diego.

"Go ahead. I'm listening," said the clerk, still looking down at his record books. "Who's missing?"

"I am," said Diego.

At that, the clerk finally lifted his head. His eyes lit up, but for only a moment. "The insane asylum is around the corner," he said, and he pointed to the exit.

"Fine," said Diego with a shrug. "I'll see you there."

At that, the clerk jumped to his feet and grabbed his visitor by the collar. "Keep that up and I'll have you thrown in jail!"

Once outside, Diego scolded himself: How could you, knowing what it is to be stateless, risk your freedom just for the fun of taunting the bureaucracy? A man without a country is someone to be despised. Don't you realize that? People throw you exiles away like old clothes, turn aside as if you smell bad. . . . Only barely do they grant you the right to talk to the birds, to the trees, to the wind, to the rocks . . . no, not the rocks. I hate rocks. So cold, indifferent, mute, they make me feel inferior: They'll still be around when I'm gone . . . and they're not afraid of that clerk in Missing Persons. Suppose the clerk had asked you for your papers, those documents you left at home? All the police in every country on earth demand your papers, in the same hostile manner, as if that were the only thing in life that interested them . . . your papers, your papers! What a world this is, Diego reflected. . . . To take a human being with all his triumphs and failures, his memories of love and war, and reduce him to a grimy piece of paper—well, only a cop or a bank clerk thinks like that. And then he remembered he had even come across a border guard who, studying his travel permit, read as if in surprise: " 'Diego Bergelson . . . stateless.' . . . That's a funny name." And Diego replied, deadpan, "Do you like it? I'll sell it to you."

When he was out on the street, Diego burst out laughing. He was laughing mostly at himself: Why hadn't he asked for French nationality when he was being discharged from the Legion? It would have been his with a stroke of a pen. Was it from a feeling of solidarity with his Spanish comrades who were still stateless? A youth in a silver-lined black leather jacket accosted him: "Hey, you, why are you laughing?"

"Because it's funny."

"Who are you talking to?"

"To my comrades who disappeared in the desert. They're the only ones I talk to. Only they know how to listen."

"Is that why you're talking to yourself?" the young man said snidely.

Diego wanted to shake his hand, but the youth had already moved on.

. . .

GAMALIEL AND BOLEK HAD MET WHEN THEY were both standing in line at that same police headquarters. Two men, one heavyset, the other scrawny, neither of them young, were quarreling over who was first in line at the window. A very tall, husky young man was trying good-naturedly to separate them. "Why are you butting in?" exclaimed the fat one. "Is it any of your business?" "Yes, it's my business," the husky young man said. "You know that mangy character?" "No, but I'm making it my business anyway." So began the friendship between Gamaliel and Bolek.

GAMALIEL ORDERS A SECOND CUP OF COFFEE. HE relaxes; it's a pleasant day. Students come and go, gulping down coffee, orange juice, a banana. Some of them seem in good spirits, others gloomy. It's exam week. Gamaliel's thoughts are far away. He is in Europe, long ago. Who could forget springtime in Paris? The carefree air of women who have cast away their winter cloaks, exuberant and attractive, their eyes sparkling with mischief or invitation. A light breeze gently caresses the trees. In playgrounds, children are dancing around and munching their chocolate snacks. In parks, people smile and talk to strangers. Under the bridges of the Seine, the clochards serenely turn their backs on the cynical ambition so prized by a supposedly normal society. The sky, so high, so clear, beckons. Oh, if only I could go up there, Gamaliel says to himself. So many are expecting me.

THERE'S A WOMAN IN A RED KERCHIEF AT THE hospital information desk. Behind her is an untidy-looking man with a thin black beard, a high forehead, and a receding hairline. He is watching me on the sly through heavy-lidded eyes. If I catch his eye, he looks away. I don't know this man; I've never met him. Why is he staring at me with what seems like disagreeable curiosity? Whom is he here for, and why: to judge, to amuse, to torment? Now he's nodding as if he knows me. I pay no attention: He is not the person for whom I chose to live. He smiles at me, and suddenly I do think I recognize him: Is he not the wandering man, that first madman of my childhood? Hardly has the thought entered my mind than it disappears when the stranger turns away.

Well, never mind. As far as I know, he's not the one my appointment is with. . . . I'm here for a wounded woman, virtually mute, who speaks only in Hungarian. Does she know me? The man who issues visitors' passes earnestly wants to know; you'd think his professional future turned on this information. He questions me as if I've come to rob the management's safe. Strange country, America, obsessed with anything having to do with security. Without a photo ID, God Himself would be denied admittance. Here, before the strait gate to paradise—or perhaps to hell—anyone is entitled to interrogate you about anything. Soon they'll be asking you if you believe in the immortality of the soul, whether you prefer Mozart or Schubert, whether your mistress is cheating on you with her second husband.

"So you're a visitor?" the man says in a tone of authority.

"Yes."

"You're here to see a patient?"

"Yes, she's Hungarian. Her name—"

"Show me your ID."

I search my pockets, but find nothing, not even a credit card or a library card. I left everything on my desk. Maybe a driver's license? But I don't own a car and I don't like to drive.

What can I say? The guard sounds impatient: "Come on, let's see that ID."

I feel around in my pockets, but still I find nothing. "I'm very sorry," I say in a tone calculated to melt the hardest of prison guards' hearts. "I must have left my wallet in my other suit."

The guard despises and distrusts me—that's obvious. He finds me offensive, or perhaps he fears me. What does he think I am? A lunatic maybe, or a criminal who's come to kidnap a wealthy patient, or to take revenge on an incompetent doctor. Is it the way I'm dressed? This old gray suit I'm wearing is my favorite. It dates back to the time of Colette—my first wife, also my last. It's missing a button and looks as if I'd slept in it. On holidays, like today, I'll change my shirt, but that's all. Do I look like a Gypsy, or some homeless man? I prefer to play the part of the absentminded professor.

"I'm sorry to say this," says the guard, imperturbable, someone whose authority is second only to God's, "but I must see proper identification. Those are the rules. You must understand why we"—who is "we"?—"must insist on those rules in times like these."

Now the stranger comes to my rescue: "I know this man. I'll vouch for him. He's practically one of us."

I gasp. Is this my guardian angel? Had our paths crossed in Hungary, in an Austrian hostel, in a shelter for refugees in France? Had he, too, been stateless? Had he, too, envied those fortunate enough to have the right papers, to be citizens of a nation that would protect them, while they sought to realize their dreams? Was there some sort of association across frontiers for onetime refugees, as there was for onetime soldiers?

"What is the patient's name?" the guard asks, still sullen.

"I told you. She's Hungarian." I stop to catch my breath and search my memory. "Lili. Lili Rosenkrantz." That was the name Bolek had mentioned when he gave me the message that had brought me to the hospital.

"I don't see that name on the list."

"I know her," says my savior.

"But I don't see her name. . . ."

"Don't worry about it; I'll see to it. You have your hands full."

"Oh yes," says the guard. "It's not as if I don't have anything to do." He glares at me. Would he never cease suspecting me? "This patient, is she a relative?"

How could I answer that? Once again, the stranger comes to my rescue: "Yes, she's his aunt."

Now the guard hands me a slip of paper. "Building four, ward three."

I go along a hall that leads to the courtyard, then to a garden. It's nice out. A peaceful morning: Spring is arriving with a smile. Doctors come and go. Two male nurses are escorting a restless, babbling patient. His features are drawn; he looks undone, as if he has been howling in silence for so long, he can no longer hear the sounds and murmurs of the world.

I look around for my benefactor. He's vanished. But he was there at the right time, as if he had lived only to appear at my side when I needed an ally. A helping hand from fate? The cynics are wrong; David Hume and Nikos Kazantzakis are right: Everything that happens in our human universe is mysteriously linked to everything else.

WHY IS THE PAST SUDDENLY WITH ME? AND WHY is my heart beating so? Gamaliel, sitting on a bench in the calm of the garden, is wondering while he waits for his appointment.

. . . A FRIGHTENED LITTLE JEWISH BOY IS CLINGing to the skirt of his distraught mother. It's dark in the bedroom where they are hidden. "Mama," whispers the small boy, who is mad about stories, "tell me a story. Tell me anything, even one I know. What matters is hearing your voice, not the story. I want to hear your voice."

"Not now," says his mother.

"But when? Tomorrow? But when is tomorrow? Are you sure tomorrow comes after now?"

His mother is weeping softly, very quietly, without tears, so as not to be heard by a suspicious neighbor or a passerby in the night. "Be a good boy, my love. Tomorrow will come; the night won't last forever."

The boy is trying to hold back his sobs. "But you . . . you won't be here tomorrow."

"I'll come back, I promise you."

"When? I want to know when you're coming back."

"Soon, my love, very soon, but now you must behave." He's willing to behave, but not to be parted from his mother. She strokes his hair, his eyebrows, his lips. "One day, you'll understand, my precious. The world is a cruel place. It doesn't want us; it condemns us."

The boy whispers in his mother's ear, "But what is the world? Where does it begin?"

"The world is a story."

"Tell it to me."

"First you have to discover it."

"Where is it?"

"In the street," his mother replies. "In the building across the way. In the passerby who looks at you suspiciously. But always you find the world in people's hearts. When their hearts are good, the world is beautiful, but when their hearts are bad, the world is poisonous, and then . . ."

The child doesn't understand the words, but he senses the menace in them. "I don't care about the world. I don't care if it loves me. It's you I want. You're my world."

"And you, my child, you're my life. Without you, the world would be a cold place."

"I don't want to live in that world if I can't be with you."

She is kissing him desperately while she struggles to explain that wars are always cruel to people, and this war is the worst of all, especially for Jews. "You must understand this, my dearest. Try very hard to understand. I know you're only eight, but you're a Jew, and today, when Death is on the lookout for him, a Jew even at eight has to understand like an old man who is three times thirty-three years old. . . . Do you hear me?" He hears, but he still doesn't understand. She persists: "Together we're lost, but if we separate, we have a chance."

He is obstinate: "No, I won't do it."

"You won't?"

"No, I won't." He has never said no to his mother. This first time leaves him feeling shame mingled with remorse. He swallows his tears: "You say I don't understand? You're the one who doesn't understand. If you leave me, I'll die."

She takes the child's head between her hands. "You're so intelligent, my son, my only love. You're clever beyond your years. But you're saying things you don't understand. What shall we do? What can we do in this awful, cruel time?"

A soft sound interrupts their whispered exchange. Petrified, mother and child hold each other without daring to breathe: It's best to play dead when the enemy approaches. Someone is knocking at the door: several light taps repeated three times. "It's all right. Relax," the mother murmurs. "The Lord be praised! It's Ilonka."

She opens the door. Her little boy closes his eyes so he won't have to look at the young woman who is entering. He decides he doesn't like her voice, though all she has said is an everyday remark: "It's nasty out, let me tell you." Nor does he like her scent: too cloying. It's an effort not to cough or sneeze. His mother says, "Here is my little boy. You'll take care of him, won't you? Never will I forget you." Ilonka replies, but he is too upset over their parting to hear what she says. His mother says again, "Say good evening to Ilonka." He obeys without opening his eyes.

A long silence follows, until the newcomer says, "Rest easy, dear lady. I'll look after your son. How handsome he is! And he looks so bright. Already I love him. And I'll take good care of him, I promise you. This war will be over soon. We'll all meet again, and we'll be happy. And we'll laugh, won't we? How we'll laugh!"

They are laughing already, but the boy does not join in. Someone inside him weeps.

And he knows this: It will be a long time before that someone stops weeping.

His mother is making tea. Their visitor has brought cakes and sweets. He cannot swallow anything. His mother tells him to try to sleep. He can't. He doesn't want to sleep. The hours pass. "It's the curfew," his mother explains. "I can't go out now." The two women are chatting. And the little boy is thinking, May the curfew last all day tomorrow, all the days of the week, and all the days of my life. Mama will talk to me in that voice like no other, and I'll be reassured. I'll wait for tomorrow without fear, and for Papa also. I'll wait for him, too. . . .

At dawn, his mother takes his hands between hers as if to warm them and looks deep into his eyes. She wishes she could make him understand how grave this moment is: They might never see each other again. It's the same anxiety she felt in 1939, when her husband went underground because the Germans had invaded what remained of Czechoslovakia after the Munich agreement. But she cannot find the words, those new and dreadful words that no mother in this world should ever have to say. She settles for simple, practical instruction. She has no choice: Time is running out of patience, and so is Death: "Listen, precious, listen carefully. I'm going away. I have to. I'm not going far, just to a house nearby. A Christian friend is taking me in as . . . as a guest. You'll stay here with Ilonka. She has a beautiful voice, and she's so clever. You'll love that in her; I'm sure you will. She knows a thousand and one tales, and she'll share them with you. If anyone asks, she'll tell them you're her little nephew from Fehérvàros—that's a village far off in the mountains, a place that no one's likely to know about. She has a document for you that's reliable. There's a new name on it, a Christian name: Péter. There—from now on you'll be Péter to every-one. You'll remember that, won't you?" When he does not answer, she repeats, "Tell me that you'll remember your new name."

In his years of exile, growing up far from his mother, he would reflect on the absolute power of such documents. Yes, though the century was in turmoil, demented, it was care-fully regulated: Your fate could turn on a single signature. If it was accepted, you could go anywhere you chose to live your life. But if it was rejected, too bad for you: You would be expelled from the land of the living.

"Yes, Mama, I'll remember, but . . ."

"But what?"

"I don't like it."

"What don't you like?" she asks in a sudden panic.

"That name, Péter. I don't like it."

"Why don't you like it?"

"Because . . ."

"Because of what?"

"Because of Papa . . ."

Once again she is sobbing.

HIS FATHER HAD BEEN ARRESTED SIX MONTHS earlier. Even before the Germans came—that was on a Sunday—the Hungarian regime's pro-fascist and anti-Semitic policy showed itself in periodic outbursts of cruelty toward Jews, especially toward those fleeing Nazi-ruled Poland. Usually, the Hungarian authorities simply drove the refugees back over the border to Galicia, where the SS were waiting to give them a "warm" reception. The luckiest refugees succeeded in getting in touch with Jewish committees, more or less tolerated by the police, and these committees provided them with false papers. The boy's father was among these. In 1939, he and his family had been able to leave occupied Czechoslovakia, thanks to the recommendation of a onetime adviser to the father of the country, Thomas Masaryk. They had lived for a time in a small town; then they moved to Budapest. The Jewish community helped the father earn a living by getting him work at one or another of their businesses, and the family was always invited for meals on the Sabbath and holidays. The family spoke Yiddish at home, but the little boy was tutored in Hungarian, and then enrolled in school, where he made Hungarian-speaking friends. His par-

ents would take him strolling in the park on Sabbath after-
noons. One day, his father said to him, "Just look at that sun,
how arrogant and masterful it is. It makes all creatures here
below kneel to him. And yet even the sun must feel contrite
and humbled when it has to set every evening. There's a lesson in that for all of us."

But the mother said she disagreed: "The sun doesn't set; it
just goes someplace else. And neither you nor we know
where that is. The sun goes to reign over other people in
other worlds, those in darkness, then to reappear the next
morning more glorious than ever."

The father stopped to kiss his wife's hand. "You're mag-
nificent. I'd marry you again any day of the week."

BY MARCH 1944, LIFE WAS RELATIVELY SETTLED
and the future looked promising. Gamaliel's father belonged
to a Jewish resistance network that helped newer refugees.
He was in good spirits. The Allies were advancing in Italy,
and the Red Army was approaching. The war wouldn't last
much longer; soon Hitler would be on his knees. The good
Lord above was watching over His people. Then things fell
apart. The Germans took Hungary's regent, Nicholas Hor-
thy, hostage at Berchtesgaden, where he'd gone to visit the
Führer. On the morning of March 19, the radio announced
that German troops were entering Hungary to help the
nation's army defend its borders. A new government of pro-
Hitler fanatics instituted a reign of terror and hate. And what
hate it was: bitter and savage, dominated by death, dedicated
to death. Roundups, arrests, humiliation: the Jewish community defenseless. Jews could no longer expect any support
from the Christian community. Government employees who

before had closed their eyes to the refugees' activities now proved fearful and powerless. Gamaliel's father was arrested on the street after being fingered by a neighbor. His documents did not impress the policeman, and at the precinct, the detective on duty did not even look at the identity card he showed him. "I know it's a fake," he said. "I can tell that much just by listening to you." True, the father spoke Hungarian with difficulty. "You're nothing but a filthy Jew," the detective continued. "We hate liars, so we teach them a lesson in honesty."

The father persisted: "But I'm not a Jew; I'm Christian."

"Then how come you take such pleasure in murdering our beautiful language?"

The boy's father tried to explain. "I have trouble speaking Hungarian. I came with Czech soldiers from our country. We came with official permission."

"So, according to these papers of yours, you're a resident of our fine country," said the detective in an irritated voice. Then he slapped the father a couple of times and ordered him to drop his pants. "You're still a Jew. Your God is not our God. It shows on your filthy body, which was born in garbage and carries the plague," he said with disgust.

"Yes, I'm a Jew, but a Czech Jew. I knew President Masaryk."

"Really? Tell us where is he now?"

"He's no longer alive."

"Well, pretty soon you're going to join him. Give him our regards, won't you?"

He was kept in prison and put through brutal bloody interrogations. "Give us the names!" they shouted at him. "Who were your accomplices? Who got you those fake papers? Who got you that apartment in Budapest?" After several endless nights of this, his ordeal was stopped by order of a higher-up who was bribed.

The boy accompanied his mother on her visits to the prison. He would wait sitting quietly on a bench in the park across the street from counterintelligence headquarters. He was terrified by the thought that his mother might never return, and each time she did, he would throw himself into her arms and desperately embrace her. He held back his tears, as she did. "Everything's all right," she would always assure him. "Papa wants you to know that." The child wanted to believe her, but with all his heart he wanted to see his father. If only once a month, once a year!

And one day, there was a miracle. That morning, his mother returned to take him by the arm. "I have good news for you: You're going to see Papa."

"When?" the boy cried out.

"Right now. In just a minute."

The boy asked no more questions. This he would later regret. He should have observed that his mother was more dispirited than usual, depressed, worse than terrorized. What had she learned that morning?

The boy would never forget the last time he saw his father. The prisoner was unshaven, emaciated, and his eyes were bright with fever. He held the boy in his arms, murmuring, "Do you know how much I love you? Will you remember it?" The boy would remember always. He would remember also how his heart ached when he saw his father suddenly grown old, enfeebled, disoriented. Until then his father had been a man filled with energy and optimism, a man who knew how to make his way through the labyrinthine world in which the unfortunate and the downtrodden dwell.

But his father said something more to him that day:

"Remember, my child, that you are a Jew." That is what his father said to him that day in the prison. The boy didn't know he was clinging to his father for the last time, but he knew now more than ever that he must obey him, must remember his father's words. The father continued, softly, and that, too, the child would remember: "You were born a Jew, my son, and a Jew you must remain. Your mother tells me she has found a wonderful charitable woman who will look after you. You must be respectful to her. And obedient. And grateful. You will use the Christian name that she gives you, but never forget that you carry the name of my own father: Gamaliel. Try not to dishonor it. You'll take it back as yours when this ordeal is over. Promise me you won't disown your name. Every name has its story. Promise me, my child Gamaliel, that one day you will tell that story."

And the child promised.

IN THE HALF-LIGHT OF THE MAID'S ROOM, DOOR and dormer windows closed, the child's mother is still trying to make him listen to reason, but in vain.

"I'm not Péter. I don't want the name Péter," the boy is repeating stubbornly. "I have a name of my own. You know perfectly well what it is. My grandfather gave it to me as a present, to remember him by. Ga-ma-li-el. I want to keep that name. It may not sound great, but it's mine. It's me. I won't let it be taken away from me. Papa didn't want that, either. I promised him. He told me its story and now it belongs to me."

"You don't understand, do you, my precious? We're all in danger. Ask this nice lady. She'll tell you: Death is on the lookout for us. Death is searching out Jews, and it won't be satisfied while it can hear any of us breathing. We have no choice, my child. For the time being, we must leave each other."

"Papa will come and save us. I know he will. He'll find some way to keep us together."

"I'm waiting for him, too. I count on him, too. But when will he come back? Not till the end of the war, and that's likely to be weeks, even months. . . ."

"Well, I'll just wait."

They fall silent. It is almost dawn. Ilonka brings him a cup of hot chocolate, bought at an exorbitant price. He goes to sleep curled up in an armchair. When he awakens, his mother is gone. Ilonka gives him a letter that he reads, distraught: "We decided to put you to sleep, my love. It was for your own good. We'll be together again; I know we will. I hope it will be soon. And then I'll tell you new stories, and none of them will be sad. My baby, my young man, one day you will understand."

But that day would never come.

I'D SEEN HIM ONCE AGAIN, THAT WANDERING MAN who had come to our door ages ago, it seemed. This time it was in the mountain village where we had found ourselves after crossing the border. Did he know that we were about to move out and go to Budapest? Once again, it was on a Sabbath afternoon. . . . Mama was asleep; my father was out. Night would soon fall. I was feeling lonely, and sad. Suddenly, the door opened. I started in fright. "My father isn't home," I said to the man standing still in the doorway.

"I know that," he said, and I recognized that distinctive voice. "You're the one I've come to see. You like stories. You really love them, don't you?"

"Yes, I do," I answered softly. "Yes, I love to hear stories, yes, always."

"Very well. Then sit down and listen."

Still standing, back-to-back with his motionless shadow, he told me the story of Hasid, a humble disciple of the Baal Shem-Tov, known as the Besht, from his initials. The disciple was worried about how he would support his family after the death of the Master. "That's simple enough," the Besht had said. "You will travel the world, telling the story of my deeds."

Of course the Hasid had no choice but to obey. With his sack over his shoulder, he went on foot from village to village, from one community to the next, from one home to the next, seeking those who were ready to hear him tell of the greatness of the Master of the Good Name. Often people were too preoccupied. They would turn him away and go about their business. The best among them would give him a few copper coins, as alms or for their own sins, and he would carefully put these away to take to his wife for Passover. Then one night that he spent in a forest, he lost his meager fortune, just when he was due to go home the following week. Tears came to his eyes, and he was still in tears when he came to the synagogue in the neighboring village. Asked what his trouble was, he replied that he made his living by telling people about his Master, that he had just lost all he had, and here it was almost Passover and his family could not afford to celebrate the traditional Seder feast. The people of the community empathized with his plight, but, being themselves almost as penniless as he, they could give him only a piece of advice. The lord of their village was rather peculiar: He seldom went out—he was never seen in either the church or the tavern—but he would admit to the castle anyone who could tell him a story. If the story was new to him, the lord would reward the teller handsomely. Let the Hasid try his luck with the lord at his castle, they suggested. The lord greeted him by saying, "They say you have some worthwhile Jewish tales in that head of yours. Is that right?" "Yes, it's true," the disciple replied. "Then what are you waiting for? Go ahead!"

The disciple and servant of the Besht began to tell of his Master's travels: how he would disappear, only to reappear in faraway places, how he conjured up the miracles his master had performed, how he saved a desperate woman, freed a hapless merchant from prison, rescued a widow, an orphan about to die, a child stolen by evil priests. After each story, the lord of the village would give him a small coin and say, "Go on." So passed that day and all the next day also. At last, the storyteller fell silent. "That's all I can remember," he said. "Try," the lord said bleakly. "Search your memory. Go on, make an effort." "I did try. There's nothing there." "Then try again," the lord insisted. "Try harder. You won't regret it." "I can't do it," said the Hasid sadly. Without a word, the lord led him to the gate, where the disciple suddenly stopped, slapped his forehead, and exclaimed, "Please forgive me, but it's just come back to me! I remember a young sinner who came to the Besht to ask his help and his advice. He had strayed too far from the right path, he had broken with his God and with his people, he had done terrible things, unforgivable things, and now he wanted with all his heart to find the path of righteousness. How could he find his way there? The Besht asked me to leave him alone with the visitor. After a few hours, he called me back. It seems that, before leaving, the young penitent had asked the Besht, 'How will I know whether my repentance has been accepted?' And the Besht had replied, 'You will know it on the day that this story is told to you.' "

The lord had tears in his eyes as he embraced the disciple, who proceeded home, his pockets stuffed, and celebrated the Seder amid the joy of his memories.

From the *Book of Secrets*

Archbishop Báranyi's heart was beating fast. Trying to shake off his nightmare, he opened his eyes, only to close them immediately. "Lord, what have I done that is so dreadful in Thy sight that Thou hast forsaken me? Why dost Thou punish me by hiding Thyself from me? What have I done that I am so blind I no longer recognize Thee?"

He got out of bed, intending to go wash his face in the basin across his bedroom. It was pitch-dark in the room; the little night-light in the corner had stopped working long ago. Usually, this did not bother the Archbishop. He had learned in the twenty years he had lived in that room to avoid the chair by his bed, then the rectangular table, and finally the earthenware stove that faced the bed. But this time he bumped into the corner of the table so hard that he groaned in pain. "Lord," he said softly, "Thy will is that I suffer. Thou striketh me there where I am most weak, in my body. I accept, from Thee I accept everything, even my suffering. . . . Ow!" He let out a cry as he bumped into the table once again. "So be it, Lord. Thou dost not wish me to wash my face, so I will not do it. Thy will be done. Amen." The Archbishop, too upset to hope for sleep, knelt and prayed: "Help me, Lord, Thou who helpeth those who believe in Thee. Save me, my Savior, Thou who rescueth sinners from the flames of the inferno. May

Thy presence never again abandon me!" Calmer now,
he lay down again and went back to sleep, only to find
himself plunged back into his nightmare. Now Satan
took an interest in him. The Archbishop recognized
the devil in the creature now man, now woman that
snickered while slapping its thighs. "You thought to
escape me, hah, hah, hah . . . fool that you are, a fool
seven times over. Did they not tell you that Christ
Himself feared me more than death? And you, you
scoundrel, you thought you could take refuge in His
bosom to avoid dealing with me? Come on, come
closer, and I'll give you a taste of my delicacies. . . .
Hah, hah, hah . . ." The Archbishop held his breath till
he was about to suffocate and made a superhuman
effort to see once again the wounded but peaceful
face of Christ. Oh, if only he could cling to Christ's
robe, kiss His wounds, His eyes, stroke His hands! Do
what his mother had done for him when he was a
child . . .

His mother had led him to his discovery of Christ. He
must have been five or six. With his father gone, he
had attached himself all the more desperately to his
mother. He suffered whenever she was far from him.
One winter morning when she was away, he
collapsed, like a toy with broken springs. She found
him lying unconscious, curled up on the floor, felled
by acute pneumonia; it was as if an evil black demon
was holding and shaking him in its immense fist.
"Water, water," he whispered, but nothing could
quench his thirst or relieve his pain. He was nauseous

and breathing with difficulty. His mother put cold compresses on his forehead and chest. "What a life! I didn't deserve what's happening to us. This evil world has it in for me . . . but everything will be all right, my child, you'll see. All will be well, and if it isn't, then I'll get even with everybody. That, I promise you." But he could reply only with a single word: "Water, water." The doctor sounded worried. Typhus was going around the region. "If he dies, I'll kill everyone and then I'll kill myself," said the mother, and she went on cursing the rotten human race. In her raving, she even cursed God the Father for not preventing His enemies from killing His son, Jesus, nor the fever from striking her own son. Indeed, she did mistrust God; He was too severe, too cruel. She hated Him. Jesus Christ was the one she loved, and it was to Him that she addressed her prayers. One night, little János felt himself sinking into an endless abyss. From far away he heard his mother's tearful, angry voice: "No, no, my son! Don't give up! I won't allow it! Hold on to the Lord. He will save you." And through half-closed eyes, he saw a man who seemed regal and calm, but very sick; his eyes were bleeding, but his upturned gaze lit up the sky. "Pray," said his mother. "Jesus will hear you. Ask Him to let you live. Promise Him that you'll grow up as a good Christian. He loves children, yes He does." Then the man with the warm, kind gaze took his hand and with infinite care drew him back from the shadows into which he was about to disappear. On that day, the child János made up his mind that he would never be without his portrait of Christ. His mother had to bring him the portrait every morning when he awakened, every night before he went to sleep, so he could kiss it, once, twice, a dozen times.

Over the years, János would examine many portraits of his Savior painted or drawn by a variety of artists in many periods of history. He became familiar with these many portrayals and was recognized as an expert. A glance was enough for him to identify the artist, and the circumstances under which he had worked. People came from afar to ask the parish priest in the remote province of Székesváros to explicate or authenticate the work of a master—or a forger's copy. He became the enemy of deception, and the defender of Christ's honor and love. For the widow Báranyi's adored son had chosen the priesthood as his vocation. She had tried to dissuade him at first; he was her only son, and she would rather have seen him father a large family, and, most of all, be happier than she had been. But he knew how to make his case: "Did you not tell me time and again when I was a child that I owed my miraculous recovery to Him? Then must I not consecrate my life to Him?" The poor woman was not able to debate him; she could only nod and swallow her tears. "Yes, my son, you're right, of course you're right. You learned in the seminary how to put words together, but still . . ." "But what, Mama?" "What's to become of us if you have no children? Someday I'll die, and then someday you'll die, and there'll be no one left of our poor family. That's why I'm weeping."

In response, he drew from the pocket of his cassock his first portrait of Jesus, the one she had given him to kiss when he was a child and dying; he was never without it. "Be not afraid, Mama. He will always be with us." "Yes, of course, of course, my son. Our good Lord Jesus will be here after we're gone. He is life. . . ." "He is life everlasting," János intoned. He was blissfully content, but his mother was torn between her good fortune at seeing her son happy and the thought that she had lost the son she adored to the beloved Son of God.

But now, in the horror-filled night that lay like a pall over the city, the Archbishop could not understand why the Christ of his dream did not resemble any of the portraits he had been looking at since childhood. And yet, the Christ of his dream had a familiar face. That made him tremble, as if he had just committed a sin for which no forgiveness could be imagined.

—∭—

Hananèl, the young Kabbalah scholar known as the "Blessed Madman," is seated at his table, a small dusty volume open before him. He is rereading the commentary in the Midrash on the section in the Book of Job that deals with the individual's responsibility to remember: "Shortly before a being is to leave his earthly existence, the Lord appears to him and says, 'Record all you have accomplished.' The man does as he is told and sets his seal to what he has written." The young scholar scratches his bushy black

beard and puzzles over the passage: Why does the
Lord have to go to the trouble of personally
reminding every individual to prepare his final
accounting? Why not send an angel to do it? Suddenly,
he glances up to see the "beadle," his friend and
faithful aide. Hananèl gives him a mildly reproachful
look: Why is the beadle disturbing him at this late
hour? But as usual Hananèl quickly dismisses the
thought. In the time they have been together—five
years, or more—the bond of affection and
understanding that joins them in the search for truth
has made them almost equals. So when Hananèl
speaks, his manner is playful. "You can't sleep,
Mendel? What's bothering you? Not your sins, I hope.
As far as I know, you don't have many of them. I've
learned to read your intentions and evaluate your
deeds, and everything in you is pure. And yet instead
of sleeping, you come here and interrupt my
studying—well, maybe *that's* your sin. . . ."

He sees that something is troubling his friend.
Usually, "Big Mendel"—as he is called, as if there were
another by that name in his circle—maintains his
outward composure. Self-assured in his words and his
actions, he always finds the way to be respectful but
frank in his dealings. He never lets himself be
humiliated or diminished, even by the Kabbalist
scholar whose voice silences the most fluent of
demons. Only Big Mendel may speak freely to
Hananèl, may tell him what his rich and powerful
visitors would rather he not know. But right now, he
seems distraught, somehow deprived of the power
of speech. All he does in answer to the questions of

the Blessed Madman, whom he insists, despite the other's protests, on addressing as "Rebbe," is shrug, as if to say, The Rebbe won't believe me. . . . What I have to tell him may seem ridiculous, but it is serious. At last, he stammers, "Hmm, Rebbe, in the waiting room, yes, down at the end of the hall—well, it's almost out-of-doors—there's a priest waiting. . . ."

The Blessed Madman makes no attempt to hide his surprise. "Did I hear you right, Mendel? A priest, you did say a priest? Outside? And he's waiting? What's he waiting for? The Messiah maybe? No, his Messiah already came, and the world's no different for it. . . ."

"He wants to see the Rebbe," Mendel says, avoiding the scholar's eyes. "He says he has a message for the Rebbe—an important message."

The Rebbe pulls out a handkerchief and sets it on the book he has been studying, to keep his place. "Mendel," he says, "if a priest comes to see a Jew, that doesn't bode well. Yet if the Jew has to go see the priest, that's far worse."

Mendel is knotting his fingers. "What must I say to him, Rebbe?"

"Ask him to come in." He sighs and adds, "May the Creator of all things—blessed be He and blessed be His name—may He have mercy on us."

Young Hananèl suddenly feels old, as if he is weighted down by all the years lived by others, by his precursors. He finds it difficult to stand. Leaning on the beadle's arm, he manages to get to his feet, then sits back down immediately. Why show even the slightest sign of weakness to a visitor who travels by night and doubtless wishes him no good? In his mind's eye he glimpses scenes long buried in the sands of time. In Paris, during the reign of Louis IX, the queen mother, Blanche de Castille, presided over a debate between the famous Rabbi Yehiel, representing the Jewish faith, and Nicolas Donin, the infamous renegade—may his name be erased forever—now become spokesman for the Christian faith. In Barcelona, Rabbi Moses ben Nahman, known by the acronym Ramban, confronted Pablo Christiani in the presence of the king and queen. The Jewish scholar won the debate but had to flee. And in the cathedral at Tortosa, Rabbi Joseph Albo and twenty erudite Jews faced Geronimo de Santa Fe in a disputation, on the one side, knowledge, on the other, slander. And what does all this have to do with the Blessed Madman? Is it now his turn to defend his people in public debate? Is he worthy, is he capable of it? In his mind he summons his ancestors to lend him their strength and their virtue. With their support, he will be able to hold his own against his adversaries, above all to preserve his dignity: the honor of a Jew serving the God of Israel. He smiles faintly. "Show the priest in, Mendel. Who knows? Perhaps he needs our help. In the world of our Lord, anything is possible. Miracles can happen even today."

Mendel leaves, and Hananèl remains absorbed by his impure thoughts. He has difficulty controlling the trembling in his left arm. Though the Blessed Madman has no idea of the reason for the priest's visit, he has been expecting it, or, rather, he has been expecting something from the outside world. He senses that some great evil is brewing for the Jewish communities of Hungary. Is this what the priest has come to tell him?

Mendel is back, but he is by himself. "Rebbe, I will show him in, but if he takes the Rebbe away, I go with you. Is that clear? I promised your worthy parents— may their saintliness protect us!—that I would watch over you. Does the Rebbe remember that?"

"I remember," the young scholar replies. Yes, he remembers the event to which Mendel is referring. His heart is beating faster. He has learned that man must not look too far, or too high.

"In that case, I'll—" Mendel starts to say.

"May the Lord above protect us," says the young Master, interrupting.

Once again, he senses that the moments he is about to live through are linked to the mystical knowledge he has acquired: the names of the angels and the powers they will confer on whoever knows to invoke them according to the manner told to Adam by the angel Raziel and transmitted by whispered word of mouth by the very few chosen ones from generation to generation. How to disarm the evil intentions of any enemy of Israel. How to act on events in such a way as to change their course. . . . And also, thanks to the backing of the old Kabbalist Rabbi Kalonimus, his guide and revered Master, he knows how to bring about the ascension of the soul to the heavenly tribunal, where the destiny of humanity is decided.

Yes, he remembers.

He even remembers what he would rather forget: the unhappy event that gave him his nickname. Before that, he was just Hananèl.

The only disciple of old Rabbi Kalonimus, he was

THE TIME OF THE UPROOTED

as attached to him as he was to his father, if not more
so. Hananèl had not hesitated a moment when the
Master of the mysteries had suggested that the two of
them, with the Lord's help, could precipitate the
ultimate events and thus hasten the Day of
Deliverance. "I am willing," he said. But the old
Kabbalist had warned him: "You realize there are
dangers, don't you?" "Yes, Rabbi, I do." "And you're
not afraid?" "Yes, I am afraid, but you taught me to
overcome fear." Rabbi Kalonimus gazed at him for a
long moment, then said, "Our forefathers are
fortunate to have begotten you." And he added,
"Receive their blessing as well as mine. Like Rabbi
Akiva, you will enter in peace into the Garden of
Knowledge, and, like him, leave in peace."

There was nothing else to do, Hananèl reflected.
The children of Israel had been too long in exile;
they could bear no more. The ordeal was too much.
The enemy was too powerful, his designs too cruel.
And the prophet Elijah was too far away. The
descendants of Abraham, Isaac, and Jacob could
no longer hold out.

Thus the Master and his young disciple entered on
a perilous ascetic journey known for its traps and
obstacles. Isolated from the world, even from their
families, they lived for three times three weeks in a
shack at the edge of the forest overlooking the village.
They followed a program of study, of intense
meditation, of prolonged fasting, of prescribed
prayers, of litanies recited without moving the lips, all
this while standing, in a state of concentration that
would leave them dizzy. Ritual baths morning and

night, chanting at midnight, carefully preparing themselves to penetrate walls, to set on fire their minds and souls and time itself. They dealt with unnameable sacrifices and ordeals performed according to rules set down in the esoteric and difficult texts of the Kabbalah. Sometimes the old Rabbi would shake himself and urge his disciple on: "Faster, my son, we must run faster; we must climb higher. Every minute counts. The danger is taking shape; the Angel of Death and Destruction is approaching. The blood of Jews will flow; it is flowing already. Only the Messiah can stop it; only He can save our people!" But Satan, the cursed devil, was on the alert. He never sleeps, and he was plotting his victory. The old Master thought that by being hasty, he was serving God, when, in fact, he was opposing His will. He was wrong. The universe of the Kabbalah has its own rhythm, its own method. Haste is dangerous: A word spoken too soon, a name invoked too late, these can jeopardize the entire endeavor by pushing humanity to the side of Evil and its destructive power. And that is what happened. The last stage in the ritual took place at dawn in the forest. It consisted of calling out the name of the angel Metatron seventy-one times, each time louder than the last, to the point of rapture, then the ineffable Name twenty-one times, then twenty-six times more, then reciting seven times a prayer known only to the High Priest. Well, the Master and his disciple were ready. They were wearing their prayer shawls as they began the ceremony, and then a torrential rain started to fall from dark, heavy clouds. They continued despite the rain. Now thunder and lightning took their turn striking at the earth. Still they persisted, in spite of the lightning, in spite of the thunder. Then during a pause in the storm, a huge wild dog appeared out of nowhere. It was black as the night, the biggest dog they had ever seen. It was foaming with rage and its baying was louder, more deafening, than the thunder itself. Jaws open, it was about to hurl itself on the two men and tear them to pieces. "Go on!" the old Master cried out. "That beast was sent by Satan to frighten us, to weaken our resolve. We must continue; it's our only chance." But the disciple was afraid, and he lost his concentration. In a moment, the dog was upon them. The old Master was knocked down. So was Hananèl, but he survived his wounds, although his Master did not. The Jewish community of the village mourned the old Master. His funeral procession stretched over streets and alleys. The old women cried their lamentation; young students wept unashamedly. Schools closed so their students could attend the funeral. Some said, "It was foolish to violate what is forbidden." And others replied, "It was foolish, but it was also holy." From then on, Hananèl was known as the Blessed Madman.

But Hananèl felt guilty. Only he knew it, but the failure of their ritual was his fault. Satan's dog had first attacked the old Master, while Hananèl was confronting another enemy, himself. At the very last minute, when the most secret portals of heaven were about to swing open, the young Kabbalist let himself be distracted. Because of the dog? Not at all: The dog had nothing to do with it. The dog had appeared only

because Hananèl let himself be distracted by an
impure vision: It was a woman he had seen one Friday
morning in the market street when he was returning
from the ritual bath in preparation for the Sabbath. It
was a beautiful summer's day. The woman, who
surely was not Jewish, so immodest in his eyes was her
dress, had looked at him, and he had seen a smile in
her gaze. But was she just a woman? Probably not.
She was Lilith, spouse of the demon king Ashmedai.
That night, she had so troubled his rest that he did not
dare close his eyes. And she came back night after
night. She would appear unexpectedly, and always she
was laughing. She laughed as she danced. She laughed
as she sang, as she climbed walls, and as she
pirouetted. She laughed as she came to the side of his
bed and bent over him so he could see her glowing
eyes. Hananèl was beside himself with fear. Suppose
she touched him with her hand, with her lips? The
more he tried to drive her from his thoughts, the more
she imposed her ungodly and provocative presence on
him. Only by weeks of pitilessly mortifying his flesh—
long fasts, self-laceration, and plunging into the cold
river—was he able to calm his spirit and drive the
vision of her from his mind. Then, at the supreme
moment when, at the side of his Kabbalist Master, he
was going to force the hand of the Lord and so bring
salvation and safety to his people—at that moment,
the woman appeared once more, voluptuous and
laughing, before his tightly closed eyes. It was then
that the raging dog had leapt at them and attacked his
Master. And so the Messiah remained in chains behind
the iron gate of his celestial prison. And it was

because of Hananèl's weakness that the children of
Israel remained in exile and now were in the shadow
of death.

Yes, Hananèl did indeed owe reparation to his
people.

Hananèl has not given up his study of the Kabbalah.
Does he, then, know the perilous art of penetrating
the dreams of others? The art is mentioned in *The
Gaze of the Abyss,* a work as old as the Sefer Yetzira, the
Book of Creation. He who masters that art has the
power to remake the dreams of others as he wishes;
he can make bitter the dreams of the irreverent and
happy those of the just. The Blessed Madman does
not know it, but sensing the coming calamity as
Passover is approaching, he invades the Archbishop's
dream to enlist him as an ally against the enemy's evil
intentions toward the Jewish community.

But hasn't the decree spelling out those intentions
already been sealed?

When Mendel returns, he is out of breath. He is
leading a young priest, a frail-looking person with a
thin face, hidden behind tortoiseshell glasses. The
man's furtive glance suggests he is nowhere at ease.
He keeps his hands in the sleeves of his cassock and
tries to overcome his nervousness. He bows
respectfully, and when he speaks, it sounds as if he is
speaking reluctantly. He starts out haltingly and keeps
interrupting himself by coughing.

"The Honorable Rabbi will please . . . will please excuse us . . . excuse us for coming . . . coming and disturbing him in the middle of the night . . . but . . . but please understand, sir. . . . It's a matter . . . it's an urgent matter. . . ." He looks down and then casts a sidelong glance at Mendel before stammering: "And to tell the truth, sir, it's a private matter. . . . The Rabbi will please understand. . . ."

As he listens to the priest, Hananèl is thinking, If he wants to be alone with me, he must be embarrassed about something. Who knows, maybe he's sick, he or someone in his family. But I'm not a doctor. So maybe he wants me to intercede with heaven for him? The young scholar signals to Big Mendel to leave. Mendel backs out of the room, obviously disapproving, as if he fears some threat to his Master.

"Now, what may I do for you?" Hananèl asks the priest in a tone he hopes is both courteous and self-assured.

"I have a message . . . a message for . . . for His Honor the Rabbi," the priest replies.

"I am not a rabbi."

"Your assistant believes . . . he believes you are. . . . And so does the person . . . so does the person who sent me."

So this is not the one who is expecting something from me; it's not about him or his personal problems. The thought worries Hananèl. Then who is it about? Who else could have need of a Jew like me? The Archbishop, that's who it must be. What's he suffering from? Insomnia perhaps? What's he afraid of?

"I'm listening," Hananèl says. "You have a message for me?"

"From . . . it is from His Eminence Archbishop Báranyi."

"And what is the message?"

"His Eminence asks . . . he asks to speak with you . . . in person."

"Well then, tell him I'll receive him."

"If I may . . . if I may make a suggestion to The Honorable Rabbi . . . His Eminence is expecting him at his residence . . . at the Archbishop's residence."

"When would he like to see me?"

"Right now."

Hananèl is about to ask why the hurry, but he holds his tongue. Any show of disrespect toward a high dignitary of the Church could cause harm to the community.

"A carriage . . . a carriage is waiting for us at the gate," says the priest.

"I'll be ready in a moment."

Hananèl buttons up his caftan, puts on his overcoat and hat, and walks to the door that Mendel is holding open. "I will accompany the Rabbi," Mendel says in a tone that brooks no contradiction. They are already seated in the carriage when Hananèl tells Mendel to fetch their prayer shawls and phylacteries. "Who knows, we may have to stay there more than just a few hours."

Mendel cannot keep from shivering. Does the Rebbe know something he doesn't? He asks, "Is that all I should bring?"

"Yes," his young Master says. "We'll look to the

Lord for whatever else we may need." His words,
though intended to reassure, sound foreboding to his
aide and friend.

The carriage, drawn by two strong horses, rapidly
crosses the streets of the small provincial town
through a newly profound darkness, to which it is
hard to become accustomed, particularly for people
who never go out at night. Since March 19, when the
Germans arrived, only an occasional streetlight has
been turned on, for fear of air raids. The young priest
sits silently beside the coachman. Hananèl is reciting
psalms. Mendel sits fidgeting. Where are they taking
us? he wonders. When will we get there? When will
we return, and in what condition? He hesitates before
questioning the priest, then does so whispering,
hoping not to be heard by Hananèl. The priest does
not answer. To prison, that's where they're taking us,
and the Rebbe has already figured it out, Mendel is
thinking. That's how he knew we would need our
ritual objects. What will become of our community?
And of my wife and children? He turns to the Rebbe,
but Hananèl is absorbed in the psalms and listens only
to their silent song.

Far away, the dawn is breaking. The sky as it
reddens is pure and delicate. Almost all the snow is
gone from the rooftops. Nature awakens as if to a
promise of life and happiness. Spring is on the
doorstep. The trees, stirred by a light wind, are tracing
their slender beauty on the horizon. "Soon it will be
time to say our morning prayers," Mendel murmurs,
but still the young scholar does not reply. His silence is
not threatening, but the priest's is. Mendel doesn't

understand what is happening, and that disturbs him. Luckily, it will soon be light. I'll see the Rebbe's face, and then I'll know, he thinks, trying to reassure himself.

After two hours of travel, the carriage reaches an outlying section of the city and pulls up in front of an impressive building that occupies half a block. The priest steps down, pulls a bell, and speaks to a watchman, who opens the iron gate. The priest respectfully asks the young Jew to accompany him. Mendel gives him his arm to lean on. In his other hand, he holds the prayer shawls and phylacteries. "This isn't a prison," he mutters. "That's something, anyway." They cross a courtyard and enter a luxurious building several stories high. Deep carpets, old paintings, lit candles everywhere. Absorbed in his thoughts, Hananèl slowly climbs the stairs to the second floor. They approach a door at the far end of a long hallway. "You stay here," the priest tells Mendel, whose objections are silenced by a gesture from Hananèl.

The door opens, revealing a room lit by a huge chandelier hanging from the ceiling. A desk is littered with books and various objects. Hananèl looks straight ahead as he enters, telling himself he will not be afraid. The man seated there, hands folded in front of him, is thin and his face is bony under the red skullcap. His gaze is icy. He waits a moment before speaking the words that have been haunting him forever: "So it is you."

The young Jew stands still and replies, "I don't know what you mean."

"Of course you do. You know perfectly well."

Hananèl decides not to insist. The prelate motions toward a chair.

"I prefer to remain standing."

The Archbishop looks down, then speaks in an anguished voice. "What do you want of me? Tell me, tell me everything. We are both men of God, you and I. We can speak from the heart."

"I still don't know what you're talking about."

"You're after me; you're pursuing me even into my dreams."

"I have nothing to do with it," Hananèl replies. "Perhaps the Lord is making use of me to address your conscience." The Archbishop is silent. Now the young scholar is inspired, and he continues in a tone that is both harsh and intense. "And if the Lord is using me, I have no right to remain concealed. Is it to please the Lord that you neither act nor speak out at this fateful time for the children of Israel? They are in danger, as you well know. The Germans are here. Will they do to us what they're doing to our brothers and sisters in Poland? My heart tells me they will. And what does your heart tell you?"

"Sit down. . . . Please be seated. . . ."

Hananèl remains on his feet. The Archbishop sits up straight: "Why are you speaking like this to me? You're hurting me, and I don't deserve it. I've never persecuted Jews. I've never preached hatred of Jews. But you're making me suffer. Why? What have I done to you that you should trouble my rest and even my sleep?" Suddenly, his tone of voice changes. "And besides . . ." He stops for a moment, as if to gather his strength. "Who do you think you are that you dare address me in His Holy Name?"

He leans forward so he can better study the face of the young visitor, who is too calm, too sure of himself. Now, just as suddenly, he is seized by panic. He cries out from the depths of his being. "No! No! It cannot be true! You cannot be . . ."

He collapses to his knees.

The young scholar helps him up and says, "Now we can begin."

THURSDAY, 10:00 A.M. "YOU'RE LOOKING FOR someone?"

Gamaliel was daydreaming. Now the voice of his self-appointed guide rouses him.

"Can I help you?"

Gamaliel pauses a moment before answering. "Yes, I'm looking for building four, ward three."

"Yes, I know where it is. Come, I'll show you."

His guide seems to know his way around. He's a stoop-shouldered elderly man with puffy cheeks and a pointed black goatee. Behind horn-rimmed glasses, his eyes light up when he speaks, but his face remains expressionless. Instinct tells Gamaliel to be cautious: There is something disturbing in the old man's manner.

"My wife's there, too. She's been there since . . . Well, I don't recall anymore since when. . . . She left me . . . all I know is I'm alone . . . have been for a long time."

The man blows on his hands. Is he cold, just when Gamaliel is beginning to feel hot? His wavering voice is shot through with remorse. Remorse over letting his wife leave him? Over forgetting what day she left? Gamaliel studies him: He's met too many people, in too many lands, not to sense a warning signal.

"It's a depressing place," the old man says. "Depressing for those who live there, and for the rest."

"The rest?"

"The rest of us." And after a pause, he adds, "You, too, are here to see your wife?"

"No." Should he tell him he's not married? Gamaliel is in no mood to confide in this man.

"Maybe she's your mother?"

"No, not that, either." This fellow is getting on my nerves with his interrogation, Gamaliel is saying to himself, but the old man backs off.

"What right do I have to be asking? We're all separated from someone we love."

Gamaliel's thoughts turn once again to his two daughters, Katya so far away, Sophie so estranged, both so hostile, and once again the pain is so sharp, it takes his breath away. Better not think about that, he tells himself. This is no time to relax his vigilance.

"Now take God, for example," the old man is saying. "He was separated from His Creation, and His Creation betrayed Him. Ever since, He's been feeling the same melancholy as the rest of us. And the same remorse."

So now he thinks he's a theologian, Gamaliel thinks morosely. They are crossing a courtyard. The quiet that meets them is so heavy, it's palpable. To Gamaliel, it's a message he cannot decode: The silence of the mad is different from our own. Is it their home, or their prison? Is it a wall, or is it the light that illuminates the wall? Do they consider themselves intruders here, just as more and more he feels himself a stranger in the so-called real world? Most of all, Gamaliel hopes the old man won't resume his chatter. If he does, Gamaliel will run away. A breeze whispers through the trees without disturbing their branches. Whence does it come? Who sent it? To stir what memories? Rebbe Nahman of Bratslav believed the wind carries messages from unhappy princes to their brides, who have been carried off by the forest spirits. In Hebrew, the word for wind is the same as for breath and spirit. But nowadays, people use the word to express disdain: "No need to listen to what he has to say; it's just wind." Gamaliel, on the other hand, takes it seriously: if only it would agree to take a message to his daughters . . .

"Let's sit for a moment," the old man suggests. "At my age, my legs will no longer do what I tell them. There . . . on that bench. It's the lovers' bench. So many lovers sat there to escape, to love, to let loose . . . and to betray. I know all about that. . . ." He pauses to take a good look at Gamaliel's features. "Have you ever sat on this bench? And how was she, that woman in your arms? Go on, tell me about it."

"I never set foot in this hospital before today."

"And she?"

"She who?"

"Are you sure she's not here, the woman you once loved, the woman you still love?"

"I'm sure of nothing."

The old man's face darkens. "I hope you didn't come here in vain."

"So do I."

After what seems like a long moment's reflection, the old man looks Gamaliel straight in the eye and says, "And what if I tell you I'm the one you came for?"

Should I take pity on him, or use my fatigue as a pretext to get away from him? thinks Gamaliel as he sits down. All is perfectly arranged here. Everything is in its place—clean, antiseptic. Not a speck of dust on the bench. Nonetheless, the old man takes out his handkerchief and diligently wipes off the seat. Gamaliel looks over at the windows on the two sides of the courtyard. They are dark and opaque. Yet he feels hundreds of pairs of curious or angry eyes watching his every move. Why are they interested in him? Do they want to warn him of some danger stalking him? Advise him to turn around and leave?

"I used to work here as a guide and gardener," the old man says, out of breath. "You can't imagine. . . . It was a long time ago. I knew all the doctors, all the nurses. The patients were my friends. I protected them from fear. Poor people, they were so afraid they'd be shaking, terrified of the electroshock treatment. You're lucky—you don't know what fear is, at least not that kind. And my poor wife . . ."

Gamaliel, more and more irritated, retreats into silence. The old man talks of fear, but what can he know about it, this solid citizen, well dressed, free to go where he wants when he wants? As for Gamaliel, the accursed refugee, it would take very little for the ground to slip out from under his feet. Should I tell this harmless well-meaning chatterbox that I've known every kind of fear? he wonders. Fear in Budapest. Fear of the Nyilas, the Hungarian Nazis, of the local police, of the German soldiers, and later, in Vienna, the fear of the unknown, the physical fear when confronted by a border guard, the fear felt by the refugee, the exiled, the hungry, the person who's been uprooted and is living clandestinely, the fear of showing one's afraid . . .

"My poor wife," the old man is saying. "How she suffered, flat on her back, thin as a rail, handcuffed to the iron cot, waiting for the first wave to hit, the first shock to shoot through her body and rip her brain apart . . ."

Gamaliel is no longer listening to the old man's soliloquy; he's thinking about the patient he's going to see. Can it be that she is someone he knows? A neighbor from back then, in Budapest? Companion of a one-night stand somewhere along the fields of flowers or dusty roads of this planet? A small shy voice somewhere inside him whispers, Suppose it's Ilonka? If it is, will she remember him? After all, it's been what seems like centuries since their ways parted. She stayed home, in her apartment, working at her trade of nightclub singer, living her life, whereas he . . . He has so many questions for her. About his mother. Who turned her in? What was she wearing? What did she carry in her pathetic little suitcase when she climbed into the cattle car? And about his father. Who tortured him in the interrogation cell at the notorious counterespionage headquarters on Andràssy Utca? Did his comrades help? What were their names? How did he maintain his Jewishness far from his own people? When and how did he die? So many things Gamaliel doesn't know but wants to find out. He can't even list them all. What questions should he ask Ilonka, if indeed it is she waiting there, to rouse her will to remember the distant and painful past? He knows only that the elusive, nebulous answers he seeks lie somewhere in a memory not his own, and that he cannot die in peace until he knows. Fortunately, Ilonka knows. For it is she he came to see. But is it she? Not necessarily. After all, that the patient speaks Hungarian means nothing; many Hungarians live in America.

"What's on your mind?"

The old man's intrusive question is exasperating. Gamaliel feels like telling him it's none of his business. He shouldn't pester a stranger like this. Let him go pick on someone else. But the old man is pitiful. Why hurt his feelings? Maybe he should just throw the question back at him.

"As for me," the old man says, as if he'd read Gamaliel's mind, "what concerns me is language—that is, language in relation to electroshock treatment." And he launches into a learned monologue on the connections between philology and semiotics as they relate to anthropology and psychiatry. "Yes indeed, you can tell if a person is in a state of advance or decline according to the words he uses to define those conditions. It's all in the language. . . . Didn't Leibniz say that language is the finest monument a people can build? Every word has its double, as does man: This double accompanies man, or denies him; it is always the aggressor. It distorts the reality that the word transmits. But where is truth? To flush it out, to corner it—there's a goal for the seeker. And then, if he digs deeply enough into the word, he will find a truth set forth by our most remote, least-known ancestors. . . ."

The old man pauses to pose the next question. "But if that word is telling a lie, is man up to the task of discovering the truth on which the word once was based? But then again, what is a lie? The opposite of the truth? But then what is truth? The Sophists, those masters of rhetoric, did not even ask the question. What interested them was the art of convincing. Now, there is conquest in conviction, and electroshock is the dreadful conqueror who convinces. But how about the conquered? Who speaks for them, for those who learned only to howl? What would we know of Plato and Confucius if their ability to express themselves had died with them? Similarly with Moses: What if the word of God had not burst forth from his lips but had sunk into the sands?"

Well, well . . . Gamaliel can't help smiling. Why didn't I have this fellow for a teacher? Who knows, I might have less trouble writing.

"It all would have been so different," the old man continues. "Yes, it would have been so very different if these great thinkers with their world-shaking ideas, these creators with their universal visions, had undergone even a minute of electroshock!"

Now Gamaliel listens more carefully. He must be a talented writer, this man obsessed, or else a frustrated orator. Suddenly, he finds the old man interesting. He'd invite him to the nearby coffee shop if he had the time and had thought to put enough money in his pocket. Gamaliel likes to draw from wells that are new to him, to be a link between people who have nothing in common. To pluck on their heartstrings, to awaken them to enthusiasm. Rescue them from boredom and oblivion. What tragedy is this cultivated, outgoing man living through with his wife, or far from her, that he is so concerned with a treatment that doctors hardly ever use nowadays? What scream is he stifling under this flood of words he pours into the ear of the first passerby he meets on his journey? Meanwhile, the old man is scratching his beard with an air of concentration and is still talking away. Now, no doubt to impress even more, he discourses on Meister Eckhart and his book on divine solace, on Pindar and his concept of silence; he is mingling Oriental philosophy, nuclear science, political gossip, and biblical exegesis, all apparently without noticing whether Gamaliel is really paying attention: "The unfortunate thing, the terribly unfortunate thing, is that the psychiatrists here put themselves on a pedestal, and so they no longer know how to listen. As for me, I know. I don't just listen to human beings; I listen to animals. I understand them; I sense what they're asking for. I listen to trees that are in fear of drought, and the wind that plays at drawing clouds, then erasing them. I listen to blades of grass that moan softly as they grow. I listen to the earth we walk on—it's resigned to being trampled. I even listen to the stones. People think a stone feels nothing, has nothing to say. Well, they're wrong. Stones have their own language. Yes, it takes them years or centuries to communicate with one another. So what? They're patient; they can wait, can't they? How old is our beloved planet? What's a century and a half compared with billions of years? I'm telling you, our caretakers should learn to listen. . . ."

How well he speaks, Gamaliel thinks admiringly. That means he's not a writer. He teaches literature—that's it. I should get his address, look him up, ask him to tell me about his theories on language.

"Luckily, the new administration here has changed everything, you understand," the old man continues. "All because of me—believe me when I say that. I could no longer stand my poor wife's suffering. I complained. I threatened. I got people in high places to put in a word. And then, my dear sir, from one day to the next, medical policy in this place did change for the better. I'm telling you this to reassure you. You have nothing to fear for that patient who is dear to you. I'm not saying electroshock treatment has been completely abolished, but that it's never practiced on people who are unable to speak for themselves. It's only used on people . . ." Here the old man, while still fiddling with his beard, stops talking in order to observe the effect of his words on his companion.

Gamaliel starts in surprise and asks, "Used only on whom?"

"On people like you," the old man replies with a chuckle. "People who claim to be innocent, and therefore sound in mind and body. But don't you understand, dear sir, that innocence makes you all sick? In this world, innocence is a disease. And I am one of those who knows how to cure it." He points to the fourth floor of the building. "Look at the fourth window on the left. Look at it carefully. It doesn't look like anything special. But that's where we take care of big shots like you."

Here's the poisoned gift of the gods, thinks Gamaliel, who has suddenly realized why he's feeling so exasperated. Great! I happened on this guide, who is bright and erudite— and crazy enough to be put in a straitjacket. How can I rid myself of him without offending him? Suppose he's violent? That's all I need this morning—some kind of incident. Gamaliel looks around and spots a pair of white coats, a man and a woman, coming out of the building facing him. The pair walk toward the bench. Gamaliel recognizes his earlier benefactor as the man in the white coat, who now addresses the old man.

"Here you are back, Martin! How was your visit with your family? But I thought you were supposed to come back last night."

"My pass was good for twenty-four hours," the old man replies, eyes down, suddenly humble.

"I know that," says the woman. "But we like you. You're our dear Mr. Johnson. We value your company. One day a month is just what you need to rest and pull yourself together. But we miss you. You know that, don't you?"

The old man has made himself even smaller.

"I think I'd better go back to my room."

Gamaliel looks over at the woman doctor. Around forty. Still attractive. Slender. Delicate features.

"You know him?" she asks.

"I just met him. What a character! I could listen to him for hours."

"Well, good luck!" She stretches out her hand, then asks, "Who are you looking for here?"

"I don't know. . . ." Quickly, he corrects himself. "Wait, I'm not like him. . . ."

"You are lucky."

"I'm looking for a woman. . . . Sorry, a woman in the hospital here . . . a patient of Hungarian origin."

"Oh, then you must be Gamaliel."

"How did you know that?"

"I'm the one who gave Bolek the message for you. Excuse me, I forgot to tell you that I'm the doctor treating that patient. According to her papers, she's named Zsuzsi Szabó, but who knows? We have no further information on her. Does that name mean anything to you?"

"No, I don't think so," says Gamaliel, "but I thought her name was Lili Rosenkrantz."

"I'm Lili Rosenkrantz," the young doctor explains, smiling.

"Oh, I see."

"But Zsuzsi Szabó—that name really doesn't ring a bell with you?"

"No, it doesn't."

The two doctors exchange a look.

"Come with us," she says.

They walk in silence. A strange thought occurs to Gamaliel: Suppose these two are also out of their minds?

They don't seem it, but who knows? A while ago, the old man didn't seem so deranged, either. And yet . . . Maybe I'd do better to go away and come back another day. But if that woman is Ilonka . . . No, it can't be. In 1956, Ilonka stayed in Budapest. In Paris, he'd gone to the Red Cross as soon as he could and asked them to make a search for her, and he'd tried other connections that he thought might find out something. It was all in vain. Hope for a miracle? Absurd. No, not so absurd if Ilonka was right. Time and again, she'd told him she believed in miracles, but she always added a warning: "My boy, if you want the Lord to help you, then you must help Him. It's too difficult, even for Him, unless you help. We mustn't expect Him to deal alone with all the madmen and imbeciles and scoundrels who make trouble in this poor little world of His, where there are so many more sinners than saints. Why should we expect Him to carry all that burden on His shoulders? You have to give Him a hand. You understand?" "But," he would complain, "how can a little boy— even a big boy—be any help to God Almighty, who is stronger than all the kings on earth?" "I'll show you how," Ilonka would say, and she'd hug him.

They are following a long, poorly lit corridor on the fourth floor when the woman doctor stops by a half-open window to whisper to a tall, imperious-looking nurse. The doctor's face darkens.

"Our patient needs emergency care," she explains to Gamaliel. "I'm very sorry. Could you come back this afternoon?"

"Of course," Gamaliel replies.

The doctor presses a button, a door opens, and she disappears. But the memory of Ilonka lingers. Gamaliel remembers how devoted she was. As if she had been his mother, she did everything to keep him busy in his mother's absence. Among her friends there was a French journalist. No doubt he was using the little boy as a pretext when he said to him, "I'll be your teacher." Always elegant, wearing a tie, his pockets filled with scraps of paper, the journalist would give the boy French lessons to pass the hours until Ilonka came home from singing in the nightclub. She was so pleased that she kissed the journalist on both checks, and then he came more and more often. So it was that Gamaliel learned enough French to get by when he arrived in Paris.

He remembers Ilonka's laugh, her delicate hands, her tenderness. She promised him she'd teach him how to live.

She was so good at it.

GAMALIEL WAS AT LOOSE ENDS AFTER HE LEFT the hospital. His thoughts turned to the sayings of his old teacher, Rabbi Zusya: "To a man born blind, God is blind. To a sick child, God is unfair. To the condemned man in prison, God is also a prisoner. On the other hand, to a free man, God is both the source of his freedom and its justification. To be free is to be made in God's image. Anyone who tries to place himself between the freedom of God and the freedom of man, between the word of man and the thought of God, is only being false to both man and God."

And also: "I no longer understand the Creator of human beings. Why did He put us on this earth? Was it to glorify Himself? These earthworms, these specks of dust, able, if not eager, to corrupt all that is noble in the soul, unfortunate mortals who need bread, water, and air to survive, how could they in their wretchedness bring forth true glory and offer it to Him? For what reason should He have need of them, He

THE TIME OF THE UPROOTED

who is the beginning and the achievement and the rebirth of all that is and ever shall be? I no longer understand."

And this: "I, Zusya, son of Rachel, I say unto Thee, God of Abraham, Isaac, and Jacob, that Thy creation is racing to its doom through a land of ashes. If Thou dost not see this, if Thou seest it and dost not intervene, if Thou hast forgotten the procession of doomed Jewish children marching through the night to the flames, God of charity, I will tell my prayer to howl. I'll no longer have the strength to invoke Thy Holy Name. I will command my mind to close Thee out of my thoughts forever."

"Péter, my child," said Ilonka, stroking his hair, "remember that your name's Péter now. Not Gamaliel, but Péter. Remember this name: Péter Kertész. You're my little nephew; you're the youngest son of my big sister, Magda. You must remember that; it's important. Your life depends on it, and so does mine. Please repeat it after me. Péter, not Gamaliel. Your mother's named Magda. Magda Kertész. And you're Péter Kertész."

At first, Péter hadn't liked Ilonka's caresses, for fear they might make him forget his mother's warm and appeasing touch. But in time, he came to accept them. Besides, she never insisted; she never pressed herself on him.

"Your mama, God save her, has become my best friend," she told him one evening before leaving for the cabaret. She continued as she prepared his dinner. "What a woman your mama is; she's all heart. We've just recently become friends, but she matters to me. I've learned a lot from her. I don't know what I'd do with my life without her. I'd die of shame. . . . My family lives far away, in the Carpathians. My parents are poor and sickly. We'll go visit them one day, maybe in July. No, that's not a good idea. They'd know that you're not Magda's son—they see her children every Sunday in church. We'll spend the summer here, and, God willing, we'll try to find a way to get in touch with your parents." She quickly corrected herself: "No, bad idea. Your papa's in prison and your mama's in hiding. Too many informers on the street. They're like mad dogs the way they sniff around, hunting out your people. May the Lord crush them like rats. You don't know who you can trust anymore."

Ilonka's sharp, insistent voice only deepened Péter's melancholy. It aroused a flood of memories that, from her first words, broke over him in waves. The meals of the Sabbath, the simple purity of the Sabbath, his mother's delicate hands lighting the candles on the table covered with a white tablecloth—that image would stay with Gamaliel forever—his father's gentle, nostalgic songs. The peace of the Sabbath: Banished were all melancholy and all passion, all worries, regrets, thoughts of failure, all remorse. The sublime meaning of the Sabbath: the final reconciliation of the Creator and his Creation, of the Jew and his soul. But now, in Ilonka's quiet home, there was no more Sabbath.

Besides, she was trying to persuade him that for the time being—only the time being, she insisted—he must forget everything that had to do with the past.

"Tell yourself you're a Christian."

"But my father . . ."

"I know, I know. Your father wants you to be a Jew, and so do I, believe me. I'd never do anything contrary to his will."

"But then . . ."

"Péter, my child, listen to me carefully. Your father wants first of all and above all for you to stay alive. If you're a Jew, the odds are against you. Your mama understood that; otherwise, she'd never have left you. If she's in hiding, it's not just for her own good; it's for yours also. That's why she put you in my care. To save both your lives. You also, you have to understand."

"But I don't want to be a Christian! I don't!"

"I'm not asking you to, not really. I'm just asking you to make believe. . . ."

She fastened around his neck a silver chain, from which hung a small cross.

"This doesn't mean anything. I mean, not for you it doesn't. In your heart you're still a Jew, just like your parents. Make believe that it's Purim. I've lived around Jews enough to know that on that day everyone wears a mask. And now you, too, are in disguise. What's wrong with that? The day will come when you'll take off your mask and everything will be the way it was before."

She taught him several prayers that every Christian child can recite by heart:

"Repeat after me: 'Our Father, who art in heaven . . .' "

Péter had no problem with that prayer. After all, it was addressed to God, not to Jesus Christ. He remembered a prayer that his father specially loved, Avinu Malkenu: "Our Father, our King, hear our voices, take pity on Thy children." And also "Our Father, our King, for Thy sake have compassion on us." He could recite Ilonka's prayer in peace without betraying his father. It was harder in the case of the Hail Mary. Who was this gentle Mary, blessed and adored, who was asked to pray for people? The mama of God? But how could God have a mother, He the invisible Creator of the heavens and of the earth? How could He have a mother, since He wasn't a man?

"Mary, holy Mary, is the mama of Jesus," explained Ilonka, patient as always. "Jesus is our Lord. Therefore, Mary is the mother of our Lord."

"And your Lord is God?"

"He is the Son of God."

"When you pray to the Lord to save us, to help us, who are you praying to? The father or the son?"

"To both of them. But also—"

"Also what?"

"Also there's the Holy Spirit."

"What? You have three gods?"

"No, three divinities."

"You mean that seriously? You're telling me that the Christians believe in two gods and three divinities? But then you must not know our Shma. I was only three when my father, sitting on my bed, taught me the most important of our prayers: 'Hear, O Israel, the Lord our God, the Lord is One.' How can you ask me to say that there's more than one God?"

Poor Ilonka didn't know which way to turn. She realized she shouldn't have spoken to him about the Holy Trinity. Now the child was even more confused. Having run out of arguments, she could only say to him what her parents had often said to her when she was a child: "Later on you'll understand."

Péter at last gave in. But from then on, he put more energy and determination into his daily recitation of the morning prayer Modeh Ani and the evening Shma Yisrael. Lying in bed with his eyes closed, he would begin his prayers by murmuring, "My name is Gamaliel. My father's name is

Pinhas. My mother's name is Ruth." Ilonka did not object. She just warned him to be careful and to be sure not to mix any Hebrew words into the Christian prayers he recited in Hungarian.

Recalling that time in his life, Gamaliel has a memory of familiarity and warmth. Brave, wonderful Ilonka. Why had she been so kind to him? What made her risk her liberty and her life—a quiet, if not very happy life—to protect a little Jewish boy who, without his parents, had no one else to turn to?

Ilonka had become more and more worried. The hatred expressed by those swine the Nyilas, the Hungarian Nazis, was too violent. The arrests too frequent. As were the roundups, which were ever more carefully organized. The net was tightening around the Jews in hiding. There were too many informers, too many police raids on nearby buildings, too many searches, too many screams and tears in the night. Not all of those arrested were able to hold out under torture. The jails were overflowing.

"Now listen, my boy," Ilonka said. "When I'm at work, you open the door for no one. You understand? No one at all. If someone knocks at the door, you stay still. Don't move. If someone calls out, you stay silent. Be careful: Don't make a sound, not even when you breathe."

No one knocked at the door that night. But the little Jewish boy did not fall asleep. He was wide-awake and on edge, sitting quietly in a corner, hands on his knees, waiting for Ilonka to come home. His anxiety grew by the minute. It became thicker, heavier; it stuck to his skin, crushed his chest. He wanted to cry; then he wanted to die. To keep himself under control, he imagined his mother's face: She was smiling at him, and it broke his heart. Where was she? "In the neighborhood," Ilonka had told him. Why so vague? She thought it was better that way. It was dangerous to know too much. But now where was Ilonka? Why was she late coming home? If she'd been arrested, who would look after him? The dawn was breaking, red and fiery, when he heard the key turn in the lock.

"If you only knew what bad luck I had," Ilonka said while she took off her coat. "This curfew was a lot stricter last night. All of us had to stay in the cabaret, including the manager, even though he's one of those filthy Nyilas."

She hugged him close and kissed him on the forehead.

"You must have been scared, Péter, my child. I'm so sorry. I'll find some other way to protect us next time if the roundups start again and those swine are causing trouble."

The little boy felt safe in her arms.

"Now let's go to sleep. I'm worn-out and you must be, too."

They stretched out on the one bed, still in their clothes, and she went right to sleep, but he did not. That afternoon, she buttered some slices of bread for him, but he couldn't eat. Anxiety had robbed him of his appetite.

Ilonka picked up a rumor the following week that the Nyilas had uncovered more information—more lists, more addresses—and, with the Germans' help, they knew just where to strike next. The Jews were in more danger than ever.

She invited the boy to sit by her on the sofa.

"I'm taking you with me tonight," she told him.

"Where are we going?"

"To the cabaret."

"What's a cabaret?"

"It's a place where people go to have a good time."

"What kind of people?"

"We used to get rich and important people, but now it's a lower class."

"Why can't they just stay home and have a good time?"

Ilonka chuckled and patted him on the head. "How intelligent you are, dear boy, but they're not that smart. They feel more at home with strangers in a cabaret than with their families in their own homes."

He thought a moment, then asked anxiously, "But you'll stay with me?"

"Of course, my darling."

"The whole time?"

"No, not the whole time."

"Where will you be? Far away?"

"No, I'll be close by."

"So we'll be together."

"No, not exactly."

The little boy drew his head down between his shoulders. "I don't understand. How can we be together without being together?"

She took his hand. "Don't worry. I won't be far away. I'll be on the stage."

"The stage? What's that?"

"You'll see. It's for the actors, the musicians, and the singers. That's what I am, a singer. You'll watch me sing."

"Can I always watch you?"

"Always."

"But it's from far away? Very far away?"

Seeing the boy's anxiety, Ilonka found it difficult to hold back her own tears. "Calm down, my dear. I'll never leave you. You'll be safe backstage while I'm singing, and the rest of the time you'll be in the audience."

With that, she drew him close. He caught his breath in astonishment when he realized he loved the warmth he was suddenly feeling. When Ilonka kissed his cheeks, they were on fire. Then he thought of his mother. He squirmed, but Ilonka was too strong for him, and he surrendered. When she let him go, he felt a strange sensation of loss.

"Don't cry," she told him as she stroked his head. "Especially not at the cabaret. I'll stay with you, always. So you mustn't cry. Only Jews cry. So even when Gamaliel feels like crying, Péter must not."

Why was she telling him not to cry, while she herself went on sobbing, as if she had a premonition?

"I won't cry," he said at last. "I'll wait for you."

He was silent for a moment, then went on: "I'll wait for you the way I'm waiting for my mama." Again he stopped; then he corrected himself. "No, not like that, it's different. . . ."

"I know, my dear, I know. We only have one mother, and you're waiting for her. And so am I. She'll come back. The good Lord of the Jews will bring her back, you'll see."

She went to the mirror to put on her makeup, as night fell abruptly on the silent, fearful city.

They hurried along a seemingly endless street, passing soldiers, gendarmes, and young fascists, but never a Jew—it was almost curfew time for the Jews. Forcing a smile, Ilonka led her friend's son into the already-crowded cabaret. She seated him at a vacant table in a dark corner, no doubt designated for run-of-the-mill customers. It was loud and smoky in the cabaret. Péter didn't know which way to look. Waiters hurried to and fro, staring straight ahead, balancing full and empty plates, bottles, glasses. Musicians on a dimly lit stand were playing slow, melancholy tunes, to which no one was listening; now and then, one of them would come down and mingle with the customers. Sounds of laughter, exclamations, greetings. Bodies intertwined on the dance floor, attracting and repelling, exchanging acceptance and rejection. Gestures of delight, and also outbursts of anger.

"Don't look," Ilonka said. "Don't watch even when I'm onstage. Promise me you won't. Don't listen when I'm singing. Close you eyes and make believe you're somewhere else, with your papa and your mama. . . ."

Péter-Gamaliel didn't understand why he shouldn't watch, but he dutifully nodded in consent.

"Never forget that you're my nephew," Ilonka continued, speaking very softly. "You're the son of my big sister. You live in Fehérvàros. Son of Magda. You go to church with me on Sundays. If someone asks you whether you're Catholic or Calvinist, say that you don't know."

"Calvinist? What's that?"

"A good Christian."

"So all Christians are Calvinists?"

"No, not all, just those who believe Calvin was Christ's most faithful disciple."

"They were friends?"

"I don't know about that. They've been dead a long time, may they rest in peace. But let's talk about people you're supposed to know, like the pastor or the priest. His name is Miklós. Say it."

"Miklós. The pastor's name is Miklós."

"And you?"

"Péter."

"What are you?"

"A Calvinist Jew named Péter."

"No, never say that!" Ilonka exclaimed in alarm.

"A Catholic Jew who—"

"No!"

"Then what should I say?"

"That you're my nephew. Say it."

"I'm your nephew."

"Where are your parents?"

"In the village. At home."

"Where's your home?"

"In Fehérvàros."

She gazed at him affectionately.

"Good, very good. You're awfully intelligent. Your parents were lucky. Someday they'll be proud of you."

She was interrupted by a very heavyset, very blond woman, who whispered in her ear, "Get a move on; you're up next."

The woman cast a curious glance at the boy and asked, "Who's that, your bastard kid?"

"He's my nephew."

"I didn't know—"

"There's a lot of things you don't know," Ilonka replied harshly.

The blonde shrugged and walked off. Ilonka joined her on the stage, which all of a sudden was brightly lit.

"Ladies and gentlemen, distinguished guests . . . ," the blonde shouted in a voice that was surprisingly hoarse, powerful, almost deafening.

Nobody was paying attention to her.

"Ladies and gentlemen," she began again, visibly annoyed. "If you please . . . Quiet down, please. . . . Pretend that your wives—your faithful and hopelessly boring wives—are with you. . . . Come on, let's behave. . . . Especially since you're going to have the good fortune and the honor of listening to a star who's admired and loved—yes, loved by real men, not idiots like you. . . ."

There were catcalls in the audience. "She's loved. Hear that, István? But how? In bed or standing up?" Unflinching, Ilonka launched into a sentimental song that was usually well received, but this time her voice was drowned out by the general hubbub. A voice yelled, "Take off your dress if you want us to listen to you." Another shouted, "Give us a look at what we know you've got." Ilonka played coy, but as she sang, she took off her red-and-green blouse. "More, more," the audience shouted in unison, applauding and making obscene gestures. I mustn't look, Péter reminded himself. She told me not to look. Did he understand that for the first time in his life he was observing a public humiliation? He closed his eyes, only to reopen them immediately. The racket had suddenly ceased. A group of armed Nyilas in uniform were standing at the cabaret's entrance. Silence had fallen like a summons to reality. All eyes except Ilonka's were on the newcomers. Ilonka, still holding her blouse, was gazing at the little boy sitting quietly at his table, a boy who didn't know where to look or what to do with himself.

"Are there any *büdös Zsidók*, any filthy Jews, here?" the leader of the Nyilas demanded.

No one spoke.

"I'll say it once more: Are there any filthy Jews here? If there are, stand up."

No one moved.

At last, a well-dressed man rose and walked over to the Nyilas leader: "Here's my ID, and my Party card. I know everybody here, and I'll vouch for each and every one of them." The Nyilas chief, a fat, surly man with jet black hair and a Hitler mustache, glanced absently at the papers and put them in his pocket. With an impatient gesture, he told his men to follow him and then scatter among the tables, stopping here and there to question a customer, leaf through a wallet, or feel up one of the bar girls' breasts. They were almost through when the leader spotted the boy sitting in his corner.

"You there, who are you?"

Péter panicked and forgot what he'd been taught.

"So maybe you're deaf and dumb? Or you're a Jew?"

"I'm a Caltho, a Calthoist," the boy stammered.

The fat Nyilas burst out laughing.

"Me, too! I'm a Calthoist, too!"

Ilonka spoke from the stage: "He's mine."

An elderly Nyilas broke in: "Aren't you ashamed of yourself? This is no place for children."

"I couldn't leave him home alone."

A bald-headed drunk seized the opening: "You live alone? Want me to come keep you company? We'll have a good time, I guarantee you. The boy? I promise you he won't bother us. We'll send him next door to stay with the neighbors."

Ilonka came down from the stage to stand behind Péter, her hands on his thin shoulders.

"If I came to see you, would you let me in?" the chief Nyilas asked with a sneer.

"Of course," said Ilonka. "All you have to do is check with the boss. He's the one who sets my working hours. And my price."

The Nyilas chief sneered and bowed.

"*Kezét csókolom, kedves aszonoyom.* I kiss your hand, my dear lady."

A moment later, the Nyilas were all gone. At a sign from the owner, the musicians launched into their repertoire of sad and boisterous tunes.

The exhausted Jewish boy went to sleep, his head resting between his arms on the table.

One day, thought Ilonka as she went back to the stage, one day I'll sing for him, I'll show him a good time, I'll make him laugh, I'll rid him of his fear, and show him the beauty of happiness. One day, I'll tell him about my childhood. One day, I'll make love to someone for love's sake. One day, the sight of a man's body won't make me sick. On that day, I'll look at myself without disgust, without remorse.

One day, I'll truly be alive, I'll live from morning to night, I'll smile when I feel like it, and I'll give pleasure to a man I like. One day, I'll wait for evening without an aching heart.

One day, one day.

But, Gamaliel muses, for Ilonka, the blessed saint Ilonka, the charitable, sensual singer who aroused the desire of her enemies and touched the heart of her little Jewish ward, that day never came.

GAMALIEL WALKS TO A SQUARE NEAR THE HOSPItal and sits down on a bench. Three hours to wait until he can meet the old Hungarian patient. How to pass the time? He could drop in on Yasha, who lives not far away, in a small apartment in Brooklyn Heights. From the street, you can see his cat, Misha, always keeping watch from the windowsill. Yasha's love for this animal is strangely touching. The cat responds to the slightest show of affection; Yasha pampers the cat, speaks to him, listens to him, treats him as a close friend. Should he telephone Yasha? Why not? From a nearby booth, he dials the number, which he knows by heart. Five rings, six: no answer. Yasha isn't home. Too bad.

Gamaliel lets himself drift off into memory. He has the

painful feeling that his childhood is fading away in the fog of those distant years in Czechoslovakia and even in Budapest. What can he do to save those years? He's overcome with fatigue. Inexplicably, his brief visit to the hospital has left his mind exhausted. His head aches, his heart is racing, and his legs feel heavy. A moment of weakness? He's sweating, though it's still cool. The days are slow, lethargic, but the years are hurrying by. Soon they'll go up in smoke. Yet they, too, weigh on him, and they keep getting heavier. No way to rid himself of them or to lessen the burden by sharing them with, let's say, a loved one. Age can neither be divided nor multiplied. Time ceases when life ceases. So does everything. Dust thou art, and unto dust shalt thou return. There lies the true mystery: The most beautiful of dreams, the grandest of conquests, all end in the silent indifferent earth.

Sitting under the curving branches of a giant oak, Gamaliel absently watches passersby laughing and arguing, heedless of one another. A yearning clings to him: Even at his age, he misses his parents. The more he thinks about them, the greater the pain in his chest; he can hardly breathe. On the High Holy Days, he always attended synagogue to say Kaddish for them, and his eyes would fill with tears. One day, Rebbe Zusya made an observation he will never forget: "Most people don't realize that the dead live among us. We only become aware of them on the eve of Yom Kippur, during the recitation of the Kol Nidre, but they are always among the living." Is it true? Gamaliel wonders. If it is, then his parents can't be far away. They're dead, but what does that mean? That they are parted from him? Is that what death is, a parting? Will they meet again, on high? Sometimes he talks to them, but they don't answer. Sometimes when he's alone, he tells them about his days, his nights, his struggles, his failures. The worst of those failures was his family life. All lost and gone. His angry wife, Colette, their defiant two daughters. How can he redeem himself in the eyes of his dead parents?

For some time now, he's been thinking about Death. Or rather, it's as if Death were thinking about him. At first, Death was a stranger to him, then it became a neutral onlooker. Now they are well acquainted; it taunts him, casts spells, trying to gain control over him. For many years, he could shake off Death's barbs, could make it back away: "Can't you see I'm busy? Leave me alone. There are things I must do. . . ." But recently his defenses are down. Death is holding on; its shadow clings to him. Last week, or maybe it was yesterday, the Angel of Death—he whom the Talmud calls the Messenger to Men—had replied with a snicker, "You say 'I'? Don't you know that in the blink of an eye I can erase that word from your vocabulary forever?" Gamaliel suddenly remembers the old Sage he'd met in Brooklyn. He, too, had referred to the ban that forbids man to say the word *I*. He showed Gamaliel the passage in the Midrash where it is written that the Ten Commandments were pronounced by Moses rather than by God. God only spoke the first word: *Anokhi*, "I." One evening, Rebbe Zusya looked deep into Gamaliel's eyes and explained, "God alone may use that word; God alone understands its fearful power. That's the sin of pride that comes from idolatry: man putting his own 'I' in the place of the Creator's." At the time, Gamaliel replied, smiling, "At least we stateless ones don't run that risk. We've been robbed not only of our nationality but also of our identity." The Sage shook his head, gently, sadly. "In a sense, but in one sense only, we are all men without a country." "Even

God?" "Yes, God, as well. Of course, God is everywhere, and it is only in the hearts of men that He sometimes feels Himself a stranger." Night had fallen. The old Sage asked his visitor to step outside with him. There, under a starry sky, he confided his only regret: that he had lived his life so far away, not from the King of Kings, the Lord of Creation, but from His creatures, for it is through man, rather than through books, that one can draw near to God. Gamaliel asked, "Why are you telling me that? And why out here on the street?" Now it was Rebbe Zusya's turn to smile as he said, "To teach you a truth that you will find to be very valuable: Regret also is part of man." Gamaliel felt like saying that, in his case, regret dominated his whole being, but he decided to remain silent.

Suddenly, Gamaliel is shivering. His thoughts have drifted away from the old Sage. He is alone again, but no, not quite. A woman is sitting on the bench. He recognizes the doctor, still in her white coat, whom he met at the hospital and who had walked away from him with hardly a word. He restrains a feeling of irritation: By what right is she interrupting his meditations? What is she looking for in his world? He steals a look at her, but all he can see is her profile. She's let down her chestnut hair, so it falls to her shoulders. In days gone by, he would have dropped everything to stroke that hair, those shoulders. But now she just troubles him, especially since he's beginning to feel vaguely attracted to her. She is much younger than he, about forty, maybe a bit older. At his age, he often thinks everyone is younger than he. He looks at her more closely. Now she turns her head slightly toward him, but still avoids his eyes. He's sure those eyes are blue and that she is somehow beautiful, beautiful inside and out. An oval face, expressive features, delicate nose. When he

looked at her that morning, he saw her as through a veil.
Now he sees her up close. Why does she seem so worried?
Her patient's condition? How about asking her? There was a
time when he would have struck up a harmless conversation,
its outcome remaining to be seen; perhaps hc would have
courted her by speaking about his novel, in which the young
Kabbalist has the power to enter into people's minds. Or
about the tzaddik in Brooklyn who knows how to cure
unbearable distress. There was a time he would have, but not
now. He's in no mood to play games that are as old as the
hills. A sudden thought makes him start: Suppose Ilonka herself sent the doctor to me? No, impossible. This doctor does
not know, cannot know the world of connections between
me and Ilonka. Should I ask her anyway, just to be sure?

But he has no time to ask, for it is the doctor who speaks
first. Or rather, she begins to weep. She remains still except
for the tears that run down her handsome features in a
stream, a tiny stream down to the corners of her slightly
parted lips. Gamaliel feels a sudden desire to get to his feet, as
if to flee from some unknown peril. But he resists the urge,
awaiting some sort of sign, a miracle—one of those miracles
that does away with all barriers and frees the soul to speak.
And the miracle does indeed happen. The doctor is still not
looking at him, but it is she who breaks the silence. "I ask
your forgiveness."

Gamaliel is immediately taken with her shy, serious voice.
She reminds him of his past, of desires now cooled.

"Don't say anything," she continues. "And above all, don't
say I've done nothing that calls for your forgiveness. I should
never have let myself go like that, bursting into tears in front
of a stranger, laying my problems on him, making him aware
of my life, of its wreckage. It has nothing to do with you. . . .

I should have given you more time this morning, or else not spoken to you at all. . . . And just now I could have sat on another bench, over there."

She falls silent, and Gamaliel comforts her by quoting a thought of Paritus the One-Eyed, one that the old Sage of the Orient repeated sometimes at nightfall: " 'We do better not to believe in luck: Our Lord forbids it. I'm old enough to draw on my own experience: Everything happens in this world because of encounters. Meaning that since we are here, you and I, brought together by a force we do not understand, we must act as though everything happened in order to make our encounter take place.' "

He moved closer to her.

" 'It may be that we've lived our separate lives just for this moment, this meeting.' "

The words are hardly out of his mouth before he regrets them. Long ago, in another life, he often used that sort of language to attract and seduce women whose misfortune it was that he found them attractive. He no longer does that. Has he lost interest? Is it because he's had enough of love won easily, too easily? Has he given up in despair over Colette's death, Esther's disappearance, Eve's betrayal? This woman beside him arouses in him a different kind of interest. Should he take her hand? No, that might spoil it all. Only their voices should meet, feed each other, become one.

"Look at me," he says. "Look and you'll trust me."

She does so. I was right: Her eyes are blue, thinks Gamaliel. She smiles shyly.

"What's happening to me is going to seem crazy to you. . . . A nightmare. Just a year ago, I was still happy. I had everything a woman could have. And now there's nothing left." She is silent a moment before resuming on a note of resignation. "I suppose that's my fate."

Gamaliel shrugs. "Fate? That's a big word. We mustn't blame everything on it. Fate has a face of its own; it has an address, an identity, a will of its own. Would you like to tell me about it?"

She does not reply at first, as if her mind were elsewhere. Gamaliel takes her hand. She smiles, but it looks like the face a child makes when scolded.

"It's a depressing story," she says. "Besides, I wonder whether you'd even understand it."

"Give it a try, and we'll see. If I don't understand, I'll tell you."

So the young woman begins to speak in a barely audible voice. Sometimes she murmurs so softly, he has to lean close to catch what she is saying. It is as if, because she spends her days inducing her patients to reveal themselves, she can no longer speak of her own problems, her private hurts, but keeps them locked away inside.

"Each of us has a secret garden surrounded by a high fence. But in the end, you have to go on living, even if you're in the crater of a volcano. . . . And what does living mean unless you're helping others come to terms with what threatens them? I was lucky. I was happy, really happy. My only anxiety," she says with a short, scornful laugh, "was at night, going to bed. I dreaded awakening the next morning and finding that my life was only a dream, quickly crushed, easily blown away, stolen by some enemy. But I loved even my fear because it let me savor the gift that life gave me every morning. Yes, I found myself at peace with every new day, and grateful to God for these blessings. No difference between my dream and my life. Indeed, I had a dream of a life. And then . . ."

She pauses, takes a deep breath, as if to muster her strength, and very quickly speaks those few short words that introduce every sad story of a life gone wrong, stricken by misfortune: "And then it happened." She pauses before saying it again. "It happened. One fine day, it happened."

IT'S EXACTLY 7:30 IN THE MORNING. SHE REMEMbers because she's just glanced at the clock on the kitchen wall. The family is having breakfast together, as usual. Orange juice for everyone. Milk for the children, black coffee for the parents. Bread and butter, scrambled eggs, croissants. Al is reading the newspaper, Pamela her book, Ron his workbook. Al looks as though he has something on his mind: the stock market? His wife is about to ask, but he speaks first.

"I'm leaving," he says without looking up from his newspaper.

The children pay no attention. Dad's leaving, the way he always does. He leaves for his office every morning at the same time. And Mom goes to her hospital. But something she hears in his voice causes his wife to put down her coffee and ask, "Where are you going?"

"Away," he says, eyes still glued to the paper.

Now Pamela asks, "Are you going on a trip, Dad?"

"Yes."

"A business trip?" asks Ron.

"Yes."

"For how long?"

"I don't know yet."

"Who's sending you?"

"Nobody."

"What do you mean, 'nobody'?"

"No one is sending me, and no one is expecting me, but I have to leave."

"But you're coming back!" Pamela says.

"Maybe. I have no idea."

Lili wonders if this is just a stupid adolescent game intended to scare them, a show of bad taste, staged to make himself more interesting. A challenge, a test by a retarded pupil. What is she expected to say or do? Burst into tears? Leave, slamming the door behind her? A crazy idea strikes her: Is there another woman in his life? She forces herself to appear calm. "Don't you think we're entitled to an explanation?"

"Yes," he concedes, "but I don't have one."

"Did something happen? Did one of us do something to offend you? Do you have difficulties at work? Do you have a problem with your health? Have you seen the doctor?"

"No, nothing like that."

"But . . . aren't you happy living with us?"

He seems at a loss: "Yes . . . No . . . I don't know. . . . I'm not sure. . . . I'm not sure of anything now."

They all fall silent. Al puts down the paper, stares at them unseeingly. He does not appear unhappy, or embarrassed, or even concerned.

"Listen to me, my love," says his wife. "You are about to wreck several lives, your own included. I don't suppose you'd do such a thing lightly. Did someone cause you to do it? Tell me who and why."

"Not you, none of you." And then after a pause, he adds, "Not even me."

The children are the first to recover. "It's male menopause," says Pamela, the budding student of psychology. "It happens. It lasts a while, and then it's over. Isn't that right, Dad?"

Pam, his beloved daughter, so smart beyond her years, she

always made him laugh. Not now. He does not reply. Ron, in turn, offers his theory: "Dad, you need a rest, to be by yourself. We understand. Go on, take a few days, a few weeks' vacation in New England, or at a ranch in Arizona, whatever. It'll do you good."

Still no response from the father. Then he stands, stretches, wipes his forehead as if to dispel a headache, clears his throat, and speaks very softly and very slowly. "I love you all. I will love you for the rest of my days. I'm the one I've stopped loving. I was happy, but now I'm not. I have no energy; I find no pleasure in living. As the poet might say, my spring has run dry; my sun has gone dark. I can't go on like this. I'm not worthy of your love. Nothing about me is real. I do everything wrong. I can't reach any of my goals. I no longer recognize myself in the man you love. I believe I have to change before it's too late. Change everything—time and place, surroundings, my own soul. Change my being. Don't judge me; just try to understand me."

He goes to the door, opens it, hesitates a moment. His wife wants to rush to him and draw him back, or at least embrace him, but she is paralyzed. It is Pamela who, followed by Ron, runs toward their father, who is already outside. He strides off at a determined pace without a backward look.

"THAT'S IT," SAYS THE DOCTOR. SHE SAYS NO more, just gives him a helpless smile.

Gamaliel wonders what he should say, and how to say it. Tell her about his own tragedies, his defeats? In order to share her pain, as if that were possible? Explain that he had suffered the same sort of blows—almost the same—during the course of his own marriage? That her Al and his Colette were kindred spirits? In earlier years, he would have distracted her by giving his interpretation of what happened. He would have told her about his life, his mistakes, his disappointments, his heartbreaks, his divorce, his wanderings, his metamorphoses, his career as a ghostwriter. Then he would carefully have courted her, told her how attractive she was, praised her finesse, spoken of her right to happiness. It's all so easy, and so promising, when one is young. But Gamaliel is no longer young. Even so, but with a kind of reticence, he tells her about his past as if it happened to someone else.

"I used to know a man who had no home and no family. Life knocked him about. He ran into one roadblock after another; the ground would give way under his feet. To make a living, he spent his time helping imbeciles who were slaves to their own vanity write nonsense that would win them a false fame, a counterfeit image. He was full of fears and complexes that he'd learned to hide, yet he felt strangely free because, being bound by no social constraints, he could take in everything and explain it all—though in fact he didn't understand anything. He'd read everything, remembered everything, but it was all on the surface. Nothing moved him deeply. Perhaps he was afraid, afraid of revealing himself, of commitment, of giving up his freedom. Without wanting to, without even being aware of it, he was sowing unhappiness all around him. Those he loved and who loved him always became his victims."

The doctor has regained her poise. When she speaks, her voice is cordial, but Gamaliel cannot tell if she is accepting or ironic. "That's all pretty abstract," she observes. "Tell me, do you have a family and children? Are you happy?"

"A family? Yes, I once had a family. They left me. As for happiness, I no longer look for it."

"What do you look for?"

The answer given by the wandering beggar in his village comes to him: He looked for stories and faces, from which he would make songs. And Gamaliel?

"I no longer know," he says to her. "Perhaps I'm seeking the reality and meaning of what I'm running from."

Somewhere, church bells are striking noon. The age-old summons is crystal clear and insistent. Gamaliel is startled to feel himself shiver. He is back in his wartime childhood, when church bells in Czechoslovakia and Hungary frightened him with their sinister and threatening message. He was afraid of everything. Fortunate that Ilonka was there to reassure and protect him. She would hold him close and whisper in his ear, calling him not "my boy" but "my big boy": "Never fear. Those bastards will be destroyed, I promise you. If God does not take care of it, I'll do it myself." Right now, it is Ilonka, of all the women who have been part of his life, whom he recalls with the greatest emotion. He recalls her warmth, her voice: Ilonka the devout Christian, faithful friend to his parents, protector of their son. Sometimes in the unfathomable depths of memory, her features dissolve into those of the most tender and sweetest woman in the world, his mother. But what about Colette? And Esther, whose name means "secret"? And Eve, whose voice both concealed and revealed her volcanic temper? Esther, whom he loved forever. Eve, his first true love, who brought together a man and a woman who needed each other to complete their lives. Why had he not urgently proposed marriage to the first? Why had he waited till it was too late with the second? They live on, in a sense, strangely joined in his thoughts. They are always there—sometimes very near, at other times far away—in the mists of nostalgia. How to explain their hold on him? His sense of guilt? But where does love come in? Is love for him anywhere but in the past? "I refuse," said Eve, shaking her head. "I refuse to bottle love up in the past when by its very nature it must transcend that past. My little family was happy because we loved one another. Time did not affect our love, and if you don't understand that, I'm sorry for you. If you don't understand that we—my husband, our daughter, and I—went on loving one another after death, it's because you've never truly loved."

Was she right? Gamaliel answers his own question: No, she wasn't. He did love Eve, yes, with a love that was total; and he loves her still, to the point that it feels like an open wound. But then why did they part?

And Esther, the wild seed, the clairvoyant who read palms, she was self-confident but never arrogant. She hid her distress and confusion behind a facade of pride, which kept admirers at a distance. Head leaning left, smiling, forever changing, she was like no one else, not even herself. What had he loved about her? The sound of her voice? Her feverish but contained sensuality? The dark flame in her eyes? That was it: He loved her for her eyes. All the depth, all the mystery of the Orient lay in her eyes, and in her smile, and in her voice. She had all the passion in the world at her fingertips. But then she vanished like a wave in the ocean.

Eve was different. When she gave herself to him, she did it as though she were making the ultimate sacrifice. Which of the two would live on within him forever? But to live forever is to cease being, is it not? He'll tell about them one day, if God grants him time. He'll make them part of his still-unfinished *Book of Secrets*. Will that erase his feeling of guilt? No, it's too late for that. He cannot rewrite the past to suit him: Its truth remains unalterable. Nonetheless, Gamaliel cannot imagine life without Eve. Nor without Ilonka.

The church bells have stopped ringing. It's a fine day. The sun, very high in the sky, remembers its duty to warm our hearts and bodies. Doors are opening and closing. The street is noisy. Young people impatiently seek refreshments, leave offices and classrooms, employers and teachers. Hurry, it's time to speak of other things. They debate, they flirt, sometimes they even love. The tables outside the nearby café are being filled at an astonishing rate. In a few minutes, they are all taken.

"Would you like something to eat?" Gamaliel asks.

"No," says the doctor, shaking her head.

"Something to drink?"

"No, thank you."

"Shall we walk a while?"

They cross the street and walk alongside a small park where children laugh as they play, or cry when they fall down or cannot retrieve the multicolored ball that a smart, nervy little dog has caught in his teeth. Oh children, do you realize the day will come when you will be grown-up like us and miserable? Where was he when little Jewish girls and their brothers were running around the yards of their homes in Czechoslovakia, trying to catch the wild beams of a sun in flames, not knowing that they were already marked for slaughter? A familiar melancholy weighs heavy on his thoughts, and on his chest, when he thinks of the children.

"Your children," he asks, "where are they?" Should he add that his own children, his two daughters, have no doubt forgotten him? No, that can wait.

"I don't know," the doctor replies. "In school, I suppose." And after a moment, she says, "I'm afraid for them."

"Not for yourself?"

"For them particularly. They're so young, so vulnerable, and their love for their father was so pure."

They have circled the park without being aware of it. They continue walking aimlessly and talking until Gamaliel halts because his legs are hurting.

"We'll see each other at two o'clock?"

"Yes, I'll be with Zsuzsi Szabó . . . the patient."

She extends her hand; he holds it in his a long moment. She murmurs, "Thanks, thanks for everything," and is gone. Gamaliel follows her with his gaze until she disappears in the crowd. Then he looks at his watch: It's almost 1:30. In twenty minutes, he will return to the hospital to see the woman whose memory may hold some flashes of his own.

IT'S TIME. AT THE HOSPITAL GATE, THE MAN ON duty recognizes him and waves him on. Gamaliel is two minutes early, but for years now he's had the strange feeling that he's always arriving late.

The nurse points him to the corridor leading to the ward where he will find Zsuzsi Szabó. He stands for a moment at the open door. What strikes him first, more than her damaged features, is the isolation of the old woman sitting on her bed in a dark corner of the ward. An invisible screen separates her from the other patients. The others are moving about, talking, complaining; not she. Impassive, motionless, as if cast in stone, she stares bleakly at some distant point in space; her gaze seems neither to focus on that point nor to avoid it. Is she Ilonka? Gamaliel tells himself that yes, somehow this must be she, she and no other, who is awaiting him. Awaiting him and no other.

No, that's impossible! The sight of her does not evoke any

memory, any event, any feeling. Had their paths crossed in another world, in another life? Maybe under another name? Then who is this Hungarian refugee over whom he's been in turmoil since morning?

It was because of Bolek, the bearded Jew from Dava-rowsk, Poland, who likes to carry news from one person to another in his own manner. Bolek is sometimes taciturn, sometimes blustering. Formerly stateless, and yet still brother to all the world's victims. Last evening when they were din-ing with their three friends, Bolek gave him an urgent mes-sage: "I met someone who asked me to tell you that there's a seriously injured woman who needs you."

"Needs me?"

"Yes, you."

"She needs me to write her book?"

"Book? Who said anything about a book? She needs someone who speaks her language."

Bolek loves a mystery. He's incapable of speaking to the point. When you question him, his answers are always vague, verbose, and useless. Conveying factual information is not what he does best. With him, one always has to guess. So, rather than ask him for details, Gamaliel went to the heart of the matter: "So she's Hungarian? But there must be a hundred thousand people in New York who speak her lan-guage. Why does she need me? And who is she?"

"No idea. I told you all I know. A woman. Injured . . . seriously. In a car accident, in a plane crash? I don't know. Maybe she was in a fire. No one can get her to answer the most basic questions. She knows nothing but that weird lan-guage that only the Hungarians understand, or at least they say they do."

"And where is this woman?"

"Where do you think she is? In the Museum of Modern Art? She's in the hospital, you idiot."

Everyone around the table burst out laughing.

"Oh, I see, a hospital? She's not in a prison, maybe in Moscow?" put in Diego, the short anarchist from Barcelona, who could never pass up an opportunity to mock the behavior of Communists wherever they might be. He had picked up the name Diego in Spain, where he went to enlist in the International Brigades. What was his real name? He claimed he'd erased it from memory. His friends suspected he was originally from Lithuania, whose melodious, intellectual Yiddish he still spoke. But his true life had started dramatically somewhere near Valladolid, in Spain. "I'll bet that patient was a Communist when she was young," he added. "Like all of us."

"Oh shut up, hombre," said Yasha, who was in a bad mood. "You have no right to insult that unfortunate woman."

"How do you know she's unfortunate?"

"If she weren't, she wouldn't be in this place that our dear Bolek can't even locate."

"Bolek, if you know where she is, say so. But be careful," said Gad, for whom "be careful" was a rule that applied to every hour of the day.

Everyone insisted, until Bolek finally gave the name of the hospital.

And that is how Gamaliel comes to be in this gloomy ward dominated by sickness and misery.

At the old woman's bedside, he asks in Hungarian, "You're from Budapest?" She seems not to hear him. In what spheres has her mind lost its way? "You are Madame Zsuzsi Szabó?" he asks. Her face remains entirely still. Her eyes never seek those of her visitor. To her, he doesn't exist. Or is it she who no longer exists?

. . .

ALL AT ONCE, GAMALIEL SEES HIMSELF IN BUDA-
pest in 1948. Ilonka was going to a hospital, a bouquet of
flowers in her hand: A Jewish friend of his mother, a survivor
of the camps, was seriously ill. When Gamaliel refused to
stay home alone, Ilonka let him accompany her. "You'll wait
for me outside, young man, promise?" He promised; he
would have promised anything to be allowed to go with her.
She disappeared into a lugubrious gray building. Time went
by; she did not return. Rain began to fall, first a few drops,
then more. Gamaliel decided to go inside. There was no one
in the corridor. He could hear muffled voices coming from
several rooms. One voice sounded familiar, so he pushed on
the half-open door. Ilonka was standing at the foot of the
bed; the flowers lay on the bedcovers. She was speaking in a
low voice to an old woman who was not answering. Ilonka
seemed to be imploring the patient, repeating again and
again, "Say something, my dearest Hegedüs Néni. I beg of
you, say something. . . . Mama was your friend, your good
friend. You remember her, don't you? Answer me, my dear,
dear Hegedüs Néni. Say something, just a few words. Do it
for me; do it for Mama. . . ."

The old woman closed her eyes, then opened them again
immediately. When she spoke, she hardly moved her dry lips,
and her voice was barely audible. "What do you want of me?
How dare you speak to me? What did I do to you? Who
authorized you to come into my grave? Who are you?"

She spoke of her "grave," Gamaliel realized, trying not to
show his dismay. She's not just sick. She's crazy.

Not knowing what to say, Ilonka reached out to stroke her
hand, but the patient withdrew it. "Go away," she went on in

the same cold, distant voice. "How dare you disturb the sleep of the dead."

She said "sleep of the dead," Gamaliel thought. So, in her insanity she considers herself dead?

"I beg your pardon, Hegedüs Néni," said Ilonka. "I—"

"You dare to beg my pardon! Oh, you people who are living, it's all so easy for you. You do awful things, horrible things; then you say 'beg your pardon,' and that's supposed to make everything all right, all the wounds healed, turn the page. Not here, dear lady, not among us. We the dead don't forgive so easily. The dead have long memories. Unlike the living."

But who was she? Gamaliel will wonder about that, with foreboding in his heart, for many years. He remembers her now as he stands before this wounded old woman. What face is hiding behind that ravaged mask? What painful truth is her silence concealing? From what danger was she fleeing, and why did she take refuge behind this barricade of indifference? What message would this woman send to the world of the living? Unfortunately, Gamaliel does not know how to make the patient speak, as Ilonka did. "I'm Ilonka, the singer," the Jewish boy's guardian had said. "Ilonka. Mama and you were friends from childhood. I would like to be able to help you."

The woman opened her mouth with difficulty: "Ilonka . . . Ilonka . . . are you Jewish?"

"No, I'm not."

The patient seemed to frown. "If you're not Jewish, what are you doing in my world?"

"I found out that you were here. I had to come."

"Can't you see I'm alone? Why did you come? To take my solitude away from me?"

"No, no . . . I swear it."

"To share it with me maybe?"

"I would like to, Madame Hegedüs, but I don't know how."

"You can never know. Try it and you'll find out. You're not Jewish; therefore, you're not dead. The Jews are all dead. Only the dead may come in here with me." Then, as if a distant memory had come to her, she sat up and pointed to a chair by her bed. "Sit down. The dead are either lying down or standing, never sitting. But you, you're living, so you may sit."

Gamaliel, in the background, looked around, as if seeking someone whom he could ask how he should comport himself. But there was no doctor or nurse in the ward. As for the other patients, either they weren't listening to the conversation or they didn't want to get involved. He saw Ilonka seat herself. He remained standing, and waited.

Suddenly, the patient's eyes lit up strangely. "Your accent." She spoke as if in a reverie. "Your accent sounds familiar. You're from Budapest. Aren't you from Budapest?"

"Yes, but I was born in Fehérvàros."

"So was I."

"I know. You and Mama were from the same village."

Even as he recalls the patient in Budapest, Gamaliel is leaning over to get a better look at Zsuzsi Szabó. "Who are you?" he asks all at once.

In his delirious imagining, the two women merge, like red flames chasing each other in a magic kaleidoscope, and their faces and their destinies become one. He knows it's impossible, but still he wonders. Suppose the two are one. At once, the boundaries of space and time vanish.

The patient in Budapest seemed suddenly seized with fear. "You don't ask such questions of the dead," she hissed.

But what was the question? For the life of him, Gamaliel can't remember. He starts when he feels a hand on his shoulder. The doctor, Lili Rosenkrantz, is standing behind him; she looks composed and interested. He had not heard her come in. "Now that you've seen her, let's go outside," she says. "We can talk better there."

"But . . ."

"Believe me, we'll be better off outside."

Reluctantly, he follows her out of the building, feeling vaguely guilty toward the patient he is abandoning to her solitude.

Once in the courtyard, they find a bench under a fruit tree that is already half in bloom. She sits down and motions to the seat at her left, but he remains standing. "I don't understand what's going on," he says. "I came here because she wanted to see me. . . ."

"I'm the one who wanted to see you," the doctor explains. "I told you. She's my patient. I thought you might be able to help me."

Gamaliel, surprised at her terse, professional tone, studies her in silence. Now he finds her less vulnerable, although melancholy. He's always been attracted to melancholy women. He was attracted to the others also, the pleasure seekers, but not in the same way.

"So it was you who wanted to see me?"

"Well . . . ," she says. She smiles and tosses her head.

He's always loved women who smile as they toss their heads. They make him want to respond with some sort of gesture of complicity.

The doctor waits for him to ask more questions, but he just gazes at her. "I see that I owe you an explanation," she says, still smiling. "I know you lived in Budapest. I know that

from our mutual friend, Bolek. I introduced him to my husband, but that didn't stop him from being a bit infatuated
with me, as he is with so many women. I thought you could
get my patient to talk. . . . Her case isn't hopeless, but it's certainly discouraging. She refuses to live because she thinks
she's already dead."

"What makes you say that, given that she's mute?"

"True, she's virtually mute. But a psychiatrist can recognize the symptoms. There are patients who believe they are
not living or have no right to live."

Gamaliel does not know how to respond. What advice
would he be given by Rebbe Zusya, the Sage who knows so
much about so many fields? A woman is convinced that she
is no longer of this world, but has gone to what is said to be
the world of truth. But hasn't Gamaliel himself sometimes
thought his true life lay elsewhere? That it is by mistake that
he was born before the Second World War in Czechoslovakia, by mistake that he came to be in Christian Hungary, by
mistake that he was saved in Budapest and then declared
stateless in Paris? Married by mistake, a father by accident.
His very identity may have been an error: Suppose he were
to discover that Ilonka was really his mother? What part does
this old patient play in his life's journey? Is it conceivable that
she alone holds the answers to some of the questions that
have been haunting him? And one day she will appear in his
thoughts and demand to be included in the narratives he
writes? No, he would send her away. Writing? At times,
Gamaliel no longer wants to go on with it. To hell with this
slave labor that is supposed to be so free and liberating. He's
written too much as it is. Too many sentences summoned to
a blank page to express the thoughts and desires that lay jum-
bled in other minds. Too many words scattered to the four

winds, seeds that neither took root nor bore fruit, wounded birds that fell to earth on land that was arid and lifeless and exhausted. Has he lived more than enough? Rebbe Zusya would shout his answer: "No, a thousand times no! You have no right to give up on life when you feel it's hopeless. Each day is a blessing; each moment gives you an opportunity for grace. Haven't I taught you anything?" Of course Rebbe Zusya would be right. But the problem is not in knowing *why* he should live, but *how*, in the midst of so much duplicity. He has an absurd impulse to tell the young doctor about his strained, complex relationship with the Just One, the Tzaddik of Brooklyn. He changes his mind, preferring to get her to talk instead. "I came here because of you, and for you. That gives me the right to know you a little better, doesn't it?"

"I've already told you about my marriage, or at least how it ended."

"And before? Where do you come from? And how did you come to be here? What made you choose medicine? You speak with an accent."

She waited before answering. "You're right. But my story is almost commonplace. Other people could tell you better stories, more colorful ones. I was born in Romania. My father disappeared in a camp near Mogilev, somewhere in Transnistria."

Her story, like that of so many others of her generation, could be told in the Book of Job or the book of survivors. A story of chance, of miracles. Her mother had found refuge in Budapest, where she married an American journalist. The little girl made the couple laugh at the way she mangled the few words of Hungarian that their housekeeper had taught her. Soon the family emigrated to America. Then a boy was born, who later would die in a car accident. Not long after that, her stepfather, in Europe on business, collapsed from a heart attack and died on a Paris boulevard. Her mother fell into a depression, from which she never recovered. "She died in this very hospital," the young woman tells him. "Fortunately, I'm a psychiatrist."

"Yes, fortunately," says Gamaliel, impressed by such a conclusion to her story.

A familiar impulse draws him to the doctor, who seems suddenly to have cast off her melancholy. Not knowing why, he hears himself asking her if she intends to get married again.

"To whom?" she replies.

Gamaliel has a crazy notion to say "To me," if only to observe the surprise on her face. She must have guessed what he is thinking, for she blushes. She tries to change the tenor of the conversation. "You really don't want to sit down?"

Now Colette's former husband, as embarrassed as a shy teenager, realizes he is still standing. "Excuse me," he says as he sits down.

They gaze at each other in silence, aware perhaps of the weight of this moment that has brought them together. Gamaliel would like to ease the tension by resuming their conversation, but it is she who wipes her forehead, as if to banish some fear, and continues in a lighter manner: "Your name was Péter, wasn't it? That's what Bolek—"

"But call me Gamaliel."

"My name is—"

"You told me. Lili. Lili Rosenkrantz. I like that name; it's beautiful. Like a melody. It makes me dream."

"Dream about what?"

"About music, about dance. Let's say about my childhood."

It's seemingly everyday conversation, an exchange of

information: polite words, cordial questions and answers, memories connected to Budapest.

"Are you still stateless?"

"Technically, no. But I've been without a country for a long time."

"Is it a difficult situation to be in?"

"Very difficult; in fact, it's unbearable."

"Like Bolek?"

"Yes, like him, and like so many others. We used to dream that we'd make a homeland for those who didn't have one, that we'd give an identity to those who'd been deprived of theirs. How about you?"

"I've always had a country. First Romania, now America, thanks to my stepfather. His ancestors were Russian Jews. You noticed that I haven't completely lost my Romanian accent. Still, I'm American enough to feel guilty about what we did to those poor Indians."

Ask her how she expresses her Jewishness? No, that's indiscreet, too personal a question. Save it for another time. But will there be another time? Better change the subject. Bolek, for example: How did she meet him?

"Oh yes, Bolek, what a fellow," she says, clapping her hands. "Some character, isn't he? Always falling in love, never twice with the same woman, always in addition to his wife. He picked me up in the subway by offering me his seat. Can you imagine? Naturally, I thanked him. At that, he asked me to have coffee with him. When? At the next station. Since he had a pleasant face, I accepted. I found him entertaining, and interesting. All these stories about being a refugee in Germany, then in France, then in the United States . . . He has a wonderful sense of humor. Everything makes him laugh. When he found out I was born in Eastern Europe during the war, he mentioned your name—or rather, your two names, and their story. As it happens, I knew about your names. My mother used to mention you sometimes while spending an evening with friends. When they talked about the German occupation and the persecution of the Jews, one of them would say he knew someone from your circle."

While he listens, Gamaliel is watching her with growing emotion. He hardly dares breathe. A thought flashes through his mind: Can that sick old woman upstairs really be Ilonka? Can it be that I did not recognize the young singer with the sparkling talent in the old woman's ravaged face? True, a lot of water has flowed under the bridges of the Danube and the Hudson since the days when she was sheltering me. Can a human being so change that her present erases every trace of her past?

The young woman's soft, lilting voice rouses him from his reverie. "Last week, our patient seemed to come out of her coma. She tried to speak. She murmured a few words, maybe names. . . ."

"What names?" Gamaliel exclaims. "Try to remember. It's important to me. Did she say a name that sounded like Ilonka?"

The doctor reflects. She turns serious, almost pained. She repeats the name several times: "Ilonka, Ilonka, a Hungarian name . . . a woman's name . . . No, I don't think so." Gamaliel, his nerves stretched tight as a bow, is watching her lips. "So who is this Ilonka?" she asks.

"A saint." And after a moment's silence, he adds, "A true saint, not the usual kind."

"One of your conquests, was she?"

"Yes, I conquered her, and I'm proud to say so. It was she who saved the conqueror."

Gamaliel falls silent. Words and pictures are swimming around in his mind. It's not the melancholy doctor whom I'm here to captivate, he realizes. It's Ilonka, that wonderful protector of mine, who would as readily weep as make love. Is it she whom I'm forever seeking in every woman who attracts me?

"This saint who wasn't the usual kind, what became of her?" the doctor asks. "Did she have a hard time of it during the war? Did she find herself a husband? Did fate reward her, as she deserved?"

"Ilonka was better at making others happy than she was at finding happiness for herself."

"Then she was unhappy!" the doctor exclaims. A wisp of hair falls over her forehead.

"Yes, much of the time. What can you expect? Everyone she loved left her."

"Who were they?"

"My mother and I. There must have been others, too."

"Why did you leave her?"

"We had to."

"You're saying that with regret, but surely it wasn't your fault."

"I know that, and she knew it, too. That didn't save her from suffering."

It was Ilonka herself who decided on their first separation. Foreseeing danger, she sent the little boy to a safe location, dispatching him with a onetime dancer to another part of Budapest.

Soon after he left, she was denounced by an anti-Semite at the cabaret and then arrested by the Nyilas. She was beaten, humiliated, raped. Her torturers tried to make her reveal under what names the Jews were hiding, and with whom.

She made up names and addresses. Each time, the sadists came back empty-handed and insane with rage. Ilonka screamed, wept, entreated; she was determined to endure anything, to withstand anything. The role of informer did not suit her, as she explained to Gamaliel when she had found him again.

"You're right: She was a saint," Lili says in a tentative manner. "But in what way was she different from other saints, whose good deeds we read about in sacred writings?"

"She was a believer, but her saintliness had nothing to do with her religion. It was all from the heart, from her great and generous heart, the kind we don't see anymore. Understand? Ilonka was human, admirably human, and to me, that places her above any saint."

The doctor looks surprised. "Why do you say that? Is the divine that much of a problem for you? Since when is being human the supreme virtue? Remember the beautiful old saying that the goal of mankind is to become god?"

"To which I would reply that to my mind the goal of mankind is to become human. Ilonka saved my life. She was a brave woman, a noble and passionate one; she was a heroic figure. That's why I think of her with love and admiration."

The doctor persists: "If a person risks life and liberty to help victims of persecution, well, that makes her a saint in my eyes. Besides, you yourself said it." Gamaliel does not answer immediately, preferring to end the discussion. The doctor interprets his silence as assent: "We agree, then, about Ilonka? Good. What sort of woman was she? Was she cultivated, intellectual? Did she like gardening, classical music? Did she read the novels of Stendhal and Victor Hugo?"

Gamaliel stares at her, wondering whether he should hurt her feelings. Should he say to her that all the intellectuals of

Europe are not worth the loving grace of this unschooled woman who did so much to save one human life, his own? He cannot make up his mind.

The doctor offers him a way out: "You were very young when she took you in, weren't you?"

"Not that young."

"Too young to understand what she really did."

"She was a cabaret singer."

"Really?"

"Yes, she sang in a cabaret."

"And that's all she did?"

Gamaliel bites his lips. Gestures, hushed voices, feelings are shooting like bolts of lightning through his mind. Ilonka leaning over the little boy curled up on the sofa. "Péter, are you asleep? Good. Sleep, my big boy. Sleep, and sweet dreams. It's better that way." She puts out the light and goes into the bedroom. But Gamaliel is not asleep. He follows her movements through half-closed eyes. She is not alone. A man is with her. Gamaliel recognizes him: It is the loudmouthed head of the Nyilas, the Hungarian fascists, whom he observed at the cabaret. He catches strange muffled sounds coming from the bedroom. He doesn't understand their cause or their meaning—or perhaps he doesn't want to understand. The same scene takes place every night, but the man who accompanies Ilonka is not always the same.

"That's all she did," he says at last to the young woman. "She was a singer. I heard her sing. She was good, very good indeed. When she sang, her voice lifted your spirits and gave you wings, and from up in the sky, you looked down at the earth as if it were a sanctuary."

Has the doctor noticed the change in Gamaliel's voice? If so, she doesn't show it. All she does is give him a supportive smile, while he tries to remember how long it was before he came to understand the nature of his protector's profession. "Tell me some more about yourself," the young woman says, and she touches him lightly, timidly, on the arm. "And if that bores you, tell me a story."

All right, a story, but which one? And why now, on this early day of spring, under this tree in bloom, so close to the hospital building housing human beings in whom the course of illness is running to its conclusion, where they completely lose their minds? Is she trying to provoke a response from him? Or is it for some professional, perhaps medical, reason? Does she see in him a disorder of which he is not aware? He decides to tell her about an incident that still embarrasses him many decades later. "At the time, I was still young, and I didn't know my way around, as the saying goes," he began in a neutral tone. "I'd just arrived in Paris. I was poor—all I had was a travel permit stamped by the French consulate—and I didn't know anyone."

At the time, late 1956, some frontiers in Europe were relatively easy to cross. It was done every day by thousands of Hungarian refugees fleeing from the Red Army tanks that had crushed their insurrection. The governments of Western Europe must have felt guilty about them, for these refugees were better received than those who had preceded them in 1945–1946. Gamaliel was not yet twenty when he stepped off the Orient Express, which had taken him from Vienna to Paris. Before he even went to the hotel where he was to join other refugees, he went on foot from the Gare de l'Est to the rue Saint-Denis. A Party comrade had sung the praises of this section of Paris while telling him everything he needed to know to achieve his desired goal. "What came first and foremost, according to my comrade? Don't laugh: He said you must make love to understand the secret of all Creation."

"I'm not laughing," says the doctor, and she squeezes his arm very hard.

"It was the first time."

"And you were almost twenty?"

"Is that so unusual?"

"For some people, everything is unusual," she says gently. "Every moment of their lives is both predictable and unexpected. And you, poor fellow, seem to be one of them."

"Please, don't feel sorry for me. I . . ." Gamaliel stops in midsentence, and his face darkens.

"Well, I'm still waiting for your story," says the doctor.

"It's not very pretty."

"I don't like stories that are too pretty. I spend my time listening to the other kind."

Walking along rue Saint-Denis that day, Gamaliel felt desire gathering in him like a thunderstorm. He didn't know where to look, or how to respond to the invitations he was hearing. Alluring, heavily made-up women were soliciting him in English, in German, never in Hungarian, but he understood French, thanks to the journalist in Budapest and the courses he had taken in school. He chose the one who promised him in French an hour in paradise, smilingly requiring only a few hundred francs as the price of admission.

The furniture and the walls of the dingy hotel room smelled of mildew. She began rapidly to shed her clothes, but Gamaliel was taking his time. "You want me to get completely undressed?" she asked in a bored tone. "That costs extra."

"Don't bother," he said in a choked voice.

"As you please. But hurry up, my boy," she said while she pulled down her red panties and tossed them on a filthy chair. "I don't have all day."

Gamaliel's cheeks were flaming as he took off his trousers and carefully folded them. The woman lying on the bed was getting impatient. "How about my present?" He didn't understand. "The money," she said, irritated. "Where's the cash you owe me?" He felt around in his jacket pocket and handed her a few bills. She counted them and kept them in her hand. "All right, come on."

"Not yet," said Gamaliel.

All he could do was stare at her, while she, stretched out on the dirty sheet, knees apart, was losing all patience. "How many times do I have to tell you, baby? I don't have the rest of my lousy life for this, you know. So come take what you paid for."

"Not yet."

"What're you waiting for? The revolution, or maybe the Messiah?"

He blushed. Like all Jews, he knew that he must always be ready for the coming of the Messiah even though He might be late, but he would never have imagined that the Redeemer would make His appearance in a place like this.

Abruptly, the woman sat up. "Tell me what it is, you little brat. You don't want me? I'm not sexy enough? Or does my body disgust you?"

"Yes . . ." He caught himself. "I mean no. Not now. Not like this."

"Say, are you some kind of pervert? No? Well then, stop wasting my time. Come on, let's get it over with."

Gamaliel saw her hard face, her folded legs; he stared at her and was seized with panic. "It's my first time," he said hoarsely.

She burst out laughing. "A virgin, imagine that! You'll bring me luck. Now come here!"

Gamaliel, unable to master his embarrassment, hurriedly threw on his clothes and fled.

"It's dangerous to look where we're not supposed to," the doctor comments. "That's why we close our eyes when we're making love. You learned that afterward, didn't you?"

"I learned a lot of things," Gamaliel replies. He'd like to touch her hand, her arm, caress her hair, her neck, her face, offer her his lips, come to terms with life and with the living, but he's afraid he'll make a fool of himself. Hell, what's the worst that could happen to me? Be rejected? My life's been nothing but a series of rejections. When I spoke, they told me to shut up. When I was silent, they wanted to make me speak. I have never been able to be myself, not even in love.

He leaned toward Lili, but she shook her head. "Not like that, not now, not here."

Then where? And when?

"NOT HERE," GAD HAD SAID.

"Why not?" asked Diego, professing surprise.

"There's a time and place for everything. It would be unseemly to talk of hatred now in this place. Be careful, my friends."

Hatred and contempt. The hatred of the world for us and man's contempt for himself. Anti-Semitism reappearing in various guises. Gamaliel often discussed it with Bolek, Diego, Gad, and Yasha now that they had found one another in New York. They had gotten in the habit of meeting at a cafeteria near the old *Jewish Daily Forward* on the Lower East Side. There, in a setting of reassuring camaraderie, they would share their nostalgia, their regrets perhaps, and also times of noisy partying. Gad, the closemouthed Israeli, who smiled only when he was playing his violin, was the youngest of the group. He was lean, well built, alert, with searching eyes. When his friends asked why he said so little, he invariably replied, "I've learned to be careful."

The five once-stateless men had met in Paris in the early 1960s, at an annual reunion of Jewish refugees, where the talk was about getting residence permits extended, obtaining working papers, and applying for visas to the United States or Canada. They had taken a liking to one another, and now that they were all living in New York, they would get together every so often.

"I know about hatred," said little Diego while he stirred sugar into his lukewarm coffee. "Back then, in Valladolid, that was all that kept us going. Sometimes I'd even pray for it. 'Our Father, who art in heaven, give us this day our daily hate.' God Himself had become the God of hate."

"That's worse than blasphemous; it's crazy," Bolek said. "God may hate, but He can't inspire hatred."

"What do you know about hate?" asked Diego in irritation. "First of all, I'm a free man! As free as God. We were created in God's image, so if He can hate, so can I. Besides, you talk about God as if He were a buddy of yours, maybe an accomplice. . . . You don't have some racket together, do you?"

"Take it easy," said Bolek. "Your nice Lithuanian accent is turning into bad Yiddish."

"Mind your own business! If I want to get mad, I'll get mad. If I feel like cursing, I'll curse. Understand? And if I feel like hating, I'll hate. I learned how in Spain. Over there, we were free—free to hate."

"Like God," Bolek said sarcastically as he scratched his head.

"Yes, just like God! Not all men may be worthy of Him, but I am, because I believe that He wants us to accept the freedom that He in His audacity offers us."

"Freedom to do anything at all?"

"In any case, anything I want to do."

"You're going too far," said Bolek.

"Be careful," Gad put in. "You're talking too much."

"And you're not talking enough!" Yasha exclaimed.

"Yasha, do you believe in God?" Bolek asked.

"That has nothing to do with it."

"How about your cat, Misha? Does he believe in God?"

"Misha is the God of cats."

Why does the conversation keep coming around to God, even though the group is made up of agnostics and unbelievers? Gamaliel wondered. He recalled Chesterton's saying that when men stopped believing in God, it was not because they believed in nothing but, rather, because they would believe in anything. Should he quote the line? He decided instead to cool the conversation down by telling a story.

"You remember Ilonka, the singer I lived with and to whom I owe my survival? 'I'm afraid,' she'd often say to me at night when she came home from the cabaret. 'I'm afraid and I'm ashamed.' One day, a Nyilas officer she knew dropped in unexpectedly. He was in a bad mood. So was she, but I understood the reason for her low spirits. The Russians were approaching Budapest, and yet the militias were still going from house to house, searching cellars and attics, flushing out hidden Jews, whom they would beat to death and toss in the Danube. Among them were neighbors she had known. All in the river. But the officer was in a bad mood for a different reason: He hadn't arrested enough Jews.

" 'You have to help me,' he told Ilonka. 'I'm sure you know people who are hiding those Yids. Give me their names and addresses; I have to come up with lists.' To distract him, she kissed him on the forehead, on the lips. They were already embracing on the bed when she saw me. 'What're you still doing here?' she shouted angrily. 'Get out of here and be quick about it! Go to your room!' I stood there paralyzed with fear. At that, the officer jumped to his feet and shoved me out of the room so hard that it hurt. That's when I came to hate him. Not so much because he was killing Jews—that was beyond me at the time—but because he was coming between Ilonka and me. I hate him to this day."

"I'm opposed to hating," said Gad, who was usually content to listen. "Anyone who gives in to hate can no longer function; he becomes stupid and vulnerable. In Israel, the commandos who went on missions with hatred in their hearts weren't likely to return in one piece." He paused, then added, "Same applies to the secret service." There were rumors, legends, about Gad. As an agent of the Mossad, he had survived any number of dangers and outwitted as many traps in order to bring vital military information to the Israeli government. It was whispered that this son of German refugees in America had traveled to Arab capitals, posing as a German businessman and former Nazi. He himself said nothing. He was married but never spoke of his wife. He preferred to talk about music. He adored his violin, his constant and faithful companion; like Yasha with his cat, Gad saw in his instrument the perfect confidant, something that would never let him down. When solitude weighed too heavily on him, he would make his violin speak low, shout, sing, tell stories, and weep without tears.

"I told you that hatred can be dangerous when we let it control us," Gad continued. "There are certain schools where they teach you how to suppress or postpone your hatred. But there's one kind of hate that's harder to tame." Contrary to his usual custom, Gad, his features tense, seemed to feel a need to unburden himself, as if his confession of vulnerability could no longer be put off after so many years of silence. "Hatred? What you're concerned about is your own hate, not the kind that hits you over the head." He stopped, hesitated a moment, as if wondering whether he had the right to go on. "Oh, I know, anti-Semitism, you've all suffered from it, even you, Diego. Well, I haven't. But to be hated for no reason at all, not even because you're a Jew, that's an altogether different thing." With that, he asked for a cigarette, this man who hardly ever smoked. Diego lit one and handed it to him. His friends, consumed with an uneasy curiosity, watched him in expectation of a dramatic tale of heroic deeds. "At the time, I was living in an Arab country," said Gad. "Think of a Nazi Don Juan—that's who I was. I was rich, single, a big spender. I kept company with a set of officials who liked me for the money I would throw around in nightclubs and jewelry stores, money that supposedly came from Jews who 'disappeared' during the war in Europe. They found that amusing.

"One night in a chic restaurant in the capital city, I was introduced to a foreign journalist, a woman who was a correspondent for a French magazine. I knew her name from reading her articles when I would pass through Paris. I knew she was gifted and intelligent, but her appearance surprised me. I don't know why, but I'd expected someone older, more solidly built, almost masculine. I certainly wasn't prepared for her inviting smile, for the challenge in her gray eyes. What was my reaction? You can probably guess. I cursed the life I was leading; I told myself that in normal times in some other place I could have fallen for her, and, who knows, made her my wife. That night, everyone was speaking English, but with different accents. Mine was German. I know she found me intriguing, because at a certain moment she turned to me and asked me who I was, where I came from, what I was doing in that city, how long I'd been there. To avoid answering her questions, I asked her if her curiosity might by any chance be connected to the fact that she was working undercover for the Jewish nation. Then one of the party, an air force major, whispered a few words in her ear. Immediately, her expression changed. She looked at me with hate in her eyes. It took my breath away. I didn't realize that such intelligence and such hatred could coexist in one person. 'Listen to me, Mr. Nazi,' she shot at me in fury. 'I'm not Israeli, I'm not even Zionist, but I am Jewish. My parents were survivors of the camps. I never knew my grandparents. They were slaughtered in Poland. I do not sit in judgment on your people; I don't believe in collective guilt. But you, you disgust me. It makes me sick to see you free and happy in this country.' She jumped to her feet and, turning to her host, said, 'Please don't hold it against me, but I refuse to sit down to dinner with this individual. I'm sure you understand.' It was the most dangerous moment of my career as a secret agent. With my entire being, I wanted to hold her back, to send her an urgent message: 'Don't go by appearances. I'm a Jew, like you. I'm entitled to love you and be loved by you.' But fortunately, I was well trained. I didn't even blush. I looked down and in a loud voice said to my best 'friend' among them, 'You see, these Jews, they live on hate.' He apologized for her and for her behavior. But as for me, that misunderstanding made me suffer such pain as I hope you'll never have to experience. So stop bothering me with your stories of hatred."

After a long silence, Diego, a romantic when he was in the mood, asked, "Did you ever see her again, that young journalist? After you left the Mossad, did you try to look her up? Tell us, did you make love to her?" Gad said nothing, but

Diego persisted: "Come on, amigo, you want me to go to my grave without knowing the rest of the story?"

"There's no more to the story."

"You didn't go back to Paris?"

"Yes. In fact, I took a plane to France the day after I resigned from the Mossad. I called the magazine where she worked and asked to speak to her. I was told it was impossible. I explained that it was urgent; then an editor came on and said, 'She cannot be reached.' When I insisted, he said, 'Where have you been, my dear sir? Don't you know that our colleague is dead?' I didn't know. 'Did she die on assignment, in the Middle East perhaps?' I asked. 'No. It was just cancer.' Yes, that editor did use the word *just*." Gad wiped his brow. "What hurts the most is that she died without knowing who I was."

Gamaliel tried to reassure him. "Someday you'll tell her."

"Are you making fun of me? I just told you she's dead."

"And I'm telling you you'll see her again, in the next world. I believe in it. I don't know if God's there, but I know my parents are, waiting for me. And that journalist is there, too, waiting for you."

Yasha was straddling his chair, as he always did when he was keyed up. He came back to the topic of hatred. "The enemy's not the one we hate the most; it's someone close to us. It's the friend who lets us down, the brother who betrays us, the neighbor who turns us in."

LATER ON, GAMALIEL WOULD RECALL, AS AN echo to what Yasha had said, Gide's line: "Families, I hate you." Had his wife, Colette, adopted the famous curse as her own? She'd loved her husband only when she thought he didn't love her, in order to make him the guilty one. Yet he had never hated her, nor their two daughters, either. Their estrangement remained a sorrow to him. Yes, only sorrow endured.

Sometimes he felt he could take no more. His cup of silent tears was overflowing. When he was younger, he'd been strong enough to pull himself together, but now that he had used up his strength, he could no longer manage it. Too much, it was too much. Too many times he'd fled, too many disappointments, too often exiled, and too much remorse, as well. Too often doubted or not understood. Too many barriers that would not go away. Too many times he'd felt powerless, as if facing a dark mass that was coming at him, sometimes to toss him in the air, at others to crush him to the ground. Too much remorse when he thought about his two daughters. To this day, they cursed him. He was sure of it.

And yet.

Sometimes the words of Rebbe Zusya would come to his mind, like lessons in solace: "The High Priest Aaron lost his two sons, Nadab and Abihu, and he remained silent.

"Job's children died, but he waited in silence seven days and seven nights before he spoke."

Or the old Sage would quote the great Rebbe Menahem Mendel of Kotsk: " 'It is when you feel that you want to cry out that you must suppress the cry.' "

Or else these words from a survivor of the camps: "To be silent is forbidden; to speak is impossible."

Another memory plagued Gamaliel. "Papa?" Sophie had asked when she was still a little girl.

"Yes?"

"Why are you sad?"

Gamaliel did not feel sad, but she was very perceptive. "How could I be sad when I have you in my lap?"

"That's just it. I'm with you, and you're sad."

"How could I be sad when you love me?"

"That's just it, Papa. I love you, and still you're sad." She stopped and put her tiny right hand on her forehead as she always did when she wanted to indicate that she was think ing. "I think I know why. You're sad because I love you."

He leaned over and kissed her eyes.

Just when did the break happen? He couldn't tell exactly. It was the outcome of a slow process, one that was impercep- tible but inexorable. Sophie, by then a teenager, had given him a strange look one overcast fall day when she was getting ready to go to school. That was when it began. He'd wanted to hug her, but she muttered, "I'm late," and hurried out the door. It was raining. He thought she might catch cold, but it was too late to call her back. Without knowing why, he felt a pain unlike any he had known. And a fear.

He'd been trying to hide it for some time. He told himself he shouldn't read too much into it, shouldn't torment him- self. Why worry over a shrug of the shoulders? It's ridicu- lous, he thought. I'm too thin-skinned, too quick to see a symptom of unhappiness or betrayal in the merest trifle. On the surface, everything seemed as usual. They went about their daily routines, exchanged everyday conversations, left home and came back, at ease with each other. Little Sophie—now no longer so little—would smile at him. As always, or almost so. But deep down, Gamaliel was no longer sure of it. Something had changed between them. Some- times she treated him as an enemy; or worse, a stranger. Should he talk to her? Ask her to explain her hostility? He vacillated for a while, waiting for the right moment. It came on a June evening. They were at home alone. Sophie was in her room doing homework, some tedious paper on the Jansenists, while Gamaliel was sitting at the big dining room table, trying to work on a manuscript but getting nowhere. Unusual for him, he couldn't seem to concentrate. Suddenly, he froze. He heard the sound of sobbing from Sophie's room. He hastened to her door, opened it as furtively as a burglar, then hesitated a moment before pushing it all the way with infinite precaution. Was that really his beloved little girl, collapsed in tears at her desk, books in front of her, head on her arms? He had never seen her in such a state. He touched her shoulder and said softly, "What's happened to you, my little duckling? You're hurting? Tell me about it. When you're suffering, I feel like dying. Who did this to you?" She went on sobbing. He stroked her neck. "Why these tears? Where does it hurt?" And then more urgently, he asked, "Who made you cry? A boyfriend? A pal who turned against you? Tell me." At once, she stopped sobbing. The silence in the room grew heavy. Sophie took a deep breath and buried her head in her arms. "It's you," she said in a low voice. "You're the one who's making me unhappy. Me and Katya and Mother—you're making us all unhappy. You're sacrificing us all. Don't you understand that?" Gamaliel staggered, as if he had been clubbed over the head. He felt as if he were suffocating. He opened his mouth to try to breathe, to stay alive. But he no longer wanted to live. To what end? he wondered. I was blind. I lied to myself. Sophie detests me. I love her and she pushes me away. So does her sister. And so does everybody. What have I been doing with my days and nights to make those I love the most in the world hate me so? Was there something lacking in my love? A more trenchant question followed: Was I the one who was first to hate, and is their hatred the bitter rotted fruit of my own? Why didn't I know enough to pay attention to what was going on around me?

ONE DAY, OUT OF PURE CURIOSITY, GAMALIEL asked Gad about the significance of his favorite saying, "Be careful." They were alone at the cafeteria, waiting for their friends. "You'd think those two words express all your philosophy of life," Gamaliel said.

"Why all of it? Isn't part enough for you?" That day, the Israeli was in an expansive mood. "It's because of my violin. If I'm not careful, it's likely to do all sorts of crazy things. Sometimes it wants to go galloping off after who knows what ears and what hearts. You see, my violin has a life of its own. Sometimes it wants to weep and cry and mourn, while I'm in a mood to sing the happiness of children and get them dancing."

Gamaliel was about to comment that Gad had all the makings of a ventriloquist, but he refrained, for fear of offending him. In any case, Gad continued: "Do you know why I come to this place?"

"For the food?" Gamaliel said, hoping to get a laugh.

"Don't be silly. It's for the people who come here. I like to hear them speaking Yiddish. I like to listen in on their conversations. They help me see into a world that for a long time was impenetrable to me—the world of my parents and grandparents." On the surface, his seemed a simple everyday story. Gad Lichtenstein, whose name was later made into the Hebrew Even-Ezer, was the only son of German emigrants, quiet, reserved people who never spoke of their past. His father worked in high finance; his mother was a doctor. He was brought up as a Zionist, did his military service, was a commando officer, and then was recruited by the Mossad. "All my life, all day long, it was drilled into me: 'Be careful. Watch out.' One wrong move in Baghdad could get you killed; one word too many in Damascus could mean prison and torture."

"You must have some great stories."

"Like everyone else. But that's just it: It's better to keep them to yourself."

"You don't mean to say you don't trust us?"

"I didn't say that."

"Well then?"

"Then nothing. It's better to listen." When he saw Bolek at the entrance, he quickly concluded: "I'm speaking from experience."

Bolek joined them, and it was the one time Gamaliel was sorry to see him.

THE DOCTOR IS TRYING TO CONSOLE ME, AND I'M grateful, but I'm barely listening to her. Can we let our minds dwell on two subjects at the same time? Yes, we can. My thoughts are still with my children and my parents, but she is reminding me of the sick woman upstairs. My intuition tells me there is some unknown connection between us, and that disturbs me. I think of the men and women whose paths have crossed my own. Some of them showed me the mystery of knowledge, others that of suffering. Whether they carried light or darkness, whether they were drawn to the service of good or attracted by evil, they all left their mark on me. It is because of them that I am who I am. The desire to share love was what inspired some, while others were determined to destroy it in favor of anger. Rebbe Zusya fascinated me with his faith in faith. But before him came the friendship of Bolek, Gad and his violin, Diego and his battles, Yasha and his regrets. . . .

Yasha was from Kiev. He came from a Jewish family that had been secretly Orthodox. His father had attended the yeshiva at Navarodok. They spoke Yiddish at home. At sixteen, Yasha enlisted in the Red Army. He was wounded and decorated; he mourned the fallen. When at war's end he returned to the city of his birth, he discovered how alone he was, and how consumed he was by hate: hatred for the enemy's occupying army, hatred for those who collaborated with them, hatred for the onlookers who let them have their way. Between Rosh Hashanah and Yom Kippur, soon after the Germans arrived, his entire family was massacred at Babi Yar. Where could he turn? He joined the Communist party. He did his university studies, was appointed a teacher in a secondary school, married Nina, an energetic and doctrinaire young Muscovite who had found work in an office that was part of the "organs"—that is, the internal security services. One day in early 1949, she told Yasha that her boss wanted to see him. His first reaction was to ask, "Should I be worried about this?" She assured him that it had nothing to do with him personally. She was right. Interrogator Pavel Borisovich questioned him about his knowledge of languages, particularly about his mastery of Yiddish. Simple questions, easy answers. Thus began an ordeal that would stay with Yasha for the rest of his life.

This was the time in the Soviet Union of Stalin's anti-Semitic mania. The killing of the great actor and director Shlomo Mikhoels was followed by the arrest of well-known Jewish writers and poets who wrote in Yiddish: Dovid Bergelson, Peretz Markish, Itzhak Feffer, Der Nister, Leib Kvitko, and Dovid Hofstein, among many others. While in Moscow the police were arresting the big names, in the provincial cities they had to make do with lesser prey. In Kiev, destiny's choice was Fishel Kleinman. Yasha knew him: They had fought in the same unit near Kharkov. He was a short, brave, quick-witted man, whose cheeriness made him popular; he had a funny story for every occasion. Kleinman called himself a poet, a writer, a journalist, and he swore with a laugh that the world would recognize his genius once victory was achieved. Not the world, in fact—that would be saying too much—but several journals had published articles and poems in which he sang his love for Stalin, of course, and for Russian Jews, loyal citizens of the Soviet Union and devoted admirers of their immortal leader. Did he know that the organs kept everything he wrote in their files? Kleinman had not yet been questioned when Yasha was asked to translate his writings from Yiddish into Russian. The meaning was clear: A case was being prepared at a higher level. "There is surely anti-Soviet material in there," said Pavel Borisovich. "Be sure to highlight it." And he added more sharply, "Be careful. This is a matter of national security! Not a word to anyone! Not even Nina, understand?" Yes, Yasha understood: You don't fool around with the organs. That same evening, Nina asked him how the meeting had gone. "Just fine," he said. "Can you tell me something about it?" "No." "Then forget I asked."

Yasha's school granted him a leave of absence. He went to the office every morning, never knowing whether he would leave it. By dint of translating Kleinman's articles and poems, he became in a sense his most faithful reader. There appeared to be nothing compromising in his writings.

Denunciation of the fascist Germans, recitation of the martyrdom of Russian Jews under the occupation, fervent eulogies of the victorious Red Army, lyrical poems to the glories of the Russian countryside, the Russian character, the Communist sky, the Communist soul, the Communist gods. Pavel Borisovich, obviously dissatisfied, was getting exasperated. "You haven't found anything that reveals the author's secret intentions, his subversive thoughts? Nowhere a deviationist word, an implied criticism of our policies? Not even an example of holding back, of hesitating?" he asked. Both his voice and his face gradually grew threatening. "I'm warning you! Don't try to protect him! Think about the risk you're running!" Yasha was indeed thinking about it. But in whom could he confide? Nina? Why implicate her in a case with unforeseeable consequences? He tried to avoid Kleinman. The latter telephoned several times to invite him to some commemorative gathering or to a dinner in honor of a visiting Jewish writer, but he always told Nina to say he was sick or not home. Yasha felt vaguely guilty: What would the prosecutor read into his Russian translations of Kleinman's Yiddish texts? All the more so since on rereading certain poems, he discovered an expression here or a misplaced comma there that could easily be misinterpreted. Then he came upon an unpublished prayer—or rather, a lament—addressed to the memory of the victims of Babi Yar, written the day after the liberation of Kiev in 1943. The author blamed the massacre on the silence of the non-Jewish inhabitants of the city, its Ukrainian Communists among them. Tears came to Yasha's eyes the first time he read the poem. Then he caught himself; a signal went off in his head. This cry from the heart might seem like a criticism of the Party! It would become a deadly weapon in the hands of the prosecu-

tor! What should he do? How could he protect his old
comrade-in-arms? The prayer was already listed in the prosecution's catalog of Kleinman's writings.

"So," Yasha told us one day when our group was recalling
Stalin's poisonous hatred of the Jewish writers, "like a fool, I
decided I'd trick that temperamental investigator in order to
protect the unlucky poet, who was guilty only of being
naïve. I didn't destroy the poem; I just set it aside without
translating it.

"Of course I expected a violent reaction from Pavel
Borisovich, but not the earthquake that shook the whole
office. He accused me of conspiring with a traitor, of trying
to sabotage Communist justice. He banged on the table with
both fists and yelled, 'Where did Prosecution Exhibit One
twenty-two disappear to? Don't tell me you ate it, or that it
flew out the window!' I replied that it was there, in the
dossier. He demanded to see it. I showed it to him. 'But it's
not where it belongs! Why did you put it at the end, out of
order, hidden under the other documents? And why didn't
you translate it?' I had my answer ready: 'I only translated his
published writings. Weren't those your instructions?' 'No,
those were not my instructions! My orders to you were
perfectly clear: Translate everything that the traitor Fishel
Yakobovich Kleinman wrote!' I answered that I'd misunder-
stood him, and that I was ready to translate the unpublished
poem on the spot. 'Never mind!' he shouted. 'I already
have a translation! Here it is.' That's how I learned that he
hadn't put his confidence in me, but had obtained another
translator, one who either didn't share my scruples or else
wasn't afraid of the consequences if he deceived the prosecutor. Now it was I who feared those consequences. I was
sure I'd never see my home again. Surely some notorious

troika was waiting in the next room to pass judgment on me. How many years would I get? And Nina, what would become of her? Now the prosecutor changed tack: 'You're going to translate that poem anyway. I intend to compare your two translations. So go ahead, get to work.' I finished the three pages in less than an hour. Later on, I was able to read the anonymous translator's version, and I was stupefied to find that, thanks to a few minor changes, his was less compromising than mine. In the end, it was because of my blunder— I, who thought I was such a hero—that the brave warrior Fishel Kleinman, wordsmith in his spare time, was sentenced to death. . . . I got seven years in prison. Nina left me; maybe they made her do it. . . . What saved me was Nikita Khrushchev coming to power . . . but ever since, I've hated poetry."

"What became of the prosecutor, Pavel Borisovich?" Bolek asked.

"As far as I know, he's still on the job."

"You still hate him?"

"Only when I hear poetry." Yasha smiled. "And yet, they say poetry cures you of hatred."

Yasha never remarried.

THE MAN WHO ENDEAVORED TO HEAL ME WHEN I no longer knew who I was—Gamaliel? Péter? Someone else?—was both gentle and strong. I don't know why, but he reminded me of Maimonides, whom a Sage once described as "the Teacher who knows."

I spent privileged, unforgettable moments with him.

I see myself facing him in his room so many years ago. He lived in the Jewish Quarter of Casablanca. I was young; I'd come there looking for a girl I'd fallen head over heels in love with. Esther, that was her name. She read palms, and cards as well; she was a fortune-teller. She was slender; her face radiant. She had an eager look, and was at times hotheaded but at others stubborn. Her parted lips were an invitation. She reminded me of Shulamit in the Song of Songs.

I had met her on a boat going to Israel. It was two days before we were to arrive. I was deep in conversation with a blond widow whose eyes were demanding and inquisitive; she encouraged flirtation with a sharp, mischievous intelligence, suggesting untold pleasures. But I realized there was nothing there for me; in short, she was a tease. Just then, my eyes fell on a young Oriental woman, and I forgot the widow. It was Esther. I liked the way she cocked her head to one side. Her penetrating gaze took hold of mine. I wanted her with every fiber of my being. My body was hungry for hers. But we shared a puerile notion of innocence, which stood like a barrier between us. So instead of seizing the moment and enjoying it to the full, we sat up all night talking, telling each other our dreams and the disappointments to come. I would say to her, "I'll tell you a story if you give me a kiss." She replied, "I always look over the goods before I buy." I said, "Do you like stories?" She replied, "Silly question. Of course I do. It's part of my work. If you only knew the stories I have to tell the people who consult me. . . . Every palm has its own story; so does every star." I took a deep breath, summoned my courage, and said, "All right, Esther, now hear a story whose ending I don't yet know.

"The dreamer was sitting and dreaming on a cloud; he was waiting for the woman he was preparing to love and whom he already loved. Had she encountered someone more handsome, younger? Had she lost her way in the alleys that led to the woods? Had she forgotten where he would be waiting for her? The dreamer's anxiety grew so heavy, it almost made the cloud tip over. So he tried to think about something else, about other beings. About the birds, who were singing and mocking one another; their chirping was pleasant to hear. He thought about the trees—how delightful to sink his teeth into ripe fruit when he was thirsty! He could still remember the young Greek or Turkish dancer who had winked at him from the distant stage. Could he have fallen for her? Maybe so, but not like this. The one he now loved, here on this cloud, he loved more, and more passionately, than all the others. He loved her for her lips; they were his sanctuary. But she was keeping him waiting. He was tiring of it, and so was the cloud he was sitting on. Should he get off? But then he might lose the one who was coming to join him. She knew these clouds; she could tell you their names and describe every one of them. Let's stay where we are, the dreamer decided. She'll come. She won't be much longer. Hadn't she said she loved him, too? That she longed for him? But time was passing, the minutes stretching into hours, and the woman of his dreams had still not arrived. So, ready to give up in despair, the dreamer decided to leave his cloud and go where broken hearts went to drown themselves. He had already gotten down when he heard a voice, the sweetest voice in the world, the voice that harmonized with his when he told her things he could tell to no one else. The voice of the woman he loved. Her name was . . ."

I paused. Should I go on? I wondered. Tell Esther I am grateful that she has convinced me I'm capable of dreaming, of making plans, of loving? "And the ending of your story, do you know it?" Esther asked. I said, "You're the one who reads the future, not I." Esther drew me to her and placed her finger on my lips. "To search for happiness is a greater gift than finding it." I started to challenge that, but she interrupted, saying, "I know what you're going to say. You'll say that you're confident of our love, that we can reaffirm it every night—but I prefer the desire to its satisfaction." Then she asked me to kiss her. I took her in my arms and caressed her, hoping she would understand that because I loved her I was accepting the limits she had set for the time being, but only for the time being.

Later on, I asked her to read our palms: Was it written there that we would meet? She demurred, saying, "That would be dangerous." I didn't understand why she was afraid. She explained that when reading a friend's palm, she had predicted a tragic event in the coming months. "What happened?" I asked. She did not answer.

The next night, I questioned her about what had happened to her friend. Again she closed herself off in an opaque silence. "I'm not afraid of dying," I told her, without knowing if it was true. She read my palms by moonlight, punctuating her findings with little exclamations that were sometimes excited, at other times sorrowful. I tried in vain to get her to say more. All she would say was, "Don't worry, you won't die young." "That's not what interests me," I said, irritated. "I want to know if we'll have a future together." She gave a deep sigh and gazed at the stars for a long time before saying in a tender, engaging tone, "You still don't understand? For me, the present lives on in the future. You want to know what I see? I won't tell you; I have no right to. It's very clear: I don't see what I would like to see, and what I see, I don't like."

Then there were words of love, fresh and new, strange and as old as time. Let's seek ecstasy together, Esther, dawn's intoxication, with all its promises, and the other kind, the ecstasy of midnight and its mournings, let's seek them out, too, Esther. Let us savor them side by side before the fall. All these words came to my lips, but I held my tongue.

I didn't stay long in Israel, nor did she. She went home to Morocco before we had a chance to meet again. I was in pain. I missed her even more than I did Ilonka and my mother. I had to find her, and as long as I was searching, there was a connection between us. But how could I go about it? I was poor and far from home. I asked Bolek if he could find me some work that would bring in enough to pay my way. Bolek wanted to know if it was urgent. Yes, it was, I told him. Everything that concerned Esther was urgent. "All right," said Bolek. "I'll see what I can do." I told myself that if Bolek came back smiling, that meant Esther was waiting for me. Well, he was smiling.

At the time, there was still a Jewish community in Morocco that, though very small, was bustling and relatively rich. I questioned one and all, but in vain. I didn't know Esther's family name, so no one could direct me to her. I told them she was a brunette, that she was gorgeous, especially when she cocked her head to one side, that her voice was beautiful when she sang that Hasidic tune about the Sabbath, about the day to come, when the Sabbath would never end. I said that she could read your palm and see in it both the immediate and the distant future. No one knew her. I followed several false leads: to an impoverished father who wanted to marry off his last daughter; to an aunt whose niece was looking for a husband so she could leave the country; to a rich man who was trying to rid himself of a mistress who was either too demanding or not demanding enough. Each such event left me more disillusioned.

One morning when I was wandering alone by the sea, toting my misery like a familiar burden, a man stopped me and said, "You're young and at loose ends; I'm older and want to help. May I help you?"

His long, bearded face and his regal bearing inspired confidence, but what especially attracted me was the warmth of his voice. It sounded as if it could unlock the gates of invisible fortresses. "I'm searching," I said, echoing the words of the beggar of my childhood.

"I, too, am searching."

"Are we seeking the same thing? The same person? The same path?" As he did not reply, I continued: "Is the man who seeks riches as worthy as the man who seeks the truth?"

"It's not the same. Riches imprison you; the truth liberates." And after a moment, he added, "Still, what matters is the search. One may start out in search of money, but on the way one's objective changes, for one's been attracted to something else."

We strolled along the shore like two old companions who like to watch the waves. I told him about Esther, and he told me about Rebbe Zusya. Coming from some ill-defined part of Eastern Europe, this singular Messenger had settled in Casablanca, where he was known to a small intimate circle as a miracle worker. Digging deep in the hidden and forgotten writings of Rabbi Haim ben Atar, the great commentator who was a contemporary and correspondent of the founder of Hasidism, known as the "Besht," this man was working in secret to hasten the coming of the Messiah. "Would you like to meet him?" he asked.

"Why not? Since he seems to know the Messiah's address, surely he'll know Esther's."

"Anything can happen," Shalom said with a wink.

The house he led me to consisted of several small rooms cluttered with disparate furnishings. Two windows gave onto a noisy street of the Jewish Quarter, but the calm that prevailed inside seemed to come from another world. In reality, it emanated from an old man, short but majestic in bearing, who sat at a large table, studying the yellowing pages of a thick volume. Had he heard us enter? His thin face was lined from many days of fasting; his shoulders were wrapped in a woolen plaid. Only his eyes seemed to move when he lifted his head to look at us with an expression of alert concern. No doubt we had interrupted his train of thought. His grimly stubborn manner intrigued me. Why did he seem so harsh and strict, this mystic who devoted his dawns and dusks to bringing the ultimate salvation to his people and to all humanity? He spoke to Shalom first: "What are you doing here at this hour? Couldn't it keep till evening? And who is this man?"

"He needs you, Rebbe."

"And how about me? You think I don't need anyone?"

He fell silent, and so did Shalom. Should I apologize for coming unannounced, for barging in? I wondered. My anxiety was such that I could not utter a word.

"My friend is suffering," said Shalom.

"What's he suffering from?"

"He's in love."

"So? He's old enough to know that love is too much like happiness not to be akin to suffering. . . . Whom is he in love with?"

"A girl from here."

"Who is she?"

"Her name is Esther."

"Yes, our beloved queen . . . She saved our people, long ago, in Persia."

I spoke up just for the sake of saying something: "This isn't the same one."

"What do you know about it? Suppose I were to tell you

that your Esther carries in her the soul of ours. Would you love her any the less?"

He seemed to be growing angry. Frightened, I stammered, "Yes, yes, I'd love her no matter where she came from."

The Rebbe calmed down. "Our Lord, blessed be He, is the matchmaker of souls. Your two souls may be apart now, but they will be joined one day. I promise you that."

"One day, one day!" I exclaimed. "But when?"

"That day will be luminous and enduring; it will be forever and forever blessed. It will be the day of salvation."

I smiled, to my own surprise, and said, "But Rebbe, I don't think I can wait that long."

" 'That long'?" Again his whole frame was shaking with anger. "Suppose it were to arrive tomorrow? What do you know of the mysteries that make time infinite?"

"Rebbe," I replied, emboldened, "what interests me at the moment is the infinite mystery of love."

"Well, it's the same mystery," he said.

I took my leave with a feeling of regret, of missed opportunity: Had I met him too late or too early? My visa was running out and I had to leave Casablanca. Later, at the time of the Jews' exodus from Morocco, he and Shalom went not to Israel but to the United States: The miracle worker was needed more by the diaspora than by the Jewish state. It was there, in Brooklyn, that our paths crossed again. I was working on a book for a Protestant theologian, whose search for his Jewish roots had led him to Hasidic circles. It was a holiday. Shalom was glad to see me. "And where is Rebbe Zusya?" I asked him.

"Not far from here. Shall we go?"

Not another word was said.

"So, what about Esther?" said the Rebbe, teasing me as he held out his hand.

"And what about the Messiah?" I shot back.

"There was a Talmudic Sage who was convinced that the Savior's coming would be brought about by accident. Not I. I believe that the Messiah's coming will be the fruit of our prayers, of our anger, and also of our struggles. If you were to insist on it, I would be willing to take an oath by all that is most sacred to us that we will win this struggle, and that we will celebrate our victory by dancing with the most illustrious and most glorious of our forerunners!"

"I don't know how to dance, Rebbe."

"You'll learn. Promise me you'll come back. Often."

"I promise, Rebbe."

I became a faithful caller at his humble quarters. Like the Blessed Madman of my *Book of Secrets*, he initiated me in the study of both the revealed and the secret texts where the Lord, like His mortal creatures, overflows with a melancholy love for the *Shekhinah*, the spirit of God, which is in exile. He seeks to deliver His spirit and His people from their exile. Each time he saw me arrive, Rebbe Zusya would call out a command: "Come closer!" I went to him as one thirsting for water, and for life.

Until the day came when my demons were too strong: They killed that thirst in me. I can see myself back then:

Sick, at the end of my rope, I am no longer expecting anything or anybody. Alone and forgotten in my small room in Manhattan, near Harlem, I am convinced I am not suited for this world; I will slide gently into death. My bowels have emptied out and so have my spirits. Were it not for the pain, I would long since have lost consciousness; but the pain keeps me awake, if not lucid. Never would I have thought my own body would become my enemy, my torturer. What did I do to it that it should attack me so ferociously?

In reality, it's not my body that is sick; *I* am. And my body is not me. Nothing about me is still me. I disgust myself. I detest myself. I find myself repugnant. I want myself dead. I've done everything to bring that about. I've scorned my friends; I've allowed myself to sink into depression and gloom. Each passing thought draws me toward the abyss that yawns before me. Each breath I take fans my despair. All those I loved were torn away from me. What good would it do to create new bonds? Why go on searching for words in the wind? And wake up to a barren world? No longer have I any desire to seek out the beauty in a face, the majesty in a tree. A hundred voices are urging me to give up. Finally, I swallow ten little white pills, then five more; it's all I have left. But Death wants no part of me. He punishes me for disturbing him. I hurt all over.

A sudden knock at the door. I no longer have the strength to ask who it is, to tell the visitor to go away, because in my condition I don't want to see anyone. The person knocks harder; then the door opens—I'd forgotten to lock it. Who can it be? "So, you like being sick?" a voice asks in a manner intended to be playful. It's Shalom. "I brought you some food. Chicken soup and hot tea—the best medicine there is." I feel like replying, Not for what ails me. But I'm too feeble to argue with him. Since I do not move, he comes over and helps me sit up, meanwhile talking about this and that, as if wanting to make sure I'm able to hear him, that I'm still alive. Slowly, I swallow a few spoonfuls of soup, a few sips of tea. Giddy at first, I then feel myself gaining strength.

"Shalom," I ask, "how did you know? Who told you? Or are you clairvoyant?"

"Not at all," he replies, laughing through his beard. "It was our Rebbe."

"How did it happen? Tell me."

Shalom clears his throat and explains: That same day, after the morning service, Rebbe Zusya asked if he had seen me recently. Shalom answered no, not for several weeks. "Last night, I had a glimpse of him," said the Rebbe. "I sensed that he was preparing to go over to the other shore. He's been avoiding me, and that's likely to do him harm. He's not well, not well at all. He's in great danger." The Rebbe ordered Shalom to go call on me immediately, and then to send me to him. It was urgent.

My vision becomes strangely sharp. All of a sudden an immense light that is warm and gentle envelops everything that my thoughts touch on or set aside. It seems to me that at last I am able to lay bare what my soul has been trying to conceal.

"When do you want me to go to the Rebbe's?"

"As soon as you feel better." Then after a pause, he adds, "We'll go together. Yes, yes. The Rebbe forbade me to leave you."

Shalom does as he is told: He does not leave me except to bring food, or hot water for tea. He recites the appropriate morning and evening prayers. When I am not dozing, he talks to me about various topics—political news of the day, the international situation, crises in Israel—but above all about what is happening in the Hasidic world, in Jerusalem, B'nai B'rak, and Brooklyn: the alliances, the intrigues in the various courts, their ambition, rivalries, marriages planned between the great dynasties. And, of course, all is intimately linked to Rebbe Zusya, the "Messenger." Few truly know him, but all who have met him are aware that he is at the center of it all, every event, all the maneuvering, everywhere. Nothing escapes him, and there is nothing to which he is indifferent.

"By the way," Shalom says with a smile, "the Rebbe doesn't understand why you don't marry."

"Is that why he wants to see me? To tell me that along with everything else he's a matchmaker? Before it was the Lord, and now it's the Rebbe? Maybe he's found a nice Jewish girl who was always intended for me? A second Colette?"

Shalom, stroking his bushy beard, becomes serious. "Think about it," he says gravely. "It may be that he has found your Esther. With our Rebbe, you never know."

Esther—alive? Esther—here? I feel my fever coming back. I'm relapsing into my sickness. Everything in me that was pushed away is reemerging. Esther and I, lovers, although neither she nor I ever spoke the word, except to postpone it until later, always later. Sharing kisses and awkward embraces but remaining chaste. Words whispered, promises offered, plans agreed to, holding each other close. David and Bathsheba, Solomon and Shulamit, Dante and Beatrice, Petrarch and Laura . . . I was floating with them in a luminous sky; then I sank into a dark well, where I found a still darker sun. And Shalom's voice, his warm voice sliding over my face and chest: "Remember this, Gamaliel. Remember that the Rebbe knows what he's doing. What's more, he knows what you're doing. The proof of that is he sensed you were sick . . . and he is going to heal you."

Suddenly irritated with him for intruding into my private hell, I deride him. "How about you, did he cure you, too? Are you happy?" Immediately, I regret the question. Why hurt his feelings? Is it not he and he alone who has cared for me day and night, who perhaps has rescued me from an illness whose name he does not know? Besides, is it his fault if the

Rebbe wants to see me and is determined to make me give up my life as a single divorced man? Why should I blame Shalom? Yes indeed, I'm being unfair to my Moroccan friend. Have I ever shown an interest in his life? Is he married? No doubt. But I've never met his wife. Do they have children?

"You still don't understand our Teacher. Wish him long life," Shalom says serenely. "First of all, healing has little to do with happiness. You have to deserve happiness. Healing also, but it's not the same thing. Besides, the Rebbe doesn't believe it's his function to cure pain, but, rather, to combat it. Healing is secondary. And his battle takes place on so high a level that only he can wage it. You and I are here only to bear witness."

I hear him, but from far away. He is speaking of the Rebbe, but the voice I hear is the voice of Esther. She is a voice, a voice with a face, with eyes, a heart that beats, a controlled passion. On the eve of our arrival in Haifa, she told me about a dream: In the infinite silence of space, she and I were two stars lost among the galaxies. We were eternally seeking each other. We were separated by innumerable clusters of light, but we spoke to each other and, miracle of miracles, each voice found the other; they alone vibrated in the silence of Creation.

It was all our happiness required.

And you, Shalom, what voices are you hearing?

The next day, we go to the Teacher, who knows how to separate and bring together, how to disturb and how to heal.

"You're too far away," he tells me. "Come closer." I step forward until I'm against the table. "Give me your hand." I reach out. The Rebbe takes my hand in his. I feel its warmth on my skin and almost in my veins.

"When one is sick, one calls out for help," says the Rebbe. "As long as one is calling, it's Life responding to Life."

"And when there is no response from anywhere?"

"Then that is because your appeal wasn't genuine."

"But it was, Rebbe. It was genuine."

Rebbe Zusya leans forward. "It was Death you called to, not Life. Am I right?" I am silent, so he continues: "By what right did you try to put an end to your days? Do they belong to you? Don't you understand yet that each life is sacred and irreplaceable? That a single life, any life, yours as well as mine, weighs more and is worth more than all that has been written about Life. And you, you dare to prefer Death? What do you know about Death to be calling for it?"

"How about God?" I ask weakly.

The Rebbe looks up and studies me with curiosity. "A good question, but a bit late and insufficient. God? A Jewish writer said that 'the silence of God is God.' I say that God is not silent, although He is the God of Silence. He does call out. It is by His silence that He calls to you. Are you answering Him?"

GAMALIEL WAS LUNCHING WITH HIS PALS ON A DANK and gloomy autumn day. They were all about the same age, retirement age. Together, they were an informal rescue committee—to needle the anti-Semites, they called themselves the "Elders of Zion"—which helped out refugees and the neediest of immigrants, those who had no one they could count on and who counted for no one.

Their usual table was off in a corner. All were present but Gad, the Israeli, who was suffering from angina. Yasha: athletic build, shaved head, bushy eyebrows over twinkling eyes. He'd made a name for himself on Wall Street. Often away on business trips, he was said to be a Don Juan. Diego: the fighter, especially for lost causes, and quick to anger, particularly when one didn't agree with him that communism was as great a danger to the world as fascism. His friends would often raise their glasses and toast in Hebrew: *"L'chayim!"* And each time, Diego would reply in French: "Death to boredom!" Bolek: bony features, high forehead, elegant, always dressed in a gray or blue suit with red pinstripes. A onetime lawyer, he was reticent with strangers, jovial with his pals. Gad and Bolek were married, more or less, had children, and were relatively happy. Gamaliel and Yasha were divorced, and Diego was a confirmed bachelor. Although they had become American citizens, they all remembered the past, the time when they were emigrants in search of paradise lost. They liked to gather together to celebrate the solidarity of the uprooted and the divine power of laughter.

They enjoyed a cozy ambiance of camaraderie. Gamaliel, closed off in what was now a willful isolation, nursed a romantic faith in friendship. It was his passion, his anchor, his reason for living, his protective circle, his barricade. The tragedy of Moses and Socrates, he would often say, was that while they had disciples and lieutenants, they had no friends. He liked to recall the beautiful passages in Cicero about friendship, or quote the Sage in the Talmud who cried out, "Friendship or death!" Or he'd quote the Hasidic Teacher, according to whom "God is not only the Judge and the Father of His creatures; He is also their friend." That was why, Gamaliel believed, no death was so awful as that of a friendship: God Himself would mourn it.

"Hey there, you!" called out Diego, draining his wineglass and already tipsy. "You look to me as if you have the blues. What's the matter, Gamaliel? Did the little boats in your bathtub sink?"

Gamaliel replied only with a shrug.

"I feel like laughing today," Diego announced. "Come on, friends—I'll buy a drink for anyone who makes me laugh."

So Gamaliel told a story he claimed to have heard recently from a Yiddish writer. "Do you know the one about the idiot father who told his son to close the door because it was cold outside? And the kid says, 'So if I close the door, will it be warm outside?' "

Yasha made a gesture of mock disgust. "Gamaliel, Gamaliel, what do you think we are—illiterates? We read Sholem Aleichem before you did."

"Let's drink to the health of Sholem Alei-Alei," broke in Diego, who pretended to have trouble pronouncing the name of the Yiddish humorist, author of *Fiddler on the Roof.*

"But he's been dead for almost a century," Bolek observed with a laugh.

"Then let's drink to his resurrection," Diego replied.

"Stop me if you've heard this one," Bolek went on. "A man dreams there's a naked woman standing by his bed. 'Who are you? And what're you doing here?' he asks her. And she says to him, as calm as you please, 'You're asking me? It's your dream, isn't it?' "

"Here's to the naked woman of our dreams," Diego declared, raising his glass.

Yasha spoke in turn: "There was a shtetl in Poland or Romania, where this poor guy finally got himself a job as the official watchman who was to inform the community when the Messiah arrived. 'Granted, it doesn't pay much,' they told him, 'but it's a lifetime job.' "

Diego poured himself another glass of wine. "Drink to the health of the watchman! And . . . to the Messiah."

Gamaliel, who was not drinking, remarked, "Isn't the Messiah right here, in all of us? Each time we help some poor refugee get his papers, isn't each of us his Savior?"

"So let's drink to all of us," said Diego. Then, wiping his mouth off with the back of his hand, he added, "I have a story, too. I remember it was in Marseilles, at the beginning of the war. We were a bunch of friends from the International Brigades, and we'd all escaped from French internment camps. We were standing in line for the various consulates. One of us, luckier than the rest, had just gotten a visa for Tierra del Fuego, in the south of Argentina. 'But that's far,' people told him. He acted surprised: 'Far from where?' "

The story brought the four friends back to their agenda. As was their custom, they compared notes on their thoughts and plans, and on the status of the cases of refugees or asylum seekers for which each of them was responsible.

Bolek read them a letter he had received from a village near Berditchev. One Zalman, the last Jew left of his community, wanted to emigrate to Israel or the United States so his children could have a Jewish education, but this was the dilemma: "If we stay here, the children will probably grow up separated from our people, but if we leave, what's to become of the cemetery and our dead, of whom I'm the only custodian?"

Yasha knew Berditchev: As an adolescent, he'd visited there with his parents. His grandparents, murdered by the SS Einsatzgruppen, were disciples of the Hasidic movement, of which Rebbe Levi Yitzhak was one of the most brilliant figures. "My grandfather wrote a paper about him," said Yasha, a confirmed atheist, in a voice half-amused, half-melancholy. "I read his paper. It was a kind of Song of Songs in honor of this Teacher who dared to bring suit against the Creator of the world for the suffering endured by His people. Once, at the Yom Kippur service, he threatened not to blow the shofar unless the Lord put an end to their suffering. He was quite a man, that Rebbe. I could believe in him, without that making me believe in his God."

Diego raised his glass. "Let's drink to his health!"

Gamaliel felt the need to speak up. "How could a Jew not love so daring a man as that Rebbe? But there's more to your story, Yasha. After having told God what was in his heart, the Teacher chanted the most beautiful, the most moving of our prayers: the Kaddish."

A long silence followed. Then Bolek asked, "What should I say to that last Jew in the village near Berditchev?" There was a long discussion among the Elders of Zion. Yasha made the case for the right of the dead to be protected, Gamaliel for that of the children to be educated. Diego proposed a compromise: They should tell the Jew to hire a local Gentile to look after the cemetery. The committee would underwrite the cost, and that of the man's emigration.

Bolek presented another case: In a small town in Georgia, a mother in distress was asking for advice and help. Her only daughter could not find a Jewish boy there to marry. If only one could be sent to her . . . She promised that her daughter would accept the boy, and so would she, her mother.

Yasha suggested they put her in touch with representatives of the Lubavitcher Hasidim. They knew everybody. Their networks operated with perfect efficiency and they were experienced in this sort of situation. If need be, they would send over a groom from Israel or from Brooklyn. It was out of the question for a Jewish girl from a good family to be left without a husband. "Who knows," said Yasha, "with God's help, their progeny might someday bring consolation to our people scattered among the nations."

If only it would be that easy to track down the whereabouts of Eve, Gamaliel was thinking.

Yasha's voice roused him from his reverie. "I don't know where your thoughts are, but they're not with us."

"Yes, I guess you're right," Gamaliel confessed.

"Don't you have a funny story to tell us? You don't like to laugh?"

Gamaliel looked down. He felt like saying he enjoyed laughter only when it was in despair, but he chose a less theatrical reply: "Yes, I like to laugh . . . but I never know when."

EVE, ATTENTIVE. EVE, HER THOUGHTS ELSE-where. Gamaliel's first true love? She, not Esther? The two were entirely different. Esther was an idea, a mirage. Nothing could really happen with her. Eve was serious, smiling, interested. She gave you the impression she was living a dream set in the real world, that she would draw you away from the daily routine to a kind of intensity you had never known, where you would experience an anxiety bordering on ecstasy.

Love at first sight? Well, why not? It must happen, since it's written about in the Bible and in novels. Gamaliel was coming to believe that now his own identity was changing: He was turning into a fictional character.

For years, as he wandered about, young and innocent, going where the wind took him, Gamaliel had believed that having lost Esther, he would never again fall in love. Colette: That was in another life, and it wasn't love. A marriage of convenience, of the moment? An unfortunate, unhappy experience. Sometimes since his divorce, he had let himself be attracted to a woman, especially if she had dark hair and a serious demeanor. He courted women, possessed them, or was possessed by them, finding in their bodies such joys that he would weep with guilt. But to reach that point, he had to deny Esther, or at least put her out of his mind for the moment. It was different with Eve. He could love her without parting from Esther, without betraying her. Thus his love for Eve was true and pure and—why not?—holy. He would never forget their first night. All was harmony, but within Gamaliel a storm was raging. Like a man possessed, unable to contain his desire, he longed to take wing and fly, to dance, to weep, to laugh, to run riot with his friends both living and dead, to get ready to die in his turn, to bid farewell to a life that from now on could only go downhill. Early the next morning, he turned to Eve and said, "I didn't realize I could still surprise myself. Just say the word and at dawn I'll light the sun; another word from you at evening and I'll put it out again."

They had met at a traditional Passover Seder at the home of Bolek and Noémie, who for the occasion had invited all their friends who lived alone. Seated next to his hostess, Gamaliel had a chance to look over the other guests as they each in turn recited the dramatic account of the exodus of the Hebrews from Egypt and the miraculous events that had made of them a free and determined people. His eyes were caught by a woman soberly dressed in blue. She was reciting in a low, melodious voice, which brought back distant memories.

"She has a nice voice," he whispered to Noémie. "Who is she?"

"Didn't I introduce you? True, you came late, when we were just sitting down. Her name is Eve. She's a remarkable woman but wounded. Don't try to seduce her; she's not for you. She doesn't look it, but she's a little older than you. She lost her husband and her daughter in a car accident. I wouldn't want you to hurt her."

Gamaliel almost said, What do you take me for? but then

he thought better of it. In any event, it was now his turn to read a page of the Haggadah, where God is speaking. " 'And I will pass through the land of Egypt, I, and not an angel. And I will strike down the firstborn in the land of Egypt, I, and not an angel of fire. And I will execute judgment against all the gods of Egypt, I, and not a messenger. I the Lord, I, and not another.' " At this point, Gamaliel stopped and, according to custom, commented on what he had read. "I don't understand that passage. God seems to be congratulating Himself on His actions in Egypt. But just what is He boasting about? Causing the death of all those Egyptian babies? Having used their suffering and dying to force the pharaoh to concede? And He expects us to thank Him for that? No, I don't understand it."

Everyone around the table was silent. They hadn't expected so critical and perhaps blasphemous a statement from Gamaliel, whose usual comments were moderate and reserved. Noémie, embarrassed, was trying to think of a quip to relieve the tension, but Eve spoke up first. "I find this passage attractive for its wisdom and its common sense. God isn't speaking just to the Hebrews in the desert, but to all their descendants, and to everyone like them. Therefore, He's speaking to us also. And what is He saying to us? He's telling us that to kill children is a crime so dreadful that only He can commit it. I mean just that: He and no living being. Looking at it that way, this short verse strikes me as very beautiful."

Surprised, the guests all applauded her. Eve, taken aback, looked at her plate, as if regretting she had spoken. Now there began a learned discussion of the relation between God and man, God's presence in history, His ability to transform immanence into transcendence. Bolek took Gamaliel's

side, citing a Sage in the Talmud to illustrate a Jew's audacity
in addressing the Lord. He believed you could say anything
to God. Did Gamaliel hear his friend's statement? He
remained silent, wondering what he found attractive about
this young widow. Nothing about her was particularly beautiful, not her roundish face, not her generous breasts. And
yet she had a certain glow, a delicacy, a quiet femininity,
qualities that Gamaliel was finding irresistible. Besides, there
were her eyes, which were a glittering blue-gray. And her
voice: inviting, low, measured, reassuring, caressing.

Noémie brought him back to earth. "Stop it, Gamaliel,
stop it. Are you staring at her because you love her, or to
make her love you? Take my advice: Look elsewhere."

"Too late," Gamaliel replied.

Noémie shook her head, smiling, both to indicate disap-
proval and as a warning.

Gamaliel enjoyed Noémie's company. She and her husband were part of his inner circle. As a couple, they were
wonderfully generous and understanding; both refrained
from criticizing or making judgments about him. The most
they would do to indicate disagreement was to frown at him,
as if surprised at what they had just heard.

They had a daughter, Leah, whom they adored. Especially
Bolek: A better father than a husband, he lived for his daughter. To watch them playing chess was an astonishing experience. At first, Bolek would try to lose; then later, he would
have to try harder in order to win. But he lost more and more
often, and then he was proud of his daughter, whose talent
exceeded his own. Gamaliel was convinced that on awakening each morning Bolek asked himself, What can I do today
to make Leah happier? She embodied both past and future
for him. She made him both vulnerable and invincible. "If

anything happened to her it would kill me," he would say to Gamaliel. There was never any misunderstanding between them, never any resentment. How did Noémie manage not to be jealous of the bond between her husband and her daughter? Sometimes Gamaliel was. He disliked himself for envying his friend—not for Bolek's good fortune but for his parental love. If he had married Esther, would he have been equally attached to their child, perhaps a son? But he hadn't married Esther. Their encounter had lasted the time of a kiss, of a crest of passion between two waves. Colette? Yes, she had been his wife. The mother of his two daughters, his misfortune. But since his family had fallen apart, he was living a virtually celibate life, determined to avoid those precarious affairs where enticements turned out to be traps. When he was with a woman, particularly one who was seductive and available, he had only to remind himself of Colette to be on his guard. He would have no heir? So be it. He would die alone, and in the earth, forever buried, would lie his memories, his hopes, and his dreams. His journey through the remembrance of God would leave no mark on that of men.

And now something in him was opening to admit a stranger.

Eve and all his vows were in question. Fate's amused wink of the eye. Eve, and the erupting of the sort of love he no longer expected.

Gamaliel was impatient for the Seder to end so he could be with the young woman who had so captivated him. What would he say to her? That he liked her voice? That he found her dress too light or too dark? That blue was his favorite color? What could he offer her, what relationship, what promise? As it happened, this year the Seder lasted longer

than usual because of the discussion set off by Eve's statement. It was long past midnight when Bolek intoned the
song of the Chad Gadya, that lovely, almost childish story
that begins with the sale of one little goat and ends with
God's victory over Death—in other words, the death of
Death.

As soon as he was on his feet, Gamaliel crossed the dining
room to Eve. "I'll keep you company."

"To where?"

"To the end."

"And then?"

"I'm no prophet."

"Too bad."

"Would you like it if I were?"

"Yes, only if you'll always laugh while making prophecies."

"To entertain you?"

"No, to make me dream."

They went to the door, where Noémie was awaiting
them. "You're leaving already? It's early," she said.

"No," Gamaliel replied. "It's late."

They walked in silence, each reflecting on the meaning
of the story they had just begun. Eve was the first to speak. "I
know nothing about you except that you frighten me."

"I know a lot about you, and you're helping me overcome
my own fear."

"Since you know so much, do you also know that I
bring bad luck?" He was silent, thinking, so she continued:
"I bring bad luck to those I love."

Gamaliel recalled the tragic event she had lived through.
"How did it happen?" he asked.

"Who told you about it? Oh, I see—Noémie. . . . Well,
they had gone out to buy me a present for my birthday. It was

raining. The car was hit by a truck; it was crushed. . . . I see the flames in my nightmares. I scream. I shout to them, 'Watch out. Watch out!' "

Should he take her hand? Reassure her? Console her? Say to her that though love can never be replaced, it can be restored? Since she was now locked in her own silence, he asked in a more pressing tone, "When did it happen?"

"Three years ago."

"And since then?"

"Since then, nothing."

"Where do you live?"

"Alone."

"When will you agree to give up your solitude?"

"Never."

"You're afraid you'd be untrue to them, is that it?"

"I'm afraid of being untrue to myself."

Then, without knowing why, he began telling her about his life—not about Colette, nor about Esther, but about his mother, his father, Ilonka.

It was pleasant out, a mild spring night. The streets were quiet, almost deserted. The stars overhead were telling one another their secrets with brief irregular flashes. Occasionally, a taxi would slow down for them, but they preferred to walk.

So began a singular encounter, one in which two lost souls thought they could rescue one another by calling on the love of those who were gone.

"Tell me more," Eve said as she took his arm.

"Do you know the life and works of Rahel Varnhagen?"

"No."

"She lived in the eighteenth and nineteenth centuries in what became Germany. She said, 'My story preceded my life.' Well, mine did, too."

"Will you tell it to me?"
"While I'm laughing?"
"While we're walking."
"If you'll help me find the words."

An old woman was sleeping on a doorstep. She was smiling. She seemed happy.

GAMALIEL COULDN'T HELP IT: HE HAD TO GO back to see the old Hungarian patient.

At the hospital, he studies her ravaged features. Where did she get all those scars? Lili, the young doctor, spoke about an accident; no one knew where or how. It was a miracle that her life had been saved. Surgeons at a local hospital, more dedicated than qualified, had labored less to restore her health than to give her a semblance of a human face and a woman's body.

"She was surely very beautiful when she was young," observes the doctor, who has just joined him. "She doesn't look it now."

What can we know of a person who refuses to communicate with us? Gamaliel wonders. Someone knew this woman; someone had held her in his arms and thanked her for the happiness she brought him. Perhaps she had had a fond husband, lively children, lovers; days of mourning and triumph had shaped her existence.

"There's such a thing as hidden beauty," he says at last.

"What use is it if no one sees it?"

"You're wrong about that. There are those who can sense it."

She glances at him with interest. "What do you sense about this woman?"

Once again, Gamaliel is back in his childhood. He had slept badly the previous night. Something was oppressing him: the uneasy feeling that signals danger ahead. Bizarre old dreams had haunted his sleep: children pursued by huge disfigured monsters. They'd all had the harsh voice and hard face of the Hungarian officer with the sour breath who had come so often and closed himself off with Ilonka in her bedroom. He had awakened with a start, his heart beating fast. He'd struggled to master his fright, and had finally been able to do so only by picturing his mother's melancholy face, her delicate hands, her gentle eyes.

A metallic voice jolts him back to the present: "Dr. Rosenkrantz, Dr. Rosenkrantz urgently wanted in ward five . . ."

The loudspeaker repeats the summons several times. The doctor gets hurriedly to her feet. "Please wait for me, I'll be right back," she says.

She's fortunate, Gamaliel reflects. She matters to someone. She can provide help and solace. A doctor's life is never useless. Not like his own: shriveled up, frittered away. He used to believe that he, too, could effectively intervene in the lives of others. Oh, yes: the years he could have made fruitful, the people whose days he could have enriched.

It was all so long ago.

When she returns, the doctor says, "A moment ago you were thinking about a woman, but not this one."

"Yes, I was thinking of a woman whose beauty moved me. She's dead now, but I can still see her beauty."

"You loved her?"

"I love her still."

"She was your wife?"

"No." He gives her a brief smile. "She was my mother. I'm not married." Then he corrects himself: "I was married. I'm not any longer." He indicates the patient with a gesture. "What about her? Is she married? Was she ever happy?"

"I'm afraid those questions will have to remain unanswered."

"Let's imagine a happy Mrs. Sisyphus," says Gamaliel.

"Yes, let's do it for her, since she no longer can," says the doctor.

Now the same burning question takes hold of him: What if it really is Ilonka on the hospital bed, already detached from the world of the living?

"Once again, your thoughts are elsewhere," the doctor says.

"It's because I'm from another world." Then he thinks, That's stupid. Anyone could say this.

"And your wife, did she live in that world?"

"No," he admits after a moment.

Colette never belonged to his world.

GAMALIEL MET HER IN PARIS IN THE MOST ordinary way, at an outside table of a café in the Latin Quarter. It was a sunny morning in spring. The streets were crowded: students hurrying to their exams, florists hawking their wares to lovers, wide-eyed tourists admiring the places where the high priests of existentialism might be glimpsed.

As he often was, Gamaliel was with his pal Bolek, whom he'd met a few months earlier, at police headquarters. Both were refugees, so they had the same problems: how to get a residency permit, how to earn a living, where to find inexpensive housing. The next day, they decided to share quarters in a cheap hotel nearby. Their favorite pastime was having a drink in a café and watching the pretty girls go by, alone or on their lovers' arms.

"Which one do you like?" Bolek asked.

"The third one," replied Gamaliel.

"You're crazy. There're only two of them."

"That's just it: I'm waiting for the next one."

"And suppose she's not alone?"

"Tough luck for whoever's with her."

She was alone.

Bolek dashed over to block her passage. "Wait, mademoiselle," he said, taking her arm, as if out of breath. "My friend needs you."

"Who are you anyway?"

"It's not about me. It's my friend. He's in despair. Only you can save him."

"Go to the devil and leave me alone!"

"Yes, but I am the devil." Bolek came back, hanging his head. "Well, she's not for you."

Gamaliel liked Bolek. His imagination would put the most gifted of novelists to shame. Tall, quick-witted, he would jump, eyes closed or open, at any chance to make a few francs. The two young men soon became friends. It would be for life. Gamaliel was entertained by Bolek's far-fetched notions and preposterous stories. It was to Bolek that he turned for help in paying his way to Israel and later to Morocco.

"Wait a minute!" Gamaliel exclaimed. "That's too easy an excuse. You let me down. Admit it."

"Well, if you insist, but still . . ." His voice trailed off. The girl had turned around and now she was taking the seat between them.

"Colette is my name," she said in a brusque manner. "Go ahead and talk. I have twenty minutes to spare. I'm listening to you. Who am I supposed to save, and why should I do it?"

"My name's Bolek, but he's the one who needs you. His name is Péter in Hungarian and Gamaliel in—"

"In what?"

"In Yiddish."

"So you're Jewish?"

"Why do you ask that question?" Bolek demanded. "We don't like to be interrogated, unless . . . well, unless you're with the police."

"Answer me."

"All right, if you insist on knowing everything. Yes, we're Jews."

She made a face. "Well, so am I."

"We're refugees. Don't tell us you are."

"No, I'm French."

"You're lucky," said Bolek.

"For you, being a refugee is a sort of disease."

Gamaliel was thinking, Yes, it's a disease, a disease that afflicts the entire world. But it must be recognized that a refugee is a different kind of being, one from whom all that defines a normal person has been amputated. He belongs to no nation, is welcome at no one's table. A leper. He can achieve nothing unless others help him.

"But as far as I know, that disease is not incurable," the young woman said.

"Well now!" Bolek cried out. "Do you happen to be a doctor? If so, do tell us what's the best remedy."

"Marriage," Colette said with a burst of laughter.

But her laughter, Gamaliel should have realized, was lacking in any gaiety or sincerity. He wasn't really attracted to her. She wasn't his type. In his fantasies, he imagined women whose beauty was concealed, who were radiant with grace, unattainable, like Esther, whereas Colette seemed available, even clinging. He was attracted to the shy ones, the dreamers; she was arrogant, businesslike. Bossy. Willful. She kept a tight rein on what she said, on what she did, and on her impulses. She wasn't just looking at the two of them; she was sizing them up.

"You," she said, turning to Gamaliel. "Yes, you, the silent one, not your chatterbox of a spokesman. Cat got your tongue? Don't you have anything to say for yourself?"

"No," Gamaliel replied, "not now."

"Then I have to wait?"

"Why not? It's all I ever do."

At that, Bolek, tactful for once, got up. "I have a feeling you can manage very well without me."

Gamaliel wasn't hearing the sounds of the busy street. He felt nonplussed. He wanted to say something, something novel or at least appropriate, but words failed him. Now the silence felt oppressive, and he had to say something. "Your twenty minutes are up," he finally said.

"I know."

Strange sort of woman, Gamaliel was thinking. Severe, hard. Who or what was she protecting herself from? She must have suffered a lot. When she was a child? Adolescent? At any rate, she seemed able to master all sorts of situations. And when did she learn how to dominate men? That meant she must be older than he. Twenty-five? In her thirties? That made her more interesting.

"How about another coffee?" he suggested. "It's on me."

Did she realize that a refugee is always short of money? Colette knew a lot about many things. She knew how to please, how to arouse desire. Her shoulders, erect but soft, invited caresses. Her expression was calmer now; her smile engaging, despite thin lips that scarcely parted to let out a word or a breath before closing with a deliberate slowness. She placed her hand on Gamaliel's, and he blushed like a kid who has just discovered that women have bodies. Coming over him was an uneasy sensation. It made him ache with anticipated pleasure. He felt hot, and he was having trouble breathing. He feared what was about to happen, while at the same time he wanted it with all the ardor in him.

"We'll walk," Colette declared. She looked him straight in the eye; she wouldn't take no for an answer. "Do you know Paris? I bet you don't. Well, like it or not, I'll be your guide. And I don't come cheap."

She paid for their coffees. Gamaliel didn't object. She took his arm and led him to the banks of the Seine. She was talking and talking; he hardly said a word. She showed him the Sorbonne, the great libraries of the Latin Quarter, the medical school, as if he didn't already know them.

"I'm going to take you in hand," she said. "Since you manage the French language so well, I'll introduce you to our literature; you'll have to read the books I get for you. We'll go to the theater, to concerts, to the Louvre. I'll make a star of the refugee you are, not in the universe of French culture, to be sure, but a star in my circles, among my friends, some of whom are well placed."

Gamaliel felt he had to say something. "But all that costs money."

"Don't worry about such things." And she squeezed his arm more insistently.

That same evening, she took him to her apartment near Parc Monceau. Gamaliel had never seen such luxury: from the living room to the dining room, from the kitchen to the bathroom. He thought she must be the daughter, sister, or niece of millionaires. What can she want with me? he wondered. What can I give her other than my awkward shyness? She offered him a drink; he dared not refuse. You never say no when you're living a fairy tale, even if the princess could be more attractive, more feminine.

"Do you like it?" she asked.

"Yes, very much."

"And me, do you like me?"

"As a guide?"

"As a woman."

"I've always dreamed of having a guide like you."

She lifted her glass and drank. When she spoke, it was in a different, more intimate register: "Well, my boy, you're in luck. This night you're going to learn a few things. That I promise you."

Her voice was lost in the whirlwind of her body. They spent the night together. Where was Esther in this? She was erased, submerged in a swamp of shame. The night was throbbing, frenetic, with stifled laughter and breathless cries, delirium and abandon, ecstasy and discovery, a night of taking wing and falling to earth.

For Gamaliel, everything was for the first time.

BOLEK WAS THE MOST DISCREET AMONG HIS friends. Even though Gamaliel had told him about his ephemeral idyll with Esther, Bolek did not try to get him to talk about his adventure with Colette. He was bound to know that Gamaliel was spending his nights elsewhere, but did he suspect that things were getting serious? Bolek asked him only once. Gamaliel shrugged. "I don't know what's going on. Colette knows everything." Bolek did not press him.

BOLEK, LIKE GAMALIEL, DID NOT LIKE TO CON-fide in others. Even in Paris his silences sometimes seemed so long and pervasive that they weighed on his refugee friends. His insistence on holding back had only increased by the time they were all reunited in New York. He married Noémie in the mid-1960s, but marriage did not make him any less moody. Sometimes he would flare up. Gamaliel and the others acted as if they did not notice and continued their conversation, waiting for him to emerge from his depression. And if he didn't, they were understanding; after all, everyone has his nightmares. Everyone carries a burden, a secret burden that sets him apart and defines him. Everyone has his no-entry zone.

As the years went by, Gamaliel thought perhaps Bolek had problems at home. Was Noémie making life difficult? They seemed an exemplary couple, despite Bolek's occasional curiosity about a well-endowed passerby. Noémie, always high-spirited, liked to entertain his friends; she gently made fun of Diego and joked with Yasha. You could see she was at peace with herself in the way she teased her husband, in the way she looked at him. But then why his moments of animosity, his violent outbursts? Was their daughter, Leah, their only child, causing him torment? Would he rather have had a son? Gamaliel didn't believe that.

Leah seemed happy living with Samaël, the son of one of

Noémie's classmates. None of Bolek's friends had met her partner, who, oddly enough, seemed to be avoiding them. But they knew Leah well and they loved her. She was beautiful, vivacious, and talented; she had been a brilliant student and now was teaching at the University of Chicago, where her colleagues valued her and her students adored her. Was it the distance between them that troubled Bolek? They spoke daily. Between them, there was a bond of mutual trust and affection. Then why these spells of melancholy in this man who, once out of his shell, was welcoming and generous, open to conversation and good cheer, ready to be surprised, to confide and be confided in? Several times when he was alone with Bolek, Gamaliel had been on the point of questioning him, but had caught himself—it was never the right time. Friendship justifies everything but prying.

Then one day when he and Bolek were returning from a visit to Yasha in the hospital, he ventured to bring it up, but in a roundabout manner. "I have a story to tell you," he said. "The other day, this poor unhappy young man, nephew of a journalist I know, came over to me in a coffee shop. He wanted my help on a matter that to him seemed serious. His fiancée believed him to be a writer, and to preserve the illusion, he wanted me to write a book for him. Otherwise, there'd be no wedding, and therefore no happiness, no reason to go on living. I knew about his situation; they weren't actually engaged, not officially, but he was miserable about it nonetheless. I asked him if he'd ever tried to write anything. Yes, he had tried, a few scribbles here, a few poems there, like everyone, but it was all worthless. Would he show them to me? I asked. He blushed and insisted he'd rather keep them to himself. 'Now listen,' I said to him. 'Go home and write something. It can be about anything, but preferably about the doubt and anxiety that you're experiencing. When you're ready to show it to me, I'll be ready to read it.' " Gamaliel stopped, then, lowering his voice, added, "When you're ready to talk, I'll be there to listen."

Bolek nodded his assent. They spoke no more till they parted.

One morning a few weeks later, Gamaliel received a call from Bolek, asking if by any chance he was free.

"Of course," Gamaliel replied. "Where and when do you want to meet?"

"In Central Park, by the Seventy-second Street entrance, at one o'clock."

"Shall we have lunch together?"

"No, not today," Bolek said.

"Very well. I'll be there."

Bolek was waiting when Gamaliel arrived at the meeting place. They shook hands. "Let's walk," Bolek said. They walked in silence along a path leading to the lake. People passing by were talking about the coming elections, the various candidates. Bolek's thoughts seemed to be elsewhere. Gamaliel wondered, Has the time come? Will he finally get it off his chest?

Central Park was teeming with people who, at lunchtime on this August day, instead of looking for a table at a crowded restaurant, had brought their sandwiches to the park; they picked up conversations where they had left off the night before, swapped gossip, and made plans. Workers on their lunch hour, students cutting their summer classes, shop girls yearning for a magical flirtation, wide-eyed tourists, artists in search of inspiration—all were admiring the work of Creation and ready to applaud its Creator.

"Let's sit," said Bolek, pointing to a bench well away from

passersby. He gazed at Gamaliel, who was wondering how his friend would go about explaining his erratic behavior. "Listen to me, but don't look at me, all right?" Gamaliel made a gesture of agreement.

"It's about a murder." Bolek stopped to see Gamaliel's reaction, but the latter swallowed and said nothing.

"Yes, I'm going to tell you about a man's death. It's on my conscience." Again he paused, and again Gamaliel remained silent.

"I'm from a shtetl in eastern Poland. Did you know that? The name of the town was Davarowsk. My father was a rabbinical judge and my mother was descended from a great Hasidic dynasty. She took care of the household. We were eight children, four girls and four boys. I was the youngest, also the most rebellious. My brothers, all outstanding students, were planning on careers in the world of the yeshiva, while I spent my days playing, daydreaming, deceiving my teachers. Now I regret it, as you can well imagine. How I must have made my poor father suffer! He was so affectionate with me, the *mezinekl*, the baby of the family: He never punished or scolded me, never even let me see his disappointment, his frustration. Naturally my older brothers envied me, like Joseph's in the Bible. I could make up any kind of story; I could go anywhere, and get away with it. My father was convinced that one day I'd straighten out and find the right way, the path that led to God, the God of Israel. I heard him say it more than once to my mother when she told him she was upset and worried about me. Years went by. The child grew up. The adolescent matured. Then history began to shake the foundations of our protected and protecting home before it destroyed it entirely. The future wore the hateful face of German power. I was fifteen. You know what happened next. You know it in your bones; you lived it in your own way. The black posters, the first decrees, the insults and public humiliation, the laws that reduced us to subhumans, to insects or microbes. The yellow star, the ghetto, the hunger, the disease, the executions, the roundups, the transports into the unknown. And I, who was young and vigorous, watched my father lose his authority and my mother her grace. At first, my brothers and sisters had the good fortune to be working in German enterprises. They were protected by their identity cards, whose colors were forever changing. As for me, I went into hiding. From time to time, I and some other youngsters would slip out of the ghetto at night to get bread and eggs and potatoes, which we'd buy from peasants at an exorbitant price or in exchange for a piece of family jewelry. Only then, when I saw how happy this made my mother—or rather, how proud she was that on this night she could feed her family, could serve a decent meal—did I come to realize how sad she must have been most of the time, how useless she must have felt for lack of being able to do her duty as wife and mother.

"Lady Luck seemed to smile on me one Thursday night, but it turned out she was setting me a trap. I'd succeeded in filling my sack with food, vegetables, eggs, and two entire loaves of bread—an offering from above for the Sabbath. I was expecting to be greeted as a hero or even a savior. I was still on the Aryan side, not far from the wall, waiting for the right moment. Then my hopes collapsed, and so did I. German soldiers and Polish police burst like a flash of lightning from the nearby streets and surrounded the ghetto like a noose of steel and death. A human wall—or rather, an inhuman one—now encircled the wall of stone and barbed wire. There was no way I could sneak through one of the usual openings. I was heartsick with anxiety at being separated from my family and ashamed of still being free. I wondered if I should come out of my hiding place and give myself up— not to help my people, for I knew I couldn't do that, but to be with them. No. Bad idea. There was still a glimmer of hope: Surely my parents were in their shelter. My brothers and sisters could get by on their own—you learned fast in the ghetto. Not our parents. Old and bewildered, they were in constant danger. That's why I had managed to find them a spot in a well-furnished bunker, at our neighbors'. The shelter was well closed off, safe from prying eyes. Dogs could have uncovered it, but the Germans were using them only rarely during that summer of 1942. They found that their voices and rifle shots were sufficient to impose their will over ours. I was convinced that the enemy could not enter my parents' hideout; That's why I stayed where I was. At least that's what I believed at the time. Now I'm not so sure. There are times when I wonder if I wasn't just scared. This notion haunts me: Didn't I just want to stay alive, as if I were standing outside what was happening? Wasn't I just using the bunker as an alibi so I could survive for a week, or even a day, by abandoning my parents when they were about to enter into eternal darkness? I no longer know. Sometimes at night, I see myself back in the ghetto, with them, part of the crowd being driven into the forest. I wake up sweating and shaking and I rub my eyes with my fists to keep from seeing.

"My parents, my beloved parents, so poorly protected, so poorly loved! I saw them when dawn came. They were with Reuven, my oldest brother, and his family in a crowd of hundreds of haggard men and women, hemmed in by heavily armed and helmeted SS men, driven along by policemen wielding clubs. As in a nightmare, I wanted to cry out at the top of my lungs so loudly that I'd move heaven and earth and the hearts of men, shout, It can't be! It can't be! The Germans couldn't have found my parents' bunker and also the one where Reuven and his small family were hiding. But then what were they doing there in this crowd of dazed people? I saw my father, Reuven to his right, my mother to his left, awkwardly holding to his sides his prayer shawl and his phylacteries—they were his pride and joy, treasures that had belonged to the great Rebbe Pinhas of blessed memory—fiercely determined not to let go of them. And my mother, and my sister Hannele, holding back her tears—I saw them, too. Or at least I thought I could make them out in the pale yellow light of dawn. I could see the fear and pain on their discomposed features, while they were herded toward the neighboring forest. Toward the common grave that the young ones, and therefore my brother Reuven, would have to dig out of the hard, dry soil.

"That's the last time I saw them. The last time I was close to them, though separate. But I still see them as I'm speaking to you.

"Don't look at me, Gamaliel. I don't want you to also see them."

The rays of the August sun were playing hide-and-seek in the foliage of the trees. Some noisy kids, their faces shining with pleasure and pride, were shoving one another and struggling vigorously over a ball as if it were a rare and precious trophy. On the lake, lovers were gently rowing, savoring the fleeting moment, seeking to hold it and make it last. Gamaliel watched them a while, glanced at the children, gazed up at the cloudless sky. He was obeying his friend's injunction not to look at him. Bolek was breathing hard; he was fighting his past, chastised by a horde of demons.

"It's been fifty years to the day," he said in a monotone. "The ninth day of the month of Av. You know as well as I do that it commemorates both the first and the second destruction of the Temple of Jerusalem, first by the Babylonians, then by the Romans. My parents were always afraid of the day; they believed it brought bad luck, that it belonged to the enemy. We're supposed to fast on this day in observance of our people's collective mourning. Back then, we fasted in our home. Now? This will surprise you: I still observe the fast. Not because of the First or Second Temple, but because of the Third, also in ruins, and I feel it burning inside me. Did you know the Germans carefully chose that date to attack our people, to annihilate our priests and pilgrims, our old people and our children? I didn't know it at the time. They'd studied Jewish history and were turning it against us, following the logic of implacable hatred, the logic of Evil and Death. Similar operations were staged that day in dozens of ghettos. Treblinka, Chelmno, and Auschwitz were already up and running. For us, the forest was the end of the line.

"One woman managed to escape from the mass grave. She was wounded but had been protected by the corpses piled up around her, as if she'd been saved to be a messenger. She came to the ghetto. She told her story. I heard her. She looked like a madwoman. Half of her hair was torn out or burned off. Most of all it was her eyes; she had practically no eyelids left. Her eyes were scorched and staring and bulging out of their sockets. She spoke in a blank, colorless voice. She described the executions; she listed the names and recited their last prayers. She spoke like some soulless machine made of cold metal. It would not have been so hard to bear if she'd sobbed, if she'd gone into hysterics. Only once did I hear her change her tone of voice. That was when she described my father's death—no, it was the last moments before it. Like the others, he'd been ordered to undress. But he took out his prayer shawl and wrapped himself in it. The Germans yelled at him to take it off; he didn't hear them. They cursed and threatened him, but he was impassive. Poor Reuven entreated him: 'Father, why suffer more? Aren't we going to sanctify the Name of the Lord? Must we have the tallith to do that?' And my father replied, 'Yes, my son, we will show the world and its Creator that we are still able to fulfill this great, this very great mitzvah. Few indeed are those in our history who have been privileged to fulfill the commandment of Kiddush Hashem, and that is why I must wrap myself in the tallith. . . .' That was the one time the woman seemed to come out of her trance and display some emotion. Her face was white as chalk as she reported my beloved father's last cry—'*Shma, Yisrael!* Hear, O Israel!'—as he tumbled into the grave. That cry," Bolek added, "it must have been heard to the ends of the earth, and beyond, in the heavens above, to the seventh heaven, and beyond. . . . It was fifty years ago to the day," he said again.

Gamaliel had never seen his friend in such a state. Other than his occasional moodiness and fits of depression, Bolek had always seemed the picture of strength and steadfastness. He let nothing bother or offend him. He didn't react even when someone bored or irritated him. He would just move on and change the subject with no more than a frown and a shrug of the shoulders. At times Noémie, always mischievous, would take him to task. "Do you have ice water in your veins? Don't you ever lose your temper? Don't you sometimes want to break a plate over someone's head? Mine, for example?" Bolek, pretending not to understand, would reply, "The plate didn't do anything to me, so why should I want to break it?" Feigning desperation, Noémie would call the whole world to witness. "My dear husband is impossible. You can't even pick a fight with him!" But on this day, the person beside Gamaliel was a man who had been flayed alive.

How long had they been there, sitting on that bench, close by the lake, where the children were amusing themselves tossing pebbles to make nonexistent fish jump from the water? A mother scolded them. The children, a dozen boys and girls, didn't seem bothered by her. Maybe she wasn't a mother—not one of theirs, at any rate—but just a strict nanny. She watched over them with a cold, unsentimental eye.

"I remember every detail of that dawn," said Bolek, resuming his account. "The first rays of the sun were casting a filthy yellowish light over the town. Sounds of footsteps on the pavement. Thick shadows retreating in a deliberate manner, as if in a ballet. And my father, my poor father, his back bent, as if he were bearing the weight of centuries on his shoulders. And my mother, I remember her face: Never had I seen her look so sweet."

Gamaliel wanted to steal a glance at his friend, but he had promised not to look at him. Why was Bolek so insistent on not being observed? Was he afraid of giving himself away, of bursting into tears? Or of taking his confession too far? Hadn't he said he had a murder on his conscience? Was he referring to the death of his family? Gamaliel decided for the time being to keep his promise to just listen.

"An hour after the doomed people had been taken away," Bolek said, "I crawled under the barbed wire and back to the ghetto. I expected to find it empty, but instead the streets resembled a hive: Dazed, disoriented people were wandering every which way, searching for a relative, a friend. They would ask one another, 'Have you seen . . .' No, no one had. 'Where are they taking them?' No one knew. 'To prison?' Perhaps. 'To a camp? To a village nearby?' Possibly. 'Will they be coming back soon?' Surely. No one could conceive of what had really happened. Here and there, people were trying to look reassuring. But most could ill conceal their happiness, even though diminished by loss, at having escaped the roundup. I, too, was joining in such exchanges. I located my other brothers and sisters, and their children, including little Moishele. We had survived for the moment, but we did not rejoice. How could we? We were alive but walled in, and that denied us any pleasure in living.

"Some time later, I was contacted by a clandestine Zionist who was with the underground movement. This group, weakened by the recent roundup of several of its fighters, was recruiting intensively. I was reluctant at first. I expressed my doubts to one Zelig, who had been sent on a moonless night to sound me out. 'You really believe you can fight the Germans? How many tanks do you have? And how many divisions? They have the best-equipped, most powerful army in the world. They're arrogant and triumphant. They crushed Poland, humiliated France. They defeated a lot of armies, conquered a lot of nations, pushed the Red Army back to the outskirts of Moscow. And you think you can hold your own against them for a week, even a day? I swear, you're out of your minds.'

"Zelig listened without reacting; then he spoke a single line, which hit me like a slap in the face: 'And what about our Jewish honor?'

"I blurted out, 'What's Jewish honor got to do with it?'

"He had his answer ready: 'It's dishonorable to let the enemy do whatever he wants, torture and torment and kill at will, without showing any will to resist.'

"That made me angry. 'In other words, according to you and your group, those they took away three weeks ago, my family among them, lived and died without honor? Explain to me what gives you the right to sit in judgment on them.'

"Perhaps Zelig was expecting such an outburst, for he did not appear to be offended. 'You didn't understand, because I didn't express myself right. It's not a question of their honor, but ours. There was nothing they could do, but we can do something, and it doesn't much matter what. Not to defeat Hitler's Germany—to hope for that would be lunacy—but to leave a mark, however faint, on our history.'

"I asked to think it over, but then I caught myself right away. What was there to think about? The danger? How could fighting in the resistance be any more dangerous than life in the ghetto? 'All right, I've thought it over. Count me in.'

"My enlistment was sealed with a handshake.

"I often met with Zelig, the other members of our cell, and our commander, Abrasha. He'd been a soldier in the Polish army and was supposed to train us to handle weapons. Trouble was, we had no weapons, or very few. A few revolvers and grenades bought on the outside, some Molotov cocktails fabricated by two chemists from Kraków, all doled out sparingly and kept in ultrasecret hiding places.

"I won't talk to you about 'my' resistance. I did nothing to garner glory. I believe we were wrong, in our ceremonies and commemorations after the war, to make such a contrast between victims and heroes. I agree with the witness who said that in those days 'the heroes themselves were victims, and the victims were heroes.'

"But I wanted to see you today to talk about something else, about an episode that even today still weighs on my conscience.

"When I was back in the ghetto, I went straight to my

parents' home, hoping to find I don't know what. Perhaps a letter, some sort of sign—from them to me. Nothing. A Bible on the table. A book of prayers open to the Lamentations of the Ninth Day of the Month of Av. On the bed, a coat my mother had forgotten. Hannele's comb. At the first alarm, they must have reacted quickly, very quickly, hurrying to the underground shelter because every second counted. Once in the bunker, there would have been a lot to do: close the trapdoor, plug holes, arrange the furniture, settle down in silence. . . . By ghetto standards, it was a safe hiding place, far safer than those where Reuven and his family were. But that was just it: Since the bunker was so well concealed, how was it that the Germans discovered this hiding place, while so many others escaped their notice?

"A disturbing, troublesome question. I spent hours with what was left of my family and a few close friends going over all the possible explanations. Had someone in the shelter coughed or sneezed or made some wrong move at a time when you had to clench your teeth and your fists until they ached? Had a baby cried? We questioned neighbors and acquaintances; they knew nothing. One of them suggested the Germans might have been using some special instruments to tap the walls and detect the slightest sound emanating from the cellar or the attic. It seemed plausible to us; after all, they were past masters at that art, and they would resort to any means to track us down and eliminate us. In the end, it was the woman, the only one to escape, who gave us the answer. I ran into her by chance on the street, in front of the *Judenrat* housing office. She seemed in a daze. Since she now had no family, they had made her move out of her room to a smaller room, in the home of strangers. 'I wonder why God spared me,' she muttered when I spoke to her. 'God has

His reasons, and we're too stupid to understand them,' I responded, surprised at myself for using one of my father's favorite lines. Since she seemed not to be listening, I persisted. 'I'm sorry to bother you, but you may be able to help me.' She snorted derisively. 'Me help you? I have nothing; I am nothing. How could I be of any use to you?' I told her my parents were in the same transport with her. For the first time, her face showed a gleam of interest. 'Who are you?' she asked. I told her. 'Oh, you're the son of the rabbinical judge? Yes, yes. Oh, I saw your father. . . .' And she repeated her account of his death. I told her I was baffled. How had his shelter been discovered? 'I've questioned the neighbors, witnesses, but no one can clear it up for me.' She looked me straight in the eye without changing expression. 'It's obvious,' she said. 'They were betrayed.' I confess that for the moment I was stunned. What, someone gave them away? So there were informers in the ghetto? Jewish scoundrels who were helping the Germans? Jews so corrupted that they'd betray their own people to the Gestapo? I couldn't bring myself to accept it. 'You're sure?' I asked her. Yes, she was sure. 'It's the same man who betrayed us all,' she said in an even tone."

Bolek stopped, and Gamaliel respected his silence. I hope, he was thinking, that I'll prove worthy of taking this testimony. And to commit it to my memory. And to protect it. For history, as they say. Is this not what Bolek wants? When he chose me, didn't he say to himself that my profession is putting all things into words? Haven't I spent a large part of my life putting sentences together? It's been easy—up till now. To write fiction or research papers that, in any case, would not be published under my name. I was free to write anything, any old way, on any subject. Any standards I followed, any rules I obeyed, were mine alone to determine. But how can I write this story of speechless agony? My words are too worn-out, too impoverished, to convey the experience that Bolek lived through. Where could I look for the right words? How could I flush them out from where they're hiding, when those I have are so tainted that they stick in my throat?

"I was astounded at the name of the person the woman identified as the informer," Bolek went on, his voice tight. "Was I too young, too inexperienced? In the ghetto, everybody had lost their youth. Was I too naïve? With what I'd seen by then, I should have been inoculated against naïveté. And I'd grown up enough to know that in extreme situations man is capable of the best as well as the worst. I could have accepted it if the swine had turned out to be a petty thief— there were some in Davarowsk—or an ignoramus—we had them, too—or a pervert, or a man desperate to help his sick wife, or an assimilated intellectual, or an atheist, or even a bum. But the traitor belonged to a respected, well-to-do family. Who didn't know the Horowitzes? They played a leading role in real estate, in business, in community affairs. Everyone respected Reb Leibish, the father, benefactor of the synagogue, who sat next to the rabbi by the sacred Ark. He presided over the association for the benefit of widows and orphans. His oldest daughter had married a well-known lawyer from Warsaw. His son . . . his son was the one who gave my parents away to the Germans. I know, you'll ask me why he did it. To save his own skin? For notoriety? For power? Because it was an easy, if repulsive, way to rebel against his father? To make a show of independence, as today's psychologists would have it? What really motivated him? What could have transformed this boy from a good family into a monster in the service of the enemy of his people? Was it a whim, a game? A moment of insanity? Had he been disappointed in love? I had no idea then, and today I still have no idea. And yet I asked him those questions. . . . I'll explain later how it came about that I saw him—or rather, saw him again. Before the war, I'd see him now and then in the house of study or in the park. He was three years older than I, always well dressed and full of himself. He wouldn't give me so much as a glance. In his eyes, I didn't even exist. But . . . Well, let's stick to the story. Back to the ghetto. My brothers and sisters were home with their children. My nieces and nephews were sitting on the floor, scared into silence. My sixteen-year-old sister, Sheindele, was off in never-never land, waiting for solace that would never come. Everyone was overwhelmed, on the verge of tears. 'We shouldn't have, we shouldn't have,' they were mumbling. Shouldn't have what? Shouldn't have left the parents in a separate hiding place? Should have stayed each in his own bunker instead of staying together? No one had the answers. Besides, what good would answers do? We promised that we'd never leave one another. And we started to say Kaddish.

"My new life occupied all my attention. I went out on many more nighttime adventures, as my commanders sent me on missions that no longer had anything to do with the black market. I was to contact certain Poles who might give me well-paid-for 'presents' for our movement. Sometimes I came back empty-handed, but then I would try again. There's no denying I believed I was on a holy mission. One night, I was almost caught by a patrol. I was crawling back under the barbed wire and I didn't notice a Polish policeman watching my usual escape route. 'Empty out your pockets,' he ordered. 'Let's see what you're bringing back.' He was looking for food. Had he found any, he would have turned me over to the Germans. But all I had on me was two handguns. 'Stolen?' he asked. 'A gift,' I said. Fortunately, he was also in the resistance, and he knew of the contacts between our two clandestine movements. He let me go.

"On those nights, I was as much impatient and worried as I was afraid of the enemy and wanting to fight them. Zelig, who had recruited me, was arrested by the Gestapo and shot. I took his place as head of our group. We held our meetings in a cellar, as did all the Jewish resistance groups. I led the discussions, in which we took up all the issues that we faced: questions of policy, strategy, supplies, underground hiding places, buying weapons, military operations. When should we come out in the open and take action? Should we wait and plan in minute detail an operation to be staged during a roundup, in order to kill as many enemy soldiers as possible, or should we attack as soon as a German showed up in the ghetto? Was it better to take action now—too soon? Or bide our time—too late? At the end of one of those meetings, I raised my hand and said, 'I have a question that's not on the agenda. It's about traitors among us.'

"My comrades were astonished. They stared at me in disbelief. Didn't they realize there was at least one informer in the ghetto?

" 'I know of one,' I said, 'but there may be others. They're dangerous, and their presence here disgraces us.'

"Mendel, the tailor, was the first to pull himself together. 'Hey, fellows, the kid is right,' he burst out. 'For all we know, Zelig fell in a trap the Germans set, thanks to one of their collaborators.' Officially, I was his superior, but to him, I was still 'the kid.'

"A porter sitting next to him, who would say 'I dunno'

as part of every sentence, was rubbing his chin. 'Well, I dunno . . . Once we start talking about traitors, I dunno, we'll end up suspecting our best friends.'

"Another said, 'But even so, we must—'

"But a girl cut him off. 'No, we must not.'

"Should I identify the stool pigeon? I wondered. Give the name of the young Horowitz? I thought it better to wait. Around midnight, I brought the discussion to a close, saying, 'I'll make my report to Abrasha. After all, he's our commanding officer.'

"Everyone agreed.

"How can I describe Abrasha to you? By his profession? Before the war, he was a *melamed*, a schoolteacher and a tutor. Medium height, but round-shouldered, so he looked shorter. An expressionless face. A fast talker. He had a habit of rocking back and forth while talking, as if he were exploring some ancient problem in the Talmud. To look at this seemingly peaceful, even serene person, you'd never have thought him capable of planning attacks on other human beings—except that in his eyes, the SS were no longer human. What impressed me about him was his way of listening. He was attentive to the smallest detail, and he never interrupted, always seeking to win the trust of the other person.

"I had requested an urgent meeting. Three days later, I met him in a small room. I could hear the mingled voices of children and adults coming from the next room. I wondered if they were his family's.

" 'So what's it about?' he asked without preliminaries.

"I reported on the debate that had stirred up my group.

" 'I know about it,' he said. 'You mean young Horowitz, is that right?'

" 'Yes.'

" 'He the one who gave away your parents?'

" 'Not just my parents.'

" 'That's true. In the ghetto, an attack on one Jew is an attack on all. What's worse, the bastard is still at it. I'm told he's hanging around the buildings where our best fighters hold their meetings. What do you suggest we do?'

" 'He must be executed.'

" 'What about his parents? They had nothing to do with it. Why make them suffer?'

" 'What about my parents? He sent them to their death.'

" 'You're right. Traitors deserve to die. But they're also entitled to a trial before a judge. Never forget who we are. We Jews believe in justice. Ever since biblical times, we've put our trust in judges.' I was about to say that our present circumstances made it impossible to follow all the rules of procedure, but he continued: 'I will arrange for a tribunal. The role of prosecutor is yours by right.'

"That's when I next saw the traitor. Two of our men, armed with handguns, roused him from his sleep and took him to a carefully hidden location where the court would meet. He was unshaven, and in his wrinkled suit and dirty shirt, he looked less like one who had been charged than one already found guilty. Three judges sitting by candlelight would decide his fate. I had a key role as prosecutor. He had no one acting as his lawyer: His kind of traitor could expect no defense. In a shadowy corner sat Abrasha.

"At first, the stool pigeon made a pitiful effort to impress us with his arrogance. 'I am the son of—' I interrupted him. 'We know perfectly well who your father is. What he doesn't know is what his son is: an informer with no scruples, a filthy collaborator with the Germans, the shame of the ghetto.'

"It was a trial such as you would seldom see. With the help of a law student's legal advice, I was calling witnesses, and the first was the woman who had exposed young Horowitz. She had agreed to testify under oath, after promising never to reveal what she would hear or whom she would see during the trial. We trusted her. Right hand on the Bible, she swore to tell the truth and nothing but the truth. Then I began to question her. 'You know the accused?'

" 'No.'

" 'No?'

" 'I don't know him. We don't travel in the same circles. But I recognize him.'

" 'Agreed. You recognize him. Tell us how and under what circumstances you saw him.'

"Speaking in her impassive voice, she recounted the brutal opening of the shelter where she and her family had been hiding. 'Going out on the street, I saw this man with the SS, off to one side. The man next to me whispered, "That's young Horowitz." '

" 'Are you sure, absolutely sure, that you are not mistaken? Don't forget that a man's honor as well as his life is at stake.'

" 'I won't forget that.'

"Two more witnesses added their recollections to the case for the prosecution. The first worked in the supply office of the *Judenrat*. He was a small, emaciated, fearful man, and he spoke so softly that I had to ask him to raise his voice. 'One evening, when I was taking documents to the Kommandatur, I saw him sitting in an office with an SS officer. They were drinking a toast.'

"His companion, a stoop-shouldered old man with a troubled expression, spoke in a low, broken voice. 'In all my life, I have never spoken ill of a Jew; it's against my principles. At heart, every Jew is good, even innocent.'

" 'But then,' I asked, 'why have you come to testify before this court?'

" 'Because from my second-story window I could see them take away the first group. I was weeping bitter tears, and all those with me were weeping, too. But that one was down in the street, leaning against a doorway, alongside an SS man. They seemed to be chatting peacefully enough. So there it is: If I could drown him in our tears, I'd gladly do it.'

" 'Are you certain it was he? Take a good look at him. . . . No, that's not enough. Look at him some more. Now tell us: Is he indeed the young man who, while Jews were being driven out of their homes to their death, was calmly chatting with an SS man, as you described it to us?'

" 'It is he.'

" 'No possible doubt about it?'

" 'None at all.'

"The accused remained impassive during the questioning of the witnesses, his head bent over, as if what the court was hearing about him were of no concern to him. Was he resigned to his fate? Was he hoping his father would come save him? I asked him several times if he wanted to question the witnesses on this point or that. He answered with a shrug of the shoulders. Contempt or indifference? I suggested he make a statement. Same silent reply. It would have come as a relief to me if he had defended himself, no matter how awkwardly. But he had closed himself off in a total denial of reality. He showed neither fear nor remorse. Nothing mattered to him.

"You can guess the outcome. After briefly deliberating, the three judges pronounced the death sentence. I had won.

My parents, my family, all those doomed people would be avenged.

"Was I proud of myself? No. Happy? Of course not. To tell the truth, I don't know what I was experiencing when two comrades led the traitor off to a secret location, where he would await his execution.

"Now I remember. I felt thirsty."

Bolek had been speaking in an emotionless tone, so softly that at times his voice seemed more to skirt than to break the silence. Then abruptly, he stopped. Was that all he had to say? Gamaliel wondered. He had spoken of a murder that was weighing on his conscience. Did he mean that because of his desire for justice and vengeance he had obtained the death of young Horowitz? Gamaliel thought of Giordano Bruno, one of his favorite philosophers. At the end of his trial, which had lasted seven years, he'd turned to his inquisitors and said, "Your sentence frightens you more than it scares me." Was the same true of Bolek and his comrades-in-arms? Did they fear that in punishing one of their own they would come to resemble their executioners?

Softly, so gently that it was imperceptible—not like the sudden nightfall in the tropics—twilight was settling over the city that says it never sleeps, calming its spirit, wrapping it in a melancholy veil of yellow and gray.

More and more people were coming and going in Central Park. Newly arrived couples were seeking cool spots under the trees or by the lake. Gamaliel wondered if Bolek noticed them, or was he still absorbed in memory? Troubled, Gamaliel wanted to look at him to see whether he was going to resume his narrative. But he had promised to listen, just listen.

"Gamaliel, do you mind if I ask you a personal question?"

His friend was as surprised by Bolek's tone of voice as he was by the question. He had been expecting anything but that.

"Go ahead."

"Why do you still live alone? Since Colette's death have you never wanted to have another family? A son to make you proud and happy?"

Colette's absurd and tragic death. It was so long ago. What could it have to do with Bolek's story? Was Gamaliel right in thinking his friend had finished with his confession? Too bad. He would have wanted to hear how the sentence was carried out in that far-off Davarowsk ghetto. Was the executioner chosen by lot?

"Oh, forget about that. This isn't the time for it, and besides, it's a long story," he replied.

"Longer than mine?"

Gamaliel wondered if he should tell Bolek about Budapest. Ilonka. The times he strayed. Esther's disappearance. His estrangement from Katya and Sophie. Their mother's suicide. The obsessive sense of heartbreak that he could not rid himself of.

"Let's just say that God didn't want my name to be carried on."

"That's too easy an answer, isn't it?"

Gamaliel wondered if he should ask what his life had to do with Bolek's. Why should Bolek's confession require him to do the same?

"Let's talk about it some other time."

"Why not now?"

"You'll have to go home soon. Noémie—"

"She knows I'm with you."

Bolek heaved a sigh. "After the war, I still couldn't put it behind me. I was constantly seeing the SS in the ghetto. They were like dogs, bristling, ready to jump on their prey. I hated their making a traitor of a young Jew. I hated all Germans. And all those who collaborated with them. And all the neutrals who stood by. I was so devoured by rage that I was ready to hurl all of Creation, damned a thousand times over by the sin of Cain, into the furnace of my hate. And yet I didn't give in to it. I would tell myself, In what way would my vengeance help my mother and father, whose loss still makes me weep?"

At one point Gamaliel turned to him. "All right, you want to know if I ever wished for a son? Yes, I did, and often. To have a son who would bear my father's name, to see him grow up, to watch him sleep, to show him the world and all that's in it, to make him a gift of all I have and all I am. What man doesn't want that?"

"But?"

"I told you, God didn't want it to happen. . . . Wait, let me finish. When I say this, I'm referring to when God's been present in history as well as the times He's been eclipsed or was absent. It's written in the Talmud that when humanity experiences catastrophes—floods, epidemics, famines—man's duty is to refrain from having children. Because, said a Sage, we are forbidden to go against the will of the Lord. If He has decided to destroy the world, we have no right to populate it."

"Well, in that case, your Talmudic Sage is wrong. And so is God."

"Possibly. But there's something else. For a long time, I've distrusted this world we live in. I told myself it doesn't deserve our children. And the proof is Auschwitz."

"No, no, a thousand times no. Look, I have Leah. She gives meaning to my life. She'll have children, and they'll

change the world. They'll make it a better place—more welcoming, more humane. Yes, humanity does have a future. It
deserves Leah. And her children will prove it."

Was that Bolek's secret? Gamaliel wondered. Was he trying to answer the philosophy of Nietzsche and Schopen-
hauer?

Bolek's face darkened. "Your argument is nihilistic," he
said after a moment, "and I've heard it before. I find it inad-
missible. Think of your parents. Your family tree will end
with you. Is that what they wanted?"

"What about the Horowitzes' son?" Gamaliel retorted,
trying to change the subject. "That's a strong argument,
isn't it?"

"The exception proves the rule, but that is not an
argument."

"Don't you have more to tell me about that traitor?"

"What do you want to know?"

"What happened next. All of it. When did he die?"

"Three days later."

"Why the wait?"

"Because of his father. He found out his son had been
arrested, I don't how or from whom. He asked to see
Abrasha. Their talk lasted several hours. The older Horowitz
was pitiful. At first, he refused to believe his son could have
sunk so low as to betray the ghetto and its Jews. Then, after
he'd read and reread the testimony of the witnesses for
the prosecution, he began to sob. 'It's all my fault, my fault,'
he said over and over, wringing his hands. 'I brought him
up wrong. I was too preoccupied with business; I thought
too much about money, about success. So is it any surprise
that he grew up without principles or values? It's my fault,
my fault. . . .' Abrasha tried to reassure him: 'It serves no purpose to blame yourself. You've been an honorable man, a

good Jew. You've done a lot for the community. If your son
didn't follow your example, it's not your fault, but his.' 'But
that's just it,' the father said. 'I gave too much time to others
and not enough to him. I blame myself; the responsibility is
mine, not his.' Abrasha said again that he was wrong to think
that. Then the older man used another argument. 'I'm on
your side; you know that. I'll give you whatever you want,
all the money you need; I'll give you what is left of my
fortune—but give me back my son! I'll punish him myself.
I'll lock him up at home, like a prisoner, till the war is over.
Or else do it yourselves—put him in your own prison, but
don't kill him! Even if he deserves it, I don't!'

"Abrasha summoned all the cell leaders to an emergency
meeting the following night. Should we accept old Horowitz's offer? he wanted to know. It was then, during the discussion, that one of us commented, 'A father like Horowitz
would have done better not to have had children.' "

"And the condemned man? What happened to him?"

Bolek looked down. He did not answer right away. He
seemed to be wondering whether he should satisfy his
friend's curiosity or leave him in suspense.

"The traitor was executed."

A wave of sadness came over Gamaliel, mingled with a
jumble of other thoughts. He had to suppress a vague sort of
fear, a sense of impotence in the face of so much sorrow,
before he could continue. "And his father?"

"He mourned his son in keeping with our law." Bolek
swallowed, then added, "Two weeks later, he and his wife
were put on a transport to Treblinka."

For a long moment, they were both silent, as if paralyzed
by the name that stopped thought in its tracks, as though to
restrain it from hurling itself into the pit of death.

"Now it's my turn to ask you a question," said Gamaliel.

"Why don't you write about what you went through back then? Don't you think it's your duty to pay homage to what your comrades did? For the sake of history . . ."

Bolek grunted in contempt. "Don't talk to me about history. Some believe in it, and others will go so far as to sacrifice their conscience to make it say what they want, for lack of the truth. As for me, I don't believe in it. History is murderous, and as set as the blank face you'd see on a hardened killer. I've heard it said that now we know everything about the Holocaust, that it's been picked apart, analyzed, demystified, that all its parts have been dismantled. Such is the arrogance of ignorance! They accumulate data drawn from the official German archives without realizing that the truth isn't found only in numbers, dates, and orders. Who knows about my father's heroic dying, my mother's silent tears? Where is their truth? And where is the truth of my brothers and sisters when they were being driven to their mass grave? We seem to know the murderers better than their victims. And they call that serving history. Well, their history isn't my history, because my truth isn't their truth!"

"Exactly, Bolek," Gamaliel replied. "Isn't that all the more reason for you to write something different, to tell another truth, that of the victims?"

"The truth of the victims went up in smoke with them," said Bolek. "How about you? Where's your testimony? You're a survivor of the Holocaust, too, aren't you? And on top of that, you're a professional writer, aren't you?"

Survivor! For a long time now, Gamaliel's reaction to the word has been that it was cheapened, made a cliché, used in all kinds of situations. Everybody wanted to be one. No need to have undergone a selection at Birkenau or the tortures of Treblinka. It was sufficient to have lived, to have survived, in a Europe occupied or even threatened by Hitler's Germany. How many times Gamaliel had heard some hapless speaker trying to win the audience's sympathy by declaiming, "We are all survivors. . . . Of course, I was born in Manhattan, but I *could* have been born in Lodz or Kraków. . . ." Didn't they realize that if everyone is a potential or virtual survivor, then no one is a true survivor? How to explain to them that, confronted with such deception, those who did indeed survive come to be ashamed of having really been there? How to tell them to let "remembrance" rest in peace, because the dead took its key with them when they disappeared in smoke?

"You have nothing to say?" Bolek asked.

"What can I tell you? It's a sensitive subject. It takes a lot of thought." If he hadn't met Ilonka, would he have survived that most cruel of wars? Gamaliel preferred the word *orphan* to *survivor*.

"May I quote you on that?" Bolek asked. "And what are you doing about what you call 'the obligation of remembrance'?"

"I believe in it, but I don't know how to go about it. I might know what to say, but not how. Sometimes it seems to me that when I use words, I get them all mixed up and they cancel one another out, instead of proceeding in a coherent order. Actually, one word is all I'd need. But it would have to be *true*. And I don't know where to go find it!"

Gamaliel often wondered what means of speech would be decent, honorable, and effective enough for him to testify on behalf of his dead parents. A prayer, or a howl? Or perhaps silence?

Gamaliel walked his friend home in silence. Never had the streets, the buildings, the passersby seemed so hostile. He tried to picture himself in the Davarowsk ghetto, but he couldn't manage it. There was a question still plaguing him. "Bolek, who executed young Horowitz? Was it you?"

"No, not I."

"Then who?"

"A member of our group."

"Did you choose him?"

"No, not I."

"He volunteered?"

"No, I had us draw lots."

"He didn't object?"

"Romek, that was his name, Romek wasn't glad, but he accepted it." He paused a moment, then went on. "Strange, but he was surely the least suited for it of us all. He wasn't a tough guy, the quickest with his fists; rather, he was an introvert, an intellectual. Romek was forever reading, studying. When we were in our shelter, worrying about a raid by the SS, or when he was waiting to go to his job as an accountant in a workshop, he would lose himself in one of the books he'd borrowed from the ghetto library. That fate should have chosen him, it was . . . well, it was unfair." He stopped, smiled awkwardly. "It's funny. . . . Afterward, he couldn't stop rubbing his hands together. . . . Well, what can you expect? It was wartime."

He made as if to open the door to his building, then halted. "I went with him," he said in a low, inward voice.

"Time stood still.

"Young Horowitz, down in the cellar, stared at us with distrust and hate. 'Well, this is great and glorious. Out there, the Germans are massacring Jews, and now you're going to assassinate a Jew in here. Tell me, doesn't that bother you?'

"He was waiting for me to answer, to speak to him, to his

despicable conscience, to the man who was somewhere in him, but I had nothing to say: The time for words was over. I was thinking, He'll take the sight of me with him into the hereafter. One part of me, forever tainted, will die with him. I was looking at him. The silence was growing heavier, and then it became unbearable. I had to break the silence with a word, but the right word was staying just beyond my reach, jeering at me. Suddenly, I saw everything with a strange clarity. I saw things and people in a new light, one that cast them in excruciating relief. I caught myself staring at Romek, and for a moment I thought I was losing my hold on reality. I recalled something my father had said: 'The Angel of Death has a thousand eyes.' So did Romek. I wondered if the condemned man saw what I was seeing. I looked at him more closely. Nothing escaped me. I noticed his right eyebrow: It was thicker than the other. There was a fever sore on his lips. His nails were dirty. That last detail bothered me: One shouldn't die with dirty fingernails.

" 'How about it?' the condemned man shouted angrily. 'You're not going to say anything? You're going to kill me without a word?'

"I said nothing, and that was driving him out of his mind. Even though his hands were tied, he moved as if trying to throw himself on me. He was like a circus animal in its cage. In fact, he was right to be angry. He was about to die, and those who are to die have rights, including the right to hear a human voice, even if it's only the voice of their judge or executioner. So should I speak to him? I wondered. But to say what? That he was a murderer? That in helping the Gestapo, in betraying us to the Germans, he had become one of them? That at this moment we represented opposite poles of humanity, the pole of Evil and the pole of those who refuse

Evil? That at this stage of our lives, in this climate of absolutes reigning in that cellar, the universe, in losing one of its beings, would be losing its equilibrium? But wasn't that true every time a German killed a Jew? All that was too complicated. Why not just tell him his fingernails were dirty and he had a fever sore on his lips. I left the cellar, leaving the two men alone. I stood with my back to the door, not daring to breathe. Then it happened. And I felt more alone than ever."

Bolek shook his head as if he didn't believe his own story. Or that it continued. Gamaliel did not ask him to go on. That evening they did not talk to one another.

But on his way home, Gamaliel couldn't help thinking that young Horowitz—in fact, what was his first name? Bolek had never mentioned it—in a strange way, he had been lucky. He had lived with his father, they had prayed together, eaten together, laughed together. Unlike Gamaliel who had of his father nothing but a faded, blurred image: a life barely sketched. How many bad memories had they shared? How many words had they exchanged? For a time, Ilonka had taken the place of his mother. But who had taken his father's place, even for a brief moment? Shalom? Too young. Rebbe Zusya? Too old. No, his father was as old as he, his son, is today. And what if I had followed him to prison, then to the camp? Gamaliel wondered. Surely I would not feel the void that, sometimes, pulls me into the blackest of nightmares.

Tired as he is, Gamaliel continues to wander the streets and green places of Brooklyn without purpose or destination. Passersby glance at him with curiosity, wondering, Who is this man who seems so preoccupied with his own cares that he talks to himself, oblivious to others on the street? Gamaliel reaches the hospital entrance, looks at his watch, and goes on walking. Suppose he were to go in to see the old woman without waiting for the doctor? She might begin to speak. Miracles can always happen; such cases are known to medicine. Patients awaken after sleeping for weeks or months. Some speak; others let their subconscious minds speak for them. The philosopher Henri Bergson, in a coma, gave a dazzling lesson before dying. Naturally, Gamaliel does not hope for as much from the wounded woman in the hospital. Should he go in anyway? The doctor promised to join him there. He finds her attractive. Her smile reminds him of Eve, and so does her voice. They might have married eventually had he been younger. But now it's too late.

For that matter, hasn't it always been too late in his life? Even with Colette?

IT HAD SEEMED SO PROMISING AT FIRST. COLETTE had the skills and the wherewithal to captivate those who attracted her. Every day, she would take presents to her new love: ties, shirts, belts, trousers, a sports jacket. He never wore them. "No offense, but please don't spend so much money on me," he told her. "If you're not interested in material things," she exclaimed, giving him a passionate kiss, "I'll give you the best I have!" Giving free rein to her imagination, she transformed their nights into enchanting hours of constantly renewed pleasure.

Yet Gamaliel would not give up the hotel room he shared with Bolek. Colette tried to persuade him. "Either you insist on wasting the little you earn, or else you're not sure of me, of us, of our future together. Are you really so afraid that you'll be out on the street tomorrow?" But Gamaliel held out. He clung to his lodgings, modest as they were, to his ways, to his freedom, to his connection to Bolek. "Besides," he observed, "it's thanks to Bolek that we met. We should at least be grateful to him." Seeing that he was irritated, Colette was quick to calm him, to act as if she agreed. As a general rule, she would give in when he held out. But she didn't accept his resistance with good grace. She would make him pay for it.

Bolek did not comment on his friend's affair. When Gamaliel came back at dawn, or after a week's absence, Bolek would greet him with a laugh. "You're happy—it shows in your face—and that's what counts." He did permit himself to give Gamaliel a bit of advice one evening when they were chatting about this and that. "Don't go too fast or too far. Keeping some distance is a good idea and can be useful. Also, you're too young to marry. And perhaps Colette isn't young enough." He thought for a moment, then continued. "I hope I'm not hurting your feelings. But think about what I'm saying. It's for your own good. It's great to make love with your mistress, so long as she's not your wife." Gamaliel teased him: "But how about the French passport I'd get?" "You can get along fine without it," Bolek replied, then added, "Besides, it'll be easier once we get to America. You won't have to sacrifice your future for a passport." When Gamaliel remained silent, Bolek became concerned. "Are you angry with me?" he asked. "Forgive me if I said the wrong thing, but you're my friend." Gamaliel reassured him, thinking, Strange that he didn't ask if I love Colette in spite of the difference in our ages.

Actually, Colette's age wasn't on his mind. What disturbed him was her willful, often authoritarian personality. She was a stranger to doubt. She was at home everywhere, always sure of herself. She never hesitated; she always knew just what to do, where to go, how to get there, and how long to stay. She seemed to enjoy keeping her lover under tight surveillance.

She introduced him to her parents and her two adolescent brothers, both lycée students. Her father was cordial. He was sixtyish, round-faced, and potbellied; he was constantly relighting his thick cigar. He owned a fancy leather business and would talk shop with Gamaliel. "Just in case," he said one day with a laugh. "You and Colette . . . you should know your way around." Gamaliel blushed and looked away. Colette's mother, always decked out in jewels and pearls, as if for a charity ball, did not hide her lack of enthusiasm. "You speak our language well, young man. What nationality are you?" she asked. Gamaliel replied that he was stateless. "Stateless?" she burst out. "Just what does that mean? Is it a nation?" "Maman," one of the boys said, embarrassed, "it's someone who has no nationality." "But then . . . ," she began. Her husband tried to silence her, saying, "Then nothing. A stateless man can easily become French like you and me. All he has to do is marry a French woman." The mother shook her head in disbelief. "It's not right, not right at all, that's what I think. It seems too easy, that's it, just too easy." "Easy?" the other son asked lightly. "What do you mean— easy to become a citizen or easy to marry?" Colette, trying to change the subject, said, "In any case, Gamaliel—sorry, Péter—hates things to be too easy." Her mother would not let go. "But just now you called him by another name, a peculiar name. . . ." "I made a mistake, Maman. His name is Péter." Her mother made a gesture of dismay. "How about your parents, young man? Where are they? What does your father do?" "Maman! That's enough!" Colette said angrily. "Péter has no parents!"

Their civil marriage was performed two months later, after the High Holy Days, by a polite but indifferent deputy mayor. A young Sephardic rabbi presided at the religious ceremony, which was followed by an ostentatious reception, complete with band, in Colette's parents' luxurious apartment. Fine leather work all over. A few poor refugees leapt at the invitation to a sumptuous repast. Over in a corner, Yasha was singing melancholy Russian songs; Diego was drinking and cursing fascist Communists and Communist fascists. Flowers and presents and wines and sweets in profusion. An amused Bolek was studying a poorly lit masterpiece. Colette was beaming. Gamaliel was saying to himself, It's only natural for all these people to be here, but where is Esther? And what am I doing here? He seemed to be participating in an occasion that had nothing to do with him. In his mind's eye he was again a child with his parents, then with Ilonka.

That same evening, he formally took up residence in Colette's apartment, but he still kept his hotel room, where he left a few books and some clean shirts in Bolek's custody.

His naturalization was expedited, thanks to her father's connections. He was happy when he went to police head-quarters to obtain his precious *carte d'identité*. "At last I'm a citizen of someplace!" he exclaimed. Colette had urged him to register himself as Péter. Certainly not Gamaliel. "Do you want people to laugh at me?" she asked. But this time, her husband did not give in. Still, Colette never called him Gamaliel.

A week's honeymoon in Nice. They went by car; Colette drove. The couple spent a day in Italy. At the border, Colette handed over two passports: her own and her husband's. Again, Gamaliel thought, I'm no longer a man without a country. I'm no longer regarded as suspect; policemen and customs officials are courteous. Yet I haven't changed; I'm still the same person. When Colette asked if he was happy, he said yes. She would ask him often, sometimes all day long. Sometimes she even awakened him in the middle of the night to ask, "Are you happy?" He would answer that he was, but then he couldn't go back to sleep.

Colette was possessive, insatiable; she was always caught up in passing fads, whims, phobias. She was prone to fits of anger or resentment. In the morning, he was forbidden to speak to her until she had put on her makeup and done her hair. In the evening, he was forbidden to exclude her from his thoughts. The sight of a bald man upset her. "The day you go bald," she told her husband, "I'll kick you out." She said the same about an unkempt beard or a bad haircut, or children who cried too loud.

Gamaliel still had not adapted to his new life after a year of marriage, with its ups and downs. He was more at home with his refugee friends. Diego would tease him, saying, "Do you still have time for us?" Yasha would say, "Forget it, Diego. We and Gamaliel will never be divorced."

Just when did Gamaliel notice the change in Colette's behavior? She was quicker to lose her temper, shouting obscenities, smashing dishes over a word, a moment's grumpiness. When Gamaliel would ask her why, she would reply, "Because you don't love me anymore." "Why do you say that?" "Because it's true." "How do you know it's true?" "Because you're not happy." He would try to calm her, to mollify her by one means or another. But with time, he came to realize his efforts were in vain.

"Listen to me, Péter my boy," she said one day. "I want to talk to you. I'll thank you not to interrupt. What I have to say to you is important. I loved you; I married you for just one reason: to give you the happiness that life has denied you. Apparently, I've failed. The only time you're happy is with your stateless pals. You have more in common with them than you do with me. Well, go back to them. Leave this house. Let's separate, the sooner the better for all concerned." Gamaliel stared at her in bewilderment. "What's wrong with you?" he asked. "Did I do or say something to displease you?" She shook her head. "No, you didn't do or say anything. That's just it—you're always there, doing nothing, saying nothing, unless I push you to it. Now I'm fed up with living like this, as strangers. Go away!" He turned toward the door. She detained him. "Just one thing more. Be aware that I know myself well. I know what's going to happen with me—

hate is going to take the place of love. That's why it's better that we part ways." She's crazy, Gamaliel thought, and he told her so. She didn't contradict him. "You say I'm crazy? It may well be. Crazy with love yesterday, today crazy with hate." She burst into hysterical laughter. "Want to hear something funny? I went to the doctor yesterday. Would you like to know what he said? He told me . . . that I'm . . . he told me I'm pregnant." She kept on laughing for what seemed a very long time. Gamaliel, standing at the door, didn't know whether he should return to her, console her, congratulate her, love her as he had before, better than before. He started back, but she stopped him, yelling, "No! Whatever you do, don't come near me! Get out of my sight and out of my life! I never want to lay eyes on you again!" Her face was distorted with contempt.

Six weeks before giving birth, Colette told him again how she hated him, how he disgusted her. She was consumed with a desire for vengeance. "Go away, quick, vanish. I can't stand you. You horrify me. . . ." But immediately she changed her mind. "No, stay here. You won't suffer so much if you're away from me. I want to see you suffer."

She gave birth to twin girls.

At the hospital, Gamaliel was dismissed by his mother-in-law, who was enraged to the point of violence. "We never want to see you again, Mr. Stateless. I always knew you were no good. My daughter gave you everything, and in return you made her miserable. Get out!" "But the babies . . . I'm their father," Gamaliel protested. "So much the worse for you and for them. They'll have a new father soon enough, I promise you that. Now clear out, or I'll call for help. Then they'll sweep you out the door." She's crazy, Gamaliel thought, crazy like her daughter.

Colette fell ill. Hate was eating at her like a disease. She lived only to give expression to her aversion to her husband. Contrary to her parents, she did not want a divorce. "I'm determined to keep him right here, so I can witness his torment." Eventually, she infected Katya and Sophie. Yet at first, they loved their father as he loved them, which only fed Colette's anger. He took them to Parc Monceau; he told them stories about happy kings and unhappy princes. He explained to them how clouds have a world of their own, and trees have their own sovereign. He lived only for them. He would accept whatever Colette said or did; a glance from Katya, a blink of the eye from Sophie helped him through the grief that day by day became heavier and more suffocating. Then everything fell apart. The twins had just celebrated their twelfth birthday. That night, Colette, disheveled, her face contorted, began hitting her husband in a fit of rage. "You're happy with the twins, and that I will not tolerate! When you're with them, you're comfortable in your skin, while with me you're a monster of selfishness and hypocrisy. You make me sick! Stop . . . or I'll call the police. . . . I'll tell them you beat me, that you want to kill me, that you've got the idea in your head that the girls aren't yours and you're planning to do away with them. . . . The police will take over. . . . You'll lose your citizenship. . . ." Was she capable of stooping so low? In any event, Gamaliel refused to be separated from the twins. The hellish scenes became ever more frequent, and they were more and more savage. Still worse, the twins could no longer bear it, and, being too young to hold their mother responsible for her own unhappiness, they came to blame it on their father. After months of one crisis after another, he had to accept the only way out: separation. Gamaliel offered to take the blame for a divorce, in order to avoid any possible scandal; Colette, stubborn to the end, refused. So ended a dismal period in his life.

In time, Katya and Sophie came to hate him. All they knew about their father, gone to the United States to join Bolek, was that he deserved to be banished because he had made their mother unhappy. They were fifteen when Colette committed suicide by swallowing an overdose of barbiturates. They, along with their grandparents, held Gamaliel responsible for her unhappiness and her death. Often he tried to get in touch with them, always in vain. His letters were returned unopened. Now he, too, felt the pain of depression, of doubt and remorse. In what way was I at fault? he would wonder in his sleepless nights. What did I do to cause so much misfortune? Was Colette right to resent my being immune to happiness, or even love? I would like someone to explain it to me.

Colette had taken her explanations with her to her prison in the sky. Gamaliel made a short trip to Paris to meditate at her grave. He spoke softly to her. He asked her forgiveness. He told her, "Maybe I didn't love you enough, passionately enough. I no longer know. Yes, I feel guilty, but I don't know why. I feel so guilty I can no longer love." He picked up a stone and placed it on her grave. On leaving, he felt that he was parting from his own self.

Poor Colette, her own victim.

And Gamaliel, hapless victim of the victim.

Then came Eve.

EVE AND HER INHIBITIONS. A LOVE DESPERATE AND despairing. Dazzling and humbling. For one as well as the other? "I'm bad luck," she would say with a clear, cool certainty that was almost superstitious. "You mustn't love me," she added, "and I'll do my best not to love you." One day, she used one of Colette's favorite phrases: "I'm telling you this for your own good." But coming from Eve, it was a warning, not a threat. "In my case," she asserted, "love always includes something evil, something harmful." And yet every moment he spent with her, when they were listening to music, or reading, or just riding the bus, had been a time of fulfillment. Then suddenly, Samaël had appeared on the scene. Had she made him unhappy, too? Gamaliel wondered later. But no, Samaël was incapable of happiness or unhappiness. What he did was make others unhappy. Eve had resisted him strongly and valiantly, but in the end she succumbed. Eve and Samaël, Eve and Gamaliel: Was she the same woman?

Gamaliel was ready to give up everything for her. Even to marry her. Despite the memory of his failure with Colette. Once again, Eve dissuaded him. "Why endanger a relationship that feels good as it is? In what way would marriage make our happiness greater?"

He persisted. "We'd do the same things, but under another name, differently."

" 'Differently'? What do you mean?"

He didn't know how to explain. In any event, they were already like a married couple in the eyes of those who knew them. No one would invite one without the other. What happened to one involved the other. Gamaliel asked her one day, "Could we live the rest of our lives like this, even though we're not married?"

"If it is written on high that we're destined to live like this till we die, it matters little whether or not we're legally or religiously joined. One has to know how to read the Book of Life, that's all."

"And I suppose you know how to read that book?" he said, trying to provoke her.

"You're the writer, not I."

"The writer writes so the reader may read. So go ahead and read it."

"But the writer has to know how to read before he can learn how to write."

So be it, Gamaliel thought. Why not let her have her way? She has her reasons, and to her they are no doubt valid. Does her reticence grow out of her first marriage? Stop! Minefield ahead: no trespassing. We will live together "as if" we are married, he thought. As long as we're in love.

Eve went on, "We'll live together, provided we're not married."

"With love?"

"No, Gamaliel, without love," she said with a smile. After a brief kiss, she added, "Love isn't everything. You should know that."

"Go on."

"There is something above love and beyond it."

"And what is that?"

"The secret."

"What secret?"

"The secret that gives us humans the ability to transcend ourselves in good as well as in evil." Another kiss ended the discussion. Gamaliel conceded defeat; Eve was superb in these debates. She always won, and that didn't bother him. Quite the contrary: With her, nothing bothered him. Besides, "winning" and "losing" had no place in their relationship. With Eve, Gamaliel was always seeking just the right word.

Wondrous days, spellbinding evenings of discovery and

sharing. Who said one can't be happy among the gigantic towers of stone that huddle together on the Manhattan skyline?

Walks in Brooklyn, picnics in Central Park, open-air musical evenings, excursions to the Catskills. Could he have known the same happiness with Colette had she not lost both her spirit and her sanity? Does happiness, like man, resemble the one who gives it birth?

"Sometimes you're off with a ghost, somewhere far away," Eve observed one day. "Tell me, can you still see me?"

"Of course I see you. In fact, you're all I see."

"Impossible. You can't see two beings at the same time with the same pair of eyes." She paused to kiss him, then asked, "Can you speak two words at the same time?"

"Yes, I can."

"Prove it."

"I can say one word that contains another within it. Some words are like Russian dolls."

"I forgot that you spend your time opening those Russian dolls."

"Not all my time. I also spend time looking at you."

"How do I look?"

"Beautiful, very beautiful, a beauty that is whole."

"That's all?"

"Almost all."

"What do you know about me?"

"I told you: You're beautiful."

"But it takes more than that to define or express who a person is," she said, pouting.

"Oh? Who told you that?"

"I don't know. I know it from people."

"So change people."

"From living."

"Change your life."

"I know it by instinct."

"You're not listening very well. You have to be a good listener in order to love. And the opposite is also true: You must love in order to be a good listener."

"Stop it!"

"I didn't say I love you; I just said I love beauty."

And they loved each other.

Gamaliel also got the upper hand when they discussed a subject on which their opinions turned out to be diametrically opposed. They never raised their voices, but their disagreement almost led to a break that would have been irreparable. Gamaliel was sitting on the sofa with Eve's head in his lap. They were talking about the news of the day— politicians' debates, AIDS, feminism, militancy—and then the conversation turned to Gamaliel's trade. Eve hated it. "Aren't you deceiving the reader when you write a book that has someone else's name on it as author? Aren't you lying to him?"

"No, Eve. I'm doing the job of a banker: I lend words to those who need them. As it happens, I have an ample supply of them in the secret drawers of my desk. I look around among them, I choose a few words, and I lend them out for a reasonable fee."

"And afterward you take them back?"

"Precisely. I take them back, and then I rent them out to other clients, but arranged in different patterns."

"But that's dishonest!"

"Dishonest? You're exaggerating."

"You're forgetting the reader; you're talking as if he didn't exist! He doesn't know about this game you're playing. He doesn't realize it's nothing but a business deal."

"So what? Provided it's a good book, will his pleasure be any the less for it?"

"Yes, obviously."

"What do you know about it? You don't read that kind of book."

"Indeed I don't. But that's just it: I want to read what you yourself write. I'd like to read books to which you're not ashamed to sign your name."

"What's more important—the book or the name on it?"

"The book, obviously. But why should I read something the author's not proud of?"

"But . . . how else would I make a living? Who cares what I have to say? You have to be realistic, Eve. Be sensible. Understand me: Yes, I live in a wonderful country. Yes, I have a passport in my pocket. But in my heart of hearts, I'm still a refugee. And maybe my words are also refugees, and that's why they hide in other people's books." According to an unspoken rule between them, he now stopped to kiss her before resuming. "But I know when I've had it, and then I take refuge in another person."

"In me?"

"Yes, in you."

"I understand you," said Eve, biting her lip. "At least I'm trying to. But I don't like it."

"What don't you like?"

"Serving as your shelter."

"Even if I need it?"

"I don't like your needing me as a place to hide. I like to think that we're free and equal human beings."

"In principle, you're right. But we can't live in principle."

"Exactly. That's just what I don't like."

"And that's what you call lying? Like ghostwriting is lying?"

The young woman's face clouded over. "I know that in the real world you're right," she said, her voice tinged with bitterness. "When we don't have the wherewithal, money becomes an obsession. But I thought you were different."

There was a sudden distance between them. It was the first rift in their relationship. Eve's head was still in Gamaliel's lap, but now she was beginning to weigh on him. In any event, Eve sat up, then moved away, as if she were preparing to leave. To relax the tension between them, Gamaliel asked her to sit down, and then he said, "I'll read you a page from what I've written. All right?"

"A page of your own? That you'd sign your name to?"

"Yes. Would you like that?"

"Of course I'd like it!"

He stood and went to riffle through the papers on his desk. He remained standing. "Here is the first page I came upon."

It was a page from the novel—so coveted by Georges Lebrun—that he had been writing over the years:

"The character who is speaking is close to me. His name is Pedro or Michael, Gregor or Paritus. He's a doctor and a philosopher. He meets a young dreamer, the 'Blessed Madman,' soon after his attempt at mysticism had resulted in disaster. The young man wants to die, and the doctor is trying to give him the confidence to go on living. Listen to what he tells him:

" ' "I know what you're experiencing. You're to blame because you're alive. Therefore you stand convicted. But didn't you set your sights too high? A little humility, my dear revolutionary mystic. It's necessary. Think of Moses, the humblest of men. Did he consider himself guilty because he had gone away at the very time his brother and his people were making the Golden Calf? You tried to overthrow the existing order of things, and you were defeated. Henceforth, try to live far from the world and its deceiving lights, far from the sight of God, in the privacy of your thoughts. I'm so advising you in order that one day you may be able to start over." ' "

Gamaliel looked for another page, then said to Eve, "Listen to my doctor. He's with a sick child in Budapest, in a Jewish hospital that the Germans have taken over. He feels overwhelmed, on the one hand by exhaustion, on the other by the need to keep fighting off the death that is hovering over the child's bed. He is thinking:

" 'What is to be done when the human condition is as evident in the remedy as it is in the ills that afflict us? Man's destiny is tragic not only because it can only end in death but also because all he does seems like a negation of the time on earth for which he is responsible. There would be no problem if it were only a matter of the body, or if it were only the soul. But man is both body and soul, body versus soul, soul the enemy of the body. So in his life—this life he was given, though he never asked for it—the two are always in contradiction. The body clings to the passing moment; the soul refuses to linger there. The soul seeks eternity, but the body cannot attain it. One can imagine a soul confined by the body; one can also imagine a body tortured by conscience. But no torture inflicted on the body will make the soul any

wiser. Body and soul: Which gives the other its
meaning? That's the quintessential question, the
question within which all others are contained.
Nostalgia is the soul's lament for a past denied it by
the laws of the body. But in fact, the soul also needs
the body: If memory does not give us back the
pleasure we once enjoyed, but only saddens us, it is
because to relive the past is once more to go on
living by the rules of a frail body and of an impossible
love.

 " 'So the soul is forever feeling bullied, dissatisfied,
unhappy. Its hunger for eternity could be appeased if
it could escape from time. But all it seeks, all it is able
to seek, is an infinite prolonging of the body's fleeting
moment. So, confined to that moment, the soul is
imprisoned by its own chains. Here is what man is as
seen by a dreamer or a visionary mystic: a stranger in
a hostile land who encounters another stranger
without realizing that it is God. And God says to
him, "Since we are alone here, let's walk together,
so we may arrive at some destination. And even if
we do not, each of us will have helped the other
not to despair." So, my child, try to resign yourself
to this: If God accepts reality, you must do
the same.' "

Eve sat still, listening, a frown on her face. "More," she
said softly. "Please go on. Was the sick child able to say anything?"

"No, he was too sick to do anything but listen. But the
reply came from a fearless old man, who, from a distance,
reprimanded the doctor: 'You picked a poor time to philoso-

phize. Don't you see that the child is suffering? While you're making speeches? You should be telling him a story!' "

"I'd like to be in that child's place," Eve observed. "Go on."

The seriousness in her voice gave Gamaliel pause. "Very well," he said. He leafed through the manuscript, first forward, then back, till he found the passage he wanted. "This is another passage from the same manuscript, my *Book of Secrets*.

" 'The door opened as if of its own accord. Big Mendel stood in the doorway, laughing. Crossing and uncrossing his arms, he kept on laughing. Shoulders, chest, face, and voice—his whole body was shaking to the point that his young Master no longer recognized him. "What's happened to you, Mendel?" he asked. "Come in and tell me about it."

" 'They had been apart since the previous evening. A surly priest had appeared in their room at nightfall and gestured to the Jew to follow him. Hananèl had stepped between them, but the priest had pushed him back so hard that Mendel said angrily, "Don't lay hands on him, understand?" The priest said nothing, and Mendel added, "I'll go with you, but don't touch him, or you'll have me to deal with." And to the young Master, he said, "No doubt they need a hand with the horses. Let the Rebbe not worry. I know how to take care of myself."

" 'Hours of anxiety had followed. Where could Mendel be? Hananèl tried to open the door, but it was locked. Heart heavy, lost in his thoughts, he paced around his prison, bumping into the walls, afraid to sit

in either of the room's two chairs. So distraught was
he that he almost forgot the evening prayer of Maariv;
it was almost midnight when he recited it. He
knocked on the door; no one answered. He knocked
harder and harder, but in vain. He tried to calm
himself so that his spirit could ask the Almighty about
his beadle's disappearance. Was he still alive? As
usual, the familiar celestial voice replied, "Yes, Reb
Mendel is alive. But . . . do not hasten to rejoice
over it." Hananèl quickly asked, "Is he in pain?"
"No," the voice answered, "he is not in pain. But
that is not a reason to be reassured." Hananèl awoke
with a start, and, as if in a trance, he began to recite,
in the order set out by a twelfth-century Kabbalist,
the Psalms of David, which rescue man from
distress.

" ' "Come in, Mendel," Hananèl said again.

" 'The beadle could hardly lift his aching limbs. He
moved slowly forward, slipping on the wooden floor.
Hananèl went to help him, and when he saw close up
the ravaged face and bloodshot eyes, he cried out,
"What did they do to you?" He led Mendel to a chair
and helped him sit. Still laughing, Mendel began to
speak.

" ' "May the Rebbe forgive me; I can't help it. There
were three of them, three priests. Two young ones,
and the old one who came for me. They wanted me to
tell lies about the Rebbe. According to them, the
Rebbe was a liar and his powers were a sham. I
shouted at them that they didn't know, they couldn't
know what they were talking about. That their
ignorance proved they were serving the Devil. Then

the old one pulled an ancient book from his pocket and showed it to me. 'It's a manual,' he said, 'a manual that dates from the Inquisition. It proved its value in Spain and Portugal. Thanks to it, you will answer all our questions. Who is this young "Blessed Madman"? From where does he derive his occult powers? Is he a sorcerer, a magician? Is he in league with Satan?' Then I started laughing to overcome my fear. 'I'm not afraid of pain,' I told them. 'I only fear the Lord God of Abraham, Isaac, and Jacob. But you, you do not fear Him, and that will cost you dearly, I'm telling you.' May the Rebbe forgive me, but I cannot describe what I underwent at their hands. But one thing is certain, and that is that I never stopped laughing. Because I knew whom I was suffering for. It was for God and His servant, my Master. But they, my torturers, did they know why they were making me suffer? I told myself that in this life sometimes we have to choose between laughing and making others laugh. Well, I made my choice."

" 'Now Hananèl kissed him on the forehead and said in a soft and gentle voice, "We've known each other a long time, Mendel. You're closer than close to me. You're part of my very being. But you came to me after the ordeals I underwent, after my defeat. Now for the first time you're experiencing real pain. Know that it is as powerful as pleasure, if not more so. Woe to the man for whom it is the only reason for living, all he cares about; nothing on earth will tear him away from it. In time, it will take him over body and soul. It becomes a deity to him, devouring all conscience and all hope. But you, you defeated that deity by rising above it."

" ' "May the Rebbe forgive me," Mendel said, "but he knows perfectly well that I'm only a beadle; my mind isn't capable of rising to such heights, so I don't understand the Rebbe's thoughts."

" 'Moved to tears, the young Master managed a smile. "Mendel, my dear Mendel. Right now, between the two of us, you're the Rebbe."

" 'The beadle's face grew somber. "No, Rebbe, a thousand times no! Is the Rebbe saying that because I didn't reveal any of his truth? But I don't understand the truth he knows. I'm just a poor servant who lives in his Master's shadow!"

" ' "I'm saying it, Mendel, because you discovered the truth not of pain but of laughter."

" 'Only then did the beadle grow calm.' "

Gamaliel stopped. Perhaps he expected Eve to ask him to continue, but she remained silent. Her eyes were half-closed, as if dozing, but she was breathing heavily, as though her heart were beating fast.

"Words," Gamaliel said. "They're just words."

"What do they mean to you?"

"I don't know. But I do know what I would like them to be. I would like them to be like fire, to leave scars on the memory of God, or at least of His creatures."

"Those words," she said very softly, "would you rent them to me?"

"It all depends."

"On what?"

"On how much you're willing to pay. Let me tell you that Georges Lebrun, that novelist of mine, who's as arrogant as he is untalented, wants to buy them from me. And he's offering me the moon."

"I'll pay better."

"Really?"

"Come here and sit."

From then on, they never quarreled. Even when Samaël's diabolical influence forced them to part, their separation was not preceded by any misunderstanding.

LIKE IT OR NOT, GAMALIEL LIVED HIS WORK night and day. He had always been fascinated by words, by the silence within a word, to which that word gives meaning. Sometimes, even when he was writing his *Book of Secrets,* he would spend hours leafing through dictionaries, for no reason other than sheer pleasure. Had he to spend ten years on the proverbial desert island with a single book, that book would be a dictionary. He was convinced that to read two words, two little words, was as serious an action as the joining of two people. For the distance that separates one word from another is, in the world of words, as great a distance from earth to a star.

What's more, each word has its own destiny. Words are born by chance, grow up, and die, drained of their blood, then can be reborn a century later, in some other place, for better or for worse, offering hope to some and sorrow to others.

A word may change in meaning and scope according to its context. The words *kadesha, kedosha,* and *kedusha,* in the Bible, are one example among many. Those same words can

mean "whore," "saint," and "sanctity." Sometimes we use the
same words to glorify what is pure and to denounce what is
not. Today more than ever, words transmit violence by
describing it. It is when he masters the word that Satan
becomes all-powerful.

Rebbe Zusya often spoke of *Galut hadibur,* the exile of the
word. "When words lose their way, when they wander off
and lose their meaning, when they become lies," he would
say, "those who speak or write them are the most uprooted
of people. And surely the most to be pitied."

WAS EVE HERSELF AMONG THE UPROOTED? NO.
Despite the loss of her husband and daughter, she had kept
her nature intact. Eve was upright, opposed to compromise.
Eve the unyielding: She had adopted as basic unspoken principles her moral values, the rules of living in a society, of
responsibility to others. No one could get her to come down
from that lofty perch. She was often right, and Gamaliel conceded that her demands, never petty or malicious, did her
credit—even when they entailed a sacrifice.

One day, a public official offered Gamaliel a particularly
lucrative contract to write his political-philosophical autobi-
ography. Gamaliel accepted, for the project presented no
major problems. Interesting topic, unusual protagonist: poor
as a child, brilliant law student, promising start as aide to
the mayor of a medium-size city, career without blemish.
Gamaliel could deliver the manuscript in a few weeks and be
paid the rest of the advance. That was when Eve asked him,
"Are you sure, absolutely sure, that this man has a clean
record?"

" 'Absolutely sure'? No, I'm not. I can't guarantee you that he never got his hands dirty one way or another. We mustn't forget he's a politician."

"And what will you do if, after this flattering book he expects from you is published, you discover some unpleasant facts about him? Will you feel morally obliged to make a public apology? If so, you won't be able to, because you've promised never to reveal that you wrote his book!"

Gamaliel tried to parry the thrust. "Intellectual honesty and moral courage aren't necessarily the same. Did you know that the great Descartes was so frightened when he learned that Galileo had been found guilty that he postponed the publication of his own treatise *Traîté du Monde?*"

"You're not Descartes. And since you know his story, you can't use his excuse."

"All right, I'll try to explain it another way. Suppose I'm a shoemaker. I make a pair of shoes for a good customer. Is it my fault if he sells them to a criminal, who then wears them to rob a bank?" Seeing the look of distrust on Eve's face, he caught himself and said sheepishly, "Forgive me. That example was unworthy of you, and of us."

And he gave back the politician's twenty thousand dollars.

There was another occasion on which Gamaliel refused a tempting offer. A rabbi, "spiritual leader" of a congregation in Detroit, asked him to write for him a refutation of the work of a certain "Rabbi Arthur." The latter had written what he considered an exposé on a Jewish Communist sect in the Ukraine. Gamaliel asked for time to think it over. "On the one hand," he said to Eve, "why should I get mixed up in the quarrel between two rabbis? On the other hand, it would pay the rent for six months."

He went out to Rabbi Arthur's town in Michigan. A quick investigation showed him that the rabbi was anything but popular. Some resented his arrogance; others mocked his ambition. But how much faith should be put in these nasty rumors? That he had been forced out of his post didn't mean all that much. It happened everywhere; one could hardly find a religious community that was free of dissension. The illustrious Rabbi Israel Salanter used to say, "A rabbi without adversaries doesn't deserve his position. But he deserves it even less if he lets them dominate him." To get a better sense of the man before coming to a decision, Gamaliel attended a public meeting where Rabbi Arthur was to speak.

The speaker was impressive only in his mediocrity. Average height, flushed face of a delayed adolescent, slack-jawed, silver-rimmed glasses over pale eyes. A tense, screechy voice, jerky movements—a comedian. That, at any rate, was what people called him: "the comedians' rabbi," or "the rabbi's comedian." Vain, self-centered, he may well have had his talents, but ideas were not among them: In that field, his speciality was borrowing. He had stayed single because, people said, he could find no woman worthy of him; he was, in a sense, married—to himself. His speech was a series of banalities laced with an underling's sense of resentment. He resented everyone—above all, his colleagues, who would not recognize his worth, his distinction, his supposed role in both Jewish and non-Jewish highbrow circles. He resented the community whose intellectual leader he aspired to be. The audience, used to his self-importance, listened with half an ear.

After the meeting, Gamaliel went to him and introduced himself as a correspondent for a major European magazine.

"You want to interview me?" the rabbi asked. "Of course, anytime, anyplace. Will you be bringing a photographer?"

The interview took place the following day in the rabbi's

study. There were many books on the shelves, but also photos of the rabbi alongside celebrities in the arts and prominent Israelis. Actually, it was a monologue, not an interview. The rabbi clearly loved the sound of his own voice. But, Gamaliel asked himself, is that reason enough to help his adversary demolish his reputation, especially since the rabbi himself seems to be doing such a good job of it? A vague feeling of pity came over him, and he decided to reject the New York rabbi's offer.

Eve tossed her head back, and, laughing, she applauded him. "I'm richer than your rabbi. I'll pay you back for what you lost by turning down his offer. But in return, you have to write a book that will be just for me."

In Eve, a sense of humor went hand in hand with a sensibility that mingled sadness with an urgent need for tenderness and calm. A book just for her? There was one: the Song of Songs.

"Someday I'll show you my manuscript," Gamaliel told her. "The book will be my gift to you. You'll read it, you'll see. I hope you'll like it. It's a book that no one else could write or even imagine. A book whose words make you dream."

In his book Gamaliel recounted his father's last words, his mother's caresses, Ilonka's great soul.

He described the first woman who introduced him to love, the first time he saw the body of a woman ready for pleasure.

He related the somber and terrible event that befell the "Blessed Madman," precursor to the Messenger, Rebbe Zusya.

He expressed what Gamaliel had heard around him: Under God's creation, to paraphrase Rabbi Nahman of Bratslav, the greatest of the Hasidic storytellers, everything that exists in this world has a heart, and that heart has a heart that is the heart of the world. According to this Sage, sound becomes voice, voice becomes song, and song becomes story. If only we lend an ear, we will hear what is all around us. The leaves of the trees speak to the grass, the clouds signal one another, and the wind carries secrets from one land to the next. One must learn to listen; that is the key to mystery.

And Gamaliel would discover that key, he promised Eve. He would find the voice and let it be heard.

"Perhaps I'm that key of which you speak so eloquently," said Eve.

Yes, it was she.

He would use that key to unlock the nocturnal gates to her body and his soul. And they would attain a happiness rooted in humanity that would flow on forever.

Gamaliel had a dream:

I am running like a madman through a town I've never seen, where everyone enjoys peace. The children speak like wise elders, the women are radiant with beauty, and the merchants are overflowing with generosity as they hand out their precious goods. Everything is free. Where have I come to, and why? I don't understand what's happening to me. Someone must have brought me here. As punishment, or reward? I stop a bearded man and ask, "What am I doing here among you?" He shakes my hand warmly and starts laughing. "Oh, how funny you are!" He stops other passersby and says, pointing at me, "See how funny he is, this visitor. Isn't he funny? Let's all thank him for being so funny!" I go to a young man and ask, "What do you think about my being here among you?" The young man reaches in his pocket, pulls out a gold piece, and hands it to me. "This is a gift for you, stranger, because you are a gift to us. But be aware that you can't use it—it's worthless here." A woman dressed with disarming simplicity signals that she wants to talk to me. She looks familiar. I know those eyelids, those lips, those gestures. But who is she? "I've been waiting for you for a long time," she says invitingly. "Yes, for a long time I've been dreaming of being in your arms. And you?" "As for me," I say in my dream, "it's a long time since I stopped dreaming." At that, she bursts out laughing and leans toward me to touch my lips. "Don't say anything, just listen. My name is Eve. I am the first and—"

Gamaliel started, then awoke, overwhelmed. Eve was sleeping restlessly, her sleep punctuated from time to time by a sigh of pain or perhaps fear; he had no way of knowing which. Should I wake her? he wondered. Better wait; maybe she'll calm down. She murmured words he could not understand. Suddenly, she cried out, opened her eyes, looked around in the half-light. Their eyes met. She seemed surprised to find him by her side.

"You were having a nightmare," he told her.

"That happens," she said in a tired voice.

"Would you like me to turn on the light?"

"No, it's better in the dark."

He told her his dream. She professed surprise. "A town where the people live in peace?"

"That can only happen in a dream," he said. He recited lines by the Yiddish poet Papiernikov:

" 'In dreams everything is better and more beautiful
In dreams the sky is bluer than blue.' "

"Yes," she said. "In our dreams."

"And you were waiting for me since the beginning of time. I loved that ending."

She did not answer. Then she whispered, "In my dream I saw my husband and my daughter."

When dawn came, they had not yet fallen asleep.

EVE GOT ON WELL WITH GAMALIEL'S PALS. SHE took an immediate interest in their activities on behalf of refugees and offered to help, financially at first, then in other ways. She had many connections among lawyers and the press, and she knew whom to call on when it could be useful.

She particularly liked Diego. The gutsy little Lithuanian-Jew-Spaniard entertained her with his bawdy stories and his memories of the Spanish Civil War, his days as an anarchist—then and in the French Foreign Legion. "Oh," she would exclaim, "I'd have given a lot to see you there!" "In Spain," Diego answered, "you'd have made war as a dancer for us or a spy against them. But that's all. They didn't take women." "I'd have disguised myself as a man," Eve shot back.

Diego had a peculiar sense of humor. He avoided opening his mouth too wide in order not to show the damage done by Franco's police, but he would laugh to the point of tears even when he was telling her how much he hated fascists and Stalinists. "Sometimes," he would say, "I couldn't tell which of them I most distrusted. The fascists killed their enemies out in the open, in street fights; the Stalinists executed their own allies in secret, in cellars, with a shot in the back of the head. Funny? You could die laughing."

One day, Diego told them this story. "I had a pal, Juan, an antifascist, like me, only a bigger model, a real giant. Actually, what we both were above all was anarchists. Power, any kind of power, that's what we couldn't stand; authority made us sick. We were ardent disciples of Nechayev and Bakunin; we wanted to live and die, make war and make love, all with joy. No long faces for us. That's what the Stalinists couldn't tolerate; they were incapable of humor. You had to see them: solemn all day long, stupidly, vulgarly serious. They were closemouthed and grim, as if they were disgusted with themselves, even when they were singing, even when they were dancing to celebrate the eternal glory of the great Soviet fatherland. You'd wonder how they made love. Juan and I were captured by Franco's forces, but we managed to escape on the very first night. The guard heard us laughing, so he wanted to know what we were doing. We dropped our voices. He came closer to hear; then he started to laugh also. He laughed so much, he stopped paying attention. So we jumped him. We disarmed him and gagged him. We never stopped laughing, but he did."

Eve kissed him on the cheek. "Bravo, Diego! I wish more than ever that I'd been there." Then, more seriously, she added, "I wonder what I would have done. I just don't know." Diego replied, "Sure you do: You'd have laughed with us." Eve leaned toward him. "And Juan, what became of him?" Diego's expression darkened. He said, tight-lipped, in a husky voice, "I'd rather not talk about it." Eve persisted.

"Come on, Diego." "Juan," Diego said, and again: "Juan." Then: "Juan is dead." "How did he die?" "Not now, some other time." Eve stared at him insistently. "Juan was tortured and killed." Diego said it all in a rush. "Assassinated. Not by the fascists. He was executed by their enemies, those brutes who were our comrades-in-arms—the Communists. On orders from Moscow." Eve took his hand and held it for a long moment. "I'm sad for you, Diego." He shook himself and said, "I told you: It's enough to make you die laughing."

Eve spent a lot of time with the little group of onetime refugees. She found them entertaining, and refreshing in their refusal to conform to the norms of society. Yasha, the shameless jokester, amused her with his funny stories about the Gulag, and Bolek, whom she had known for many years, had become her friend and confidant. With Yasha, she shared a love of cats. Yasha's was named Misha, and he was so quick and intelligent that when he was playing, it seemed as if he had his master's sense of humor. Yasha's beaming face when Misha, purring, would lick his cheek was a sight to behold. "Yasha," Eve said to him one day, half-joking, "women would all be yours if you loved them as much as you do that little cat." "They already are mine," Yasha said, "because of my cat." He was convinced that Misha was the reincarnation of a medieval clown, a dwarf known as Srulik the Giant, whose mission it was to cheer up the sad at heart.

For some time, Eve had been paying particular attention to Bolek. She guessed that he had a secret, which piqued her curiosity. "He's a purist at heart, and so he's in distress," she explained to Gamaliel. "He's in search of himself," Gamaliel replied, "but in other people." His friends were always impressed with how unruffled Bolek was in his calm state, and how disconsolate he could be when he was depressed.

Sometimes he would be full of energy and enthusiasm. Gamaliel pointed out how happy he was with Noémie, and his joyous pride when he talked about their daughter, Leah. "True," Eve acknowledged, "but even so . . . might he have a mistress?" Gamaliel laughed. "No, not Bolek. He's easily infatuated, but it never goes any further." "Problems with his health?" "No, at least I don't think so." "Money problems?" "No, not that, either." Eve persisted. "Nonetheless, my instinct is seldom wrong. I know how to decipher the look on a person's face. I can sense it when someone is going around with a secret."

Bolek told Eve about the tragedy in his life one day when she invited him to lunch. Gamaliel was away. Bolek came to her apartment, where every piece of furniture testified to wealth and a restrained, unerring taste. She poured him a drink. They sat chatting of this and that in the living room, sitting in front of a chessboard, on which the pieces were arrayed in an unfinished game. Abruptly, Eve leaned forward and looked him in the eyes. "We have half an hour before we should leave for the restaurant. Do you want to talk now, or after?"

"Why not now?" Bolek said, unsuspecting.

"Fine." Eve took a deep breath, as if to gather her strength. "Now listen to me, Bolek, and don't interrupt," she said in a voice that she knew how to make persuasive. "Let me say some things that you may find annoying. Your friends love you and are loyal to you. As for me, I have never felt so close to you. You know that you mean a lot to me. The fact that I'm talking to you like this proves it." Eve paused a moment. "You can put on an act with others, but not with me."

"Why do you say—"

"I asked you to hear me out. Then it'll be your turn to talk. I sense something, but I don't know what it is. Like everyone, you wear a mask, and I want to tear yours off. Are you suffering? I believe you are. Why do you hide your pain from those around you? Don't tell me I'm wrong. I know about suffering. And the need to hide it, I know about that, too."

Bolek stiffened. He gazed at her without trying to avoid her eyes. Then all at once, he gave in. "Eve . . . you're incredible," he said in a low voice, suddenly stammering, he who always expressed himself so clearly. "Really and truly . . . insightful . . . perfect vision . . . How do you . . . You're the only one in the world . . . the only one to sense it . . . to guess. Even my closest friends, even Gamaliel, they don't know about it. . . . Noémie, she doesn't know, either. I mean, she doesn't know everything. It's better that way. . . . I've been like this . . . since the war. . . . Why depress her? Besides, there's nothing she could do. I know, I'm keeping her in the dark. . . . It's unfair. . . . Actually, I'm denying her the right to participate, to take . . . I can't help it. I love her too much. I fear for her. I pretend all's well. I keep my worries to myself. . . . You all have your own troubles; why should I add mine? But you . . ." And now Bolek told Eve what was haunting him: Leah, his child, his treasure, his joy, his life—well, she was in great difficulty, and that was making him, her father, unhappy, too.

With Bolek's permission, Eve told Gamaliel his story. Later on, he would say to Gamaliel that if he was able to tell Eve this most intimate and painful of secrets, it was because of the conversation they had had about Bolek's experience in the ghetto. Also, there was his liking for Eve. Besides, Eve knew how to listen, and a woman understands some things better than a man.

Leah, Leah's story, Leah's suffering and her misfortune, how could her father keep it to himself without breaking his own heart?

Leah had had a car accident, then spent several weeks in a hospital, where they gave her painkillers. Soon she needed the pills to sleep, to eat, to read, to watch television, to talk to her parents, to her friends. Morphine became her daily bread. By the time she left the hospital, she was addicted. Then there was cocaine, heroin, failed detox programs. This university teacher, who had been headed for a brilliant career, had to resign her position: Her prolonged absences had become unacceptable. Journals returned her manuscripts. She was no longer invited to international conferences. Her career shattered, she abandoned herself to the abyss, encouraged by her partner, whom Bolek could no longer abide. He was convinced that Samaël's one objective was to gain control of the family's wealth.

Samaël. Malevolent, shady, unsettling, a man without a soul. But when he met him, Gamaliel had no idea that Samaël was going to pillage his life.

Eve introduced them. She had met Samaël as a favor to Bolek, who was trying to detach him from his daughter. "Have lunch with him when he comes to New York," Bolek asked her. "Then tell me what you think of him." Out of kindness, Eve agreed. Gamaliel would never find out what happened at that first meeting. No doubt it was not unpleasant, since the two began meeting more and more often. Gamaliel did not worry about it, asking her only what was so special about this person whom she spent so much time with. "Tell you what," she said. "Join us next time."

At their first meeting, in a restaurant, Samaël did not arouse Gamaliel's suspicion. Indeed, he found him interestingly provocative. He was elegant, well-spoken, courteous, and very virile; Gamaliel thought he must be successful with women. In his dark gray suit, white shirt, and blue tie, he looked like a Wall Street banker. Self-confident but not condescending, he commanded respect with his fluent speech and his almost encyclopedic knowledge. Whatever the topic—history, literature, or music—Samaël had something to say about it. He enjoyed pleasing people and winning them over.

At the time, Gamaliel didn't know what Samaël did for a living, only that business brought him frequently to New York. Eve saw him more and more often, and Gamaliel did not object: They respected each other's freedom. Besides, the purpose was to help Bolek by helping his daughter. Eve did not as yet know what form that aid might take, but after each lunch with Samaël, she reported in detail to the anxious father. The topic at these lunches was always Leah: the state of her health, the possibility she could recover. "I'm her best chance," Samaël would say. "She loves me and I love her." When she told Bolek this, he commented, "He's her bad luck. He's her curse." He was convinced Samaël was destroying his daughter by keeping her addicted to drugs and trading on her heightened emotional susceptibility. Bolek said he would be eternally grateful to Eve if she succeeded in separating the two, for then anything would be possible. Leah's rescue could come only through Eve.

"Bolek may well be right," Gamaliel said to Eve. "Your role in this tragic business strikes me as useful—indeed, fundamental. But in that case, isn't Leah the one you should be seeing? She's the one who's sick, who needs help." Eve agreed but said she had to start somewhere. Later on, she would go to Chicago; she would speak with Leah. She considered herself on a sacred mission, and indeed she was gone more and more frequently, visiting both Samaël and Leah. Where was Gamaliel in all this? He missed her. He loved her, whatever she believed. Eve was his last love. She brought him what Esther had denied him: sensual satisfaction, joy and pleasure to the point of exhaustion. With Esther, it had been the joining of two souls in love with chastity. With Eve, it was the satisfaction of two beings' appetites, two who could not imagine leaving each other. That, too, is love, Gamaliel thought. A different kind of love, yes. But after all, each kind of love is as unique as each kind of suffering. To compare is to make them commonplace.

Still, he was not so blind he did not realize that, despite the evidence of love she gave him at night, Eve was beginning to drift away from him. When she would remain silent, it was not because she was reflecting, but because her thoughts had turned to Samaël, and when she looked at Gamaliel, it seemed to him she was just verifying that he was still there. Could he, should he, have said something to warn her, to point out the risk she was running? That she was going to have to choose between two men—the one who was making their friend's daughter miserable, and the other, who gave the most beautiful of offerings, self-denial and fidelity in love? But she could not love as much as she was loved. Was she afraid of love because she had been widowed? Gamaliel had no idea. Would Eve prefer to call it an affair or a friendship? She refused to use any of those words. "Words limit our existence by claiming to define it," she would say. "Let's leave them where they are, in the dictionary." Gamaliel had his own views on that—he knew the subject all too well. But, to lighten the mood, he reminded her that Diogenes also distrusted words. He criticized Plato's dialogues as too long, and Plato himself detested books because one couldn't ask them questions. They were both wrong, in Gamaliel's opinion. And what did Eve think about that? She made a gesture, indicating that this was not a time for Gamaliel to be showing off his erudition, not a time to be discussing dead philosophers, but Leah, who was alive, and Bolek, who was alive. So Eve went on seeing Samaël. Out of pride or resignation, Gamaliel decided to stay out of the way. He kept telling himself, naïvely, that things would work out eventually, that he must be patient, wait for a miracle. So, mistakenly, he waited, and he paid dearly for his mistake.

NOW, LOOKING BACK, GAMALIEL TELLS HIMSELF he should never have allowed Eve to encounter Samaël. He should have argued, fought, called on her mind and on her heart, told her that he, too, needed her. Maybe nothing would have happened. If she had not tried to uncover Bolek's secret, if she had not forced it out of him, had not learned the truth about his daughter, she would not have felt obliged to help Leah, would not have met Samaël. . . . He and Eve would have remained together and would have lived happily who knows how many years.

I didn't fight. Gamaliel has been thinking this for a long time. I didn't say no to destiny. I bowed to my fate and returned to my solitude, which, after all, is my natural condition. After my parents, after Ilonka, after Colette—I remain alone. A writer once said that God alone is alone; a human being is not alone and should not be. But I interpret that thought in my own fashion: If man is created in God's image, then he is as unique as God, and therefore alone, like God. Not necessarily in death, but alone in life. In happiness as in despair. Excuse me, did I say *happiness*? Since Budapest, that word has no meaning for me. It's as if happiness is seeking out someone far away to touch on the lips, in the heart. As for me, it flees or ignores me.

Was I happy with Eve? Let's say that I learned the taste of happiness. Suddenly, a crazy idea came over me: Suppose that unknown patient is Eve? No, Eve would be younger than she. But how can one tell, since the fire so destroyed her features? No! Eve would have recognized me, and I would have recognized her. . . . How silly I am! Eve didn't know a word of Hungarian.

Eve. Straightforward and plain-speaking. Her vision reached beyond time, without overlooking the present.

It was she who made known to me the change in our relationship, indeed its ending, and therefore my return to solitude.

It was a winter afternoon. The city was snowed in. Life was slowed down, as in a state of siege. The airports were paralyzed, most offices closed. Only one in ten taxis was out negotiating icy avenues. Ambulances had a clear path. Their sirens taunted drivers mired in the unreal, phantasmagoric landscape. Most of the news on the radio was about the weather. Nature was inclement—no hope of a thaw. Eve was late. I was growing more worried.

"Nasty weather out," she said as she shook the snow off her boots. She hung up her coat and came into the living room, where I was waiting for her. Usually, I would ask about her lunch with one or another of her friends. This time, I remained silent. She was returning from a rendezvous with Samaël. It was up to her to speak. She sat in her favorite armchair across the table from me and fixed her gaze on me.

"I believe the time has come for us to talk," she said.

It felt as if she had struck me: The time has come. The

solemn proclamation of a disaster. I nodded and said, "All right, let's talk." I could guess what she was going to say. She was going to tell me it was all over between us. The time had come for us to part. Farewell, all the lovely promises, if promises there had been.

I was stunned; there was something in this situation I could not grasp. Eve, who could read what she called "the inner face" and could decipher the best-kept of secrets, the deepest reaches of a person—why had she not seen through Samaël? What had happened to her intuition, to what she had learned from life over the years? Why had her insight not enabled her to see Samaël for what he really was: a genius of a liar, a genius also in his cruelty, a jealous egotist unable to admit that there could be any goodness or any purity in the human heart?

"The time has come," Eve said again, unhesitating. "It's never been my style to play the fool. We were too close not to tell each other the truth."

She said "we were," I thought, trying not to show how distraught I was. I was right: All that remains to us is the past.

"And the truth is," Eve continued, "that I'm going to marry him. I must."

"Is it because you love him?"

"If there's one man in this world who shouldn't ask me that question, it's you. Anyone else can use that word, but not you. You know perfectly well what I think about it."

"But then . . ."

"Then nothing. I have to marry him to help Bolek and to save Leah. It's as simple as that."

There again, I could have debated, argued, reminded her of what she herself had said about marriage. But I remained silent. So did she. I got to my feet, opened a few drawers, put my books and bathroom articles in a bag, set the keys on a table. Hardly an hour had passed since Eve's return. Without a useless gesture, without a word too many, I closed the door behind me.

I never saw Eve again.

From the *Book of Secrets*

Big Mendel's apprehension proved to be well-founded. The Rebbe and he did not return to Székesváros that day. It was obvious that they were being detained by Archbishop Báranyi. "We still have many things to say to each other," he had explained to them.

"Just what does that mean?" Mendel shouted angrily, after they had been confined for three days, alone in a room at the far end of the hall. "What is this Christian talking about? Me, they tortured. Are they also going to torture the Rebbe? I beg the Rebbe to perform a miracle, and the sooner the better! The Rebbe must use his powers, for the love of God! We mustn't stay in this Christian prison. Let's leave. The community is waiting for us. Let's go right away, even on foot!"

The young Master, standing at the window, which gave onto a huge garden, was absorbed in his thoughts and did not reply. Mendel knew his nagging was in vain, but he went on nonetheless. At last, Hananèl, still gazing out at the garden as it emerged slowly from the night, advised his friend and servant not to persist. "What happens on earth is decided in heaven. We are here to accomplish some purpose. It may be that the Archbishop is right. He and I have things to say to each other."

There was a knock at the door. The monk who had

come to get them in Székesváros entered with two cups of hot tea. Mendel dismissed him. "Leave us. We must say our morning prayers."

The priest left. Hananèl, still standing at the window, gave a sigh and said, "You see, Mendel, we were right to bring our tallith and our tephillin. We already knew we would not return so soon."

Mendel thanked him for the compliment. "It was the Rebbe who knew, not I. I would have preferred it had the Rebbe been mistaken." He started to take the prayer shawls and phylacteries out of their bags, then stopped in the middle and said, "Rebbe, I forgot— I should have asked you the first day: Do we have the right to pray in a house ruled by the cross?"

"Close your eyes and face Jerusalem," the Rebbe replied.

Mendel prayed faster than usual, Hananèl more slowly. Neither touched the tea.

"We will fast today," Hananèl said finally. "Remember this, Mendel: In the old days, each time a Sage had to confront a representative of Christianity, all the members of the community accompanied him in their thoughts and they purified body and soul by prayer and fasting. How could we swallow anything at all when the lives of our brothers and sisters are at stake? In this most grave of times, we must abstain."

The two friends spent the day meditating and reciting psalms. Hananèl was standing, lost in his thoughts. Mendel was pacing back and forth, wringing his hands; now and then he would stop and sigh, as if in pain. The young Master, deep in concentration, was breathing soundlessly. The church chimes sounded the hours without disturbing them.

That evening, the Archbishop came to get Hananèl
and took him to his office. Hananèl remained
standing, as before, while the Archbishop sat in his
armchair. "Shall we continue?" he asked.

Hananèl nodded assent.

"What do you want of me?"

Hananèl had his answer ready. "Save us," he said.

"You think you are all in mortal danger?"

"I do."

"How do you know it?"

"I know it."

"Heaven told you, is that it? Well then, if heaven
wants your death, why should I save you?"

"Nebuchadnezzar, the Babylonian, said the same
when he destroyed the Temple, and God punished
him for it."

The Archbishop started. "You compare me to that
pagan Babylonian?" he shouted, red with anger.
"Perhaps the Jews were innocent at that time, but they
are not now. God sent them His Son as their Savior
and they denied Him. And you still do, every day you
treat him as an impostor, a renegade. How can you
expect God the Father to continue to love you?" Then
a daring idea came to him and he continued. "You
want me to save your life? I'll do it." He paused; when
he resumed, his voice was harsh and he spoke as if to
an inferior. "Yes, I'll save your life and your family's.
But on one condition: You must let me save your soul.
Understand? I'm offering you salvation in exchange
for your sinful faith. The others matter less; they can
remain in sin. But you're different. Your soul belongs
with the Savior."

Hananèl leaned toward the Archbishop. "Look at

me," he said very softly. "No, not like that. Look at me closer."

The Archbishop felt a mysterious, irresistible force take hold of him and lift him to his feet. "Are you trying to frighten me, Jew?" he said. "You cannot defy . . . you cannot threaten the Lord's most Holy Catholic Church, certainly not without punishment. Who are you to defy me? In whose name are you speaking? Who sent you?" Suddenly, his voice caught in his throat. "You look like . . . you resemble . . ."

Without losing his calm or looking away, Hananèl replied, "You know perfectly well who I am. You've known it since the first morning." Then, after a silence that was heavy with meaning, he said, "With every Jew you kill, you put your Lord back on the cross. Does that not frighten you? Tell me, man of the Church, do you know what you are doing to your Lord when you allow these murderers to massacre the descendants of Abraham, Isaac, and Jacob? And you dare to speak of saving my soul when it is your own that is in perdition?"

The Archbishop sat down, took his head in his hands, and, without looking at the other man, conceded defeat. "I'm prepared to keep you here. Your servant also. Under my protection you'll be safe."

"No," Hananèl replied.

The Archbishop looked up in amazement. "I don't understand you. Did you not say—"

"What I require from you has nothing to do with me or my own survival. I demand that you save my entire community."

"You're mad! Where would I put this community of yours?"

"It's everyone or no one."

"But there isn't enough room here." Seeing Hananèl's determination, he spoke more gently. "How many souls are there in your community?"

"A few hundred."

"Including children?"

"Yes, counting the children."

In despair, the Archbishop began thinking about how and by what means he could comply with this absurd demand.

As for Hananèl, he was wondering where he had found the strength and the will, the audacity even, to face up to a man who incarnated the power of the Church. Then he recalled the failure of his mystical undertaking. I owe this to the community, he reflected. Yes, I owe them at least this much.

IN AN HOUR OR TWO, I'LL BE BACK WITH THE tormented old woman in the hospital.

All these beings doomed by a cruel fate . . . I no longer know where I stand in the face of their overpowering reality. The people of my *Book of Secrets,* the people of my childhood. All these men, all these women, all these children, victims of the Angel of Death and Punishment.

Why lie to myself? I wander around, sorrowful, beaten down. Why do the wicked win so many battles? I recall what the Rebbe of Kotsk said: "This world is rotten." Yes, it's a loathsome place, this world that men have made, unreliable and unstable. Enough to break your heart. So what should I do? Give up on it, leave it? Go back to my apartment and take an overdose of sleeping pills, the way I did once before? Say good-bye to a humanity that permits a Samaël to do so much harm? Is that the response to Eve's farewell of so long ago?

So long ago? It seems like yesterday.

I feel empty. I am wandering, briefcase in hand, along streets that now seem as if they, too, are hostile. By an entryway, I stumble upon some blankets piled up in a mound. This is a human being, a homeless man. He is sleeping, detached from his surroundings; nothing disturbs his stupor. What have we in common, he and I? If I touch him on the arm, will he answer me? Will he see me as friend or foe? What is he hiding from? As for me, I'm dragging myself around like an old vagabond in search of shelter that is nowhere to be found.

I reach the railroad station. Travelers dash in all directions, as if fleeing an enemy. I sit down on a bench, pick up a crumpled newspaper. Plane crash, a dozen killed. Political cover-up. Sexy photos. Articles about the end of the century. King Solomon foresaw it all: One generation passes away, and another generation comes, but the earth abides forever. Woe to a generation that knew how to discover absolute Evil but not absolute Truth: so a philosopher said of the dictators whose triumphs debased humanity in the twentieth century. But can we overlook the achievements of science? The conquest of space, the miracles of medicine and communications, and the hope they give us? How does it add up? Evil and Good are racing side by side. In my head, images and ideas intermingle and become confused. No longer can things be clearly identified. And where am I in all this? And Eve? What did I do wrong that caused her to leave me? What am I doing among these strangers this hostile or indifferent world has rejected? I could almost feel sorry for myself. Above all, not that, I tell myself. What right have I to complain? No one owes me anything. Surely not Eve. Nor Colette, nor our daughters gone astray on the lost roads of the planet. I'm unhappy. So what? Aren't others unhappy, too? Happiness is a rare gift in this cursed and dreadful century. Faces haunt my feverish mind: a starving child in Africa, eyes bulging, in its mother's arms; another child, in tears, in Asia. In Rwanda, a man stands dazed over the bodies of his slaughtered sons. Corpses piled in a ditch in Bosnia. A universe of smoke and barbed wire under a bloodred sky. When one of our little group of eccentrics dared to mention happiness as a goal, an obligation, or a possibility, Diego burst out laughing and shouted, "Hey, you guys, listen to him! At last we find someone who believes in happiness! Give the man a prize—the world's grand prize for fools." And yet with Eve, I felt at home, at peace. I may not have known it then, but I do now: Even when I was with Colette, I was waiting for Eve. Even when I recalled Esther and her mysterious body, which I often saw in my dreams, even when I remembered Ilonka and her limitless generosity, even when I thought of my parents, whose faces were engraved in my memory, if I just embraced Eve, I was glad to be alive and to have lips to kiss her. I would stroke her hips, her shoulders, and be grateful for an appetite that could still be aroused.

Parted now from Eve, I see myself long ago in Budapest. The station, the trains whistling. The stores, the pastry shops . . . The century was young and I was a child. Snow, thick and soft, on the bridges of Budapest. The snow was pure. Then in Paris, a lot of rain, not much snow. Very little was pure.

LATER, MUCH LATER, BOLEK GAVE ME NEWS OF Eve. Though he was grateful to her for what she had done for Leah, now restored to a normal life, he saw Eve less and less often. It was still the same enemy: Samaël. Bolek hated him more than ever; he couldn't mention his name without getting angry. "Poor Eve," he would say. "I knew Samaël would hurt her. It was inevitable. She may have known it, but she was determined to rescue Leah, to sacrifice herself for Leah."

But suppose all that was just a pretext? I came to think that perhaps Eve really did love Samaël. Was she happy? Was she still living with him? Bolek did not know, but he had heard she had left New York, and that Samaël had put his destructive talent to work driving her out of her mind. He was unfaithful. He mocked and humiliated her, had even gotten her started on drugs.

The bastard.

I'M NOT SURE WHY, BUT ONE DAY I TOLD THE whole story to Rebbe Zusya. We were talking of time and its passage. Does a man fulfill himself in a single moment, or over the course of a lifetime? Then we turned to the role of Evil in the search for Truth. I said that if Evil could be incarnated in a single person, I thought I had met him. I told him the beautiful, the exhilarating story of Eve, of my love for Eve. I had told it to no one, for fear of diluting it, making it commonplace. In any case, no one would have understood our story. Except perhaps a mystic like the Rebbe, who would be the first to see that some love stories can only be conceived in the most esoteric of terms. I thought that perhaps, with a word or a glance, he could even restore her to me. It was very late, of course, but surely the Rebbe was more powerful than Samaël.

"Samaël? You did say Samaël!" the old Sage exclaimed, and a hint of fear crossed his face. "I sense that this is a dan-

THE TIME OF THE UPROOTED

gerous person, and you enter into relations with Evil person-
ified at your own peril, unless you can immediately disarm
him." He stroked the beard that hung down to his chest.
"Tell me what happened. Tell me the whole story—don't
leave anything out. I must know every detail if I'm to help
and protect you."

I made a full report, though, to avoid offending him, I
omitted the intimacy of our relations. I just said we were
very close.

He approved, saying, "You told me she lost her husband
and only daughter, is that right? God considers Himself the
protector of widows. He who comes to their aid is the messenger of God. . . ." I expected him to question me further
about Eve's life, about her character and personality, but he
just scrutinized me a moment, then resumed. "And anyone
who does them harm is the envoy of Satan."

I accepted that, though I'm not sure I believe in a power
that can be identified by the name of Satan. Evil is to be
found in every person who allows himself to be dominated
by it. But Rebbe Zusya believed in Satan, and that was
enough for me. I thought, If Satan exists, it is surely someone
like Samaël, or indeed Samaël himself.

"What do you know about him?" Rebbe Zusya asked.

"Not much, Rebbe. Very little. Next to nothing."

"Where is he from? What's his background? What is his
business? What does or did his father do? You don't know? Is
he miserly? Does he speak deliberately, thinking over every
word, or rapidly? Does he move his head while speaking?
Does he stammer? His hands—what does he do with his
hands while speaking?"

How could I reply? My recollections were too vague. "All
I know, Rebbe, is that there's something fascinating about

him, but also something repellent, and I don't say that lightly. You listen to him, you try to pay attention, and at the same time you want to get him out of your presence, out of your sight, for fear of being infected by contact with him."

The old Rebbe nodded in concern. "There is Evil in many things. It can find a place anywhere."

"Even in the Good?"

"Even in the Good. That is where it's most pernicious, most dangerous. It steals in behind a mask, pretending it wishes to serve the Lord and come to the rescue of those He created. Oh, how difficult it is to unmask him, to make him reveal himself. To do it, you must have *siata dishmaya,* the grace of God. . . ." I was silent, straining not to miss a word the Rebbe was saying. "Sometimes Satan wears the mask of one of the Just. He speaks like him, behaves like him, recites the prayers as he does, and he does it so well that naïve and pious Jews may be duped into becoming his adepts and disciples. Then, once he dominates and leads them, he suggests they help him to hasten the coming of the Messiah. He tells them how to go about it: The Talmud declares that Redemption will come only when humanity is either entirely innocent or entirely guilty. Now, many Sages and Teachers have chosen the first option, and everyone knows they failed. So why not try the second way? And how is that done? Simply by violating the commandments of the holy Torah. Break the Sabbath, insult your father and your mother, steal, covet your neighbor's wife, lie about your neighbor, commit adultery and incest, preach violence, kill. In short, call pure what is impure, and impure what is pure—and all supposedly for the well-being of our people and of all peoples, in the name, that is, of the ultimate Deliverance. . . . Is that the goal that this Samaël is trying to achieve?"

The Rebbe's eyes never left me, as if he were afraid he would lose me forever if my attention were to stray even for a moment from his words and his vision. He kept rocking back and forth as he spoke.

"This Samaël you've told me about is dangerous because he resembles Satan himself in all he undertakes. His evil is contagious. He is corrupt, so he seeks to corrupt others. His poisoned soul is never satisfied unless it can poison others. Are you afraid for your own soul?"

"No, Rebbe, not for mine, but for Eve's."

The Rebbe's gaze was severe and piercing. "You're a widower. You're alone, aren't you? Why didn't you marry her? Is it because of your first wife?"

"Perhaps, Rebbe. Colette made me suffer too much, especially after her death. She took my two daughters away from me. For years, I was afraid of making the same mistake again."

"God is present in every union of two people."

"Not in mine with Colette."

"What do you know about it? Some philosophers hold that man was God's mistake. I don't accept that. It's just that at times a man has to make his own mistake before he can find his way with more self-respect and humility."

What could I say to that?

"And Esther?"

There again, I did not answer, but the Rebbe persisted. "Are you still searching for her?"

"No, Rebbe. Excuse me, that's not right. Yes, I am searching for her, but as you would for an old melody, a forgotten word, a flavor, a moment, a feeling you once had. Esther has nothing to do with Eve."

"Well then," the Rebbe asked once more, "why didn't you marry her?"

"She chose someone else."

"Samaël?"

"Yes, Rebbe."

The old Teacher heaved a sigh. "Let us hope she hasn't fallen so low that she cannot be rescued."

"I don't know, Rebbe. When I think about her, I no longer understand anything."

Our eyes met. His were sadder than ever.

On my way out, I met Shalom. Seeing my dejected mien, he took my arm and gave it a squeeze. "You're having another problem with a woman? Don't let it get you down. The Rebbe is on your side; that's all that matters."

All that matters? Easy to say.

AN ETERNITY LATER, I HALTED A MOMENT BEFORE the door in the hallway, whose gray walls were stained with humidity. I was shivering in spite of the heat. I was cold in the depth of my being. I knew I must turn the knob, but I could not bring myself to take that simple action. What was holding me back? In truth, I knew perfectly well what it was. Old Rebbe Zusya, who had once again urgently summoned me, was sick and perhaps dying. He would die, and his life's work—like that of the hero of my novel, the Blessed Madman—would remain unfulfilled: He would not witness the coming of the Messiah. I was afraid to face him in his despair. Should I knock, or leave? I wondered. As always, I decided, it was too late to back out. There, in the room, one of the Just awaited me, one of the thirty-six men to whom the world owed its continued existence. He was waiting for me. Was it so he could die in peace after entrusting me with the reply to unanswerable questions, the secrets whose meaning I had been forever seeking? Perhaps the future of others besides me depended on my last meeting with this man who understood everything. The curtain was up; I was facing those others. I could not leave the stage before the end.

Still I hesitated. Was I looking for an alibi, an excuse for my fear? So that one day I could say, In the hour before the death of Rebbe Zusya of blessed memory, my hand trembled and my heart beat fast?

It was beating very hard indeed. A frightened small voice inside me said, Suppose he is already dead? You did wrong to wait so long. When one who is dying summons you, you must hurry to him and, above all, waste no time. . . .

My fingers felt damp and sticky. I was sweating. I was breathing slowly, noisily. I was hot, or was I cold? I was freezing.

I pushed the door open abruptly, as if in panic. The pale, dusty light made me still more uneasy. I glanced around the room. It looked abandoned. Stains here and there marked the walls like black geometric frescoes. On the table lay books, a prayer shawl, phylacteries. The bed was in a corner. Was Rebbe Zusya asleep? No, he was watching me. I felt impure, unworthy, as if I were covered with mud. The same small inner voice rebuked me: Is this any way to bid farewell to your Teacher? I saw my shadow on the wall to my right, an elongated caricature. It had parted from me, as if to dissociate itself from what was to happen. Shadows also need alibis.

"Come closer," said the old Rebbe in an astonishingly strong voice.

I took a step toward his bed.

"No doubt you're thinking my life is going to end in defeat. Isn't that what you're thinking?"

"I no longer know what to think, Rebbe."

Now, at what was to be our last meeting, he repeated, "Come here." But this time I did not move. "So what are you waiting for? Come here! Are you afraid? Afraid of seeing me beaten, defeated by death?"

"Yes, I'm afraid."

"But I'm not beaten! I'm still alive. With my last gasp, I can change the course of events. Don't you know that yet? Haven't I taught you anything?"

Actually, my fear was different. Vague and undefinable, it did not grow out of any premonition, nor was it connected to any particular event. It had seeped into my soul and now weighed on my life and my thoughts as if to paralyze them. I was afraid I had omitted something. A deed—but which? A word? Perhaps I should have recited a prayer. The dying man was saying a prayer. Should not his companion do as much? Did not the dying man and his witness feel the same need to bring God into their last moment together?

"Come closer," said the Rebbe.

I was standing right at his bedside. Did he not see me? Or did he mean something else? Was I to interpret his command as purely symbolic? Perhaps mystical? *"Ta khazzi"*—"Come look"—is an invitation that is often found in the Zohar, the Book of Splendor. Was he preparing to give me his secret as testament?

And I, to whom would I leave mine? When I die, I thought, I will leave nothing behind, no trace of me on this earth. My daughters? If they had given birth in their turn, surely that too put me even further out of their thoughts. Why had I never told Rebbe Zusya about this? He whose vision encompassed the universe might at least have been able to tell me where they were living.

I remained silent. Was the Rebbe expecting me to question him? I felt vaguely disappointed. I was hoping for a revelation, perhaps about Esther. I had never forgotten Esther; I never would. Even when I'd loved Eve, and I'd loved her with all my heart, Esther had been strangely present in my love. Esther was beginning and promise; Eve was parting and loss. Should I speak of it to the Rebbe now? I wondered. It would be my last chance. There would surely be no more, for old Rebbe Zusya, descendant of the great Master by the same name, a pillar of the Hasidic movement, was at death's door.

I would have liked also to have told him more about Colette and our unhappy marriage. The Rebbe liked to quote the Talmud, which says all marriages are arranged by God. Then ours, stormy and ridden by our inner demons, had surely been a blunder on God's part. I had mentioned it in an earlier discussion, no point bringing it up now. Besides, this was no time to make the dying old Master unhappy.

"Come closer," he said in a suddenly feverish tone.

"I'm here right by you, Rebbe."

I could draw no closer than I was to his bedside.

"Tell me the truth: You think I summoned you because I'm going to die, isn't that right?"

"Yes, Rebbe, that's what I think."

"Well, you're mistaken. If I wanted to see you today, it was to talk about this heretic acquaintance of yours, Samaël. Are you still in touch with him?"

"No, Rebbe, I've completely lost track of him."

"But you know how to reach him?"

"No, Rebbe, I don't."

The sick man was sweating. He closed his eyes and sighed. "Too bad. I want to see him, and I need to talk to him. It's important. You must find him and bring him to me. Go, my son. May the Lord guide you to him. But watch out: Don't let him involve you in any long conversation, or you may be lost. Just tell him that you have a message for him: I wish to speak with him. That's all. Do you understand me?"

Rebbe Zusya sat up to extend his hand to me. To bid me farewell? Perhaps to bless me?

"Know this, my son: I will go on fighting. I will fight to my last breath, to the end and far beyond."

Exhausted, his eyes closed and his head fell back on the pillow.

I backed out of the room.

AFTER HIS ENCOUNTER WITH THE REBBE, GAMA-liel spent long hours reflecting on the subject of lies. The word buzzed around in his head like a bee trapped in a bottle.

Gamaliel knew that Samaël's lies carried deadly poison. But what about his own lies? Wasn't his whole life a series of deceptions? He had married Colette without truly loving her. He had not invested enough energy and determination in restoring his relationship with his two daughters. He had to admit that Esther had vanished from his life because he lacked the strength and intelligence to hold on to her. As for his work—all those pages filled with symbols, those ideas, those plots, those conflicts that he invented and that others appropriated—was this not still another perversion of the truth? And in that case, what was the difference between him and Samaël? Was it conceivable that a Samaël exists in each human being, and therefore in himself, too? But then how could he destroy that Samaël in himself without dying in the act? Paritus the One-Eyed, in his earliest text, wrote that life consists of nothing but appearances, temporary interchangeable illusions; only death is real.

Gamaliel told himself that one day, God willing, he would revise Calderón's play *La vida es sueño*—life is not just a dream. If a dream is a lie, then is life a lie? he wondered. But what does that make death? The truth, reality, perhaps the only one? Unless there are many realities? Mine is not necessarily Bolek's, which, in turn, isn't Diego's. Rebbe Zusya himself recognized how difficult it is to distinguish what is true from what is not. So my truth could be Samaël's lie. God alone knows how to quarantine one and liberate the other, even though the truth is fleeting, as is everything that concerns human beings. A great Hasidic Sage wrote that even the Just have different time spans during which their spiritual qualities are manifest: Some are just throughout their lives, others for only an hour. Is that how it is for truth and those in whom it reveals itself?

One day . . . but when? Gamaliel at times was painfully aware of his age. Once past sixty, the knees gave way more easily; the back was stooped. The body that had once been a source of surprise and pleasure now threatened to become his fearsome, invincible enemy, receptacle of a life that was proceeding inexorably toward its end. Philosophers say that the meaning of life is life itself, he mused. Preachers go further, saying that to be true to himself, man must transcend that self. But how can I achieve that? Doesn't going beyond mean going against oneself? God is capable of that, but is man?

Inevitably, Gamaliel found himself thinking about death, more specifically his own. He didn't fear death itself; its approach was what distressed him. Bearing the burden of his years. Growing old too fast. Sickness, debilitating disease, his powers ebbing. Decrepitude. Fading intelligence. The slow, implacable loss of dignity, then of memory. Words getting confused and sticking in the throat. Awkward, clumsy gestures. Always dropping things. If he could choose, he knew that he would prefer a quick, unexpected stroke of the sword from the Angel of Death. This in the ancient texts is called *Mitat neshika,* the kiss of God. Thus did Moses die: God kissed him on the mouth and received his last sigh.

But that was Moses, the only prophet to speak to the Lord face-to-face. No one else could claim to have changed the course of History by teaching a system of ethics that would endure as long as human awareness. What trace would he, Gamaliel, leave behind? He thought bitterly that with his daughters gone, his line would end with his death. He regretted to the point of despair that he had not married Esther or Eve. Sometimes he would imagine the son one of them could have given him. Once, he'd made the mistake of speaking of it to Eve.

"You're beautiful, but pregnant you'd be still more beautiful. Did you know that according to Jewish tradition we must show our respect to any pregnant woman by giving her our seat? Normal courtesy, you'd say? No, Eve. I must stand for a pregnant woman because—who knows?—she may be carrying the Messiah in her belly."

Eve had flared up. "The Messiah in my belly? Please, stop talking nonsense!"

"That's not what I meant to say. . . ."

He'd wanted to explain that he would have loved her as the mother of his son, but Eve's offended expression told him he would do better to hold his tongue.

Nonetheless, he often dreamed of a child to whom he would leave his name and his memories, since that was all he possessed. Now it was too late. At his death, all he had been would be buried with him.

Like the old woman in the hospital?

THIS UNKNOWN WOMAN HAUNTS ME. WHO IS SHE? How much does she know about her condition? This will be the third time I've come to see her. It's late; night is falling, sooner than I'd expected. Usually, I interrupt my work or my reading to greet the twilight, so moved am I by its solemn or shining beauty. Not this evening. It is heavy, pallid, hostile.

I no longer need anyone to show me to the patient's room. Here is the garden, with its formal paths. Hanging over it are dark gray clouds. The trees look as if they're girding themselves to ward off an attacker.

Here is the building, the ward. A wan, almost dusty light accentuates the shadows on the walls. A glance at her bed and I start: The bed is empty. I'm about to panic. Is she . . . dead? Away for some emergency treatment? No, there she is, sitting crouched on the floor, hair undone, staring emptily into space. Who helped her out of bed? I go to her, kneel to speak to her, without knowing what to say. Does she hear me? I doubt it. She seems even further away in her thoughts than she did earlier. If only I could see what she sees, touch what she touches, feel what she feels. If only I could go with her, follow her, keep her company. I am ever more certain that she could answer many of my questions. But I don't know which to ask, nor how to frame them—and that, too, is part of the mystery that draws me to the old Hungarian woman even as her muteness keeps me far from her. A harsh voice rouses me from my reverie. "What are you doing here?"

A nurse. I hadn't heard her come in. She seems sure of her power and of my culpability. "Who gave you permission to enter? And to move the patient? Who gave you the right to disturb her?"

I get to my feet and start to say, "Excuse me, but—"

She doesn't let me finish. "Do you know her?"

"That's just it: I don't know her, but—"

"But what?"

She towers over me. Strangely, her face is not as severe as her voice. I hardly know what to say. I'm rescued by the doctor's arrival. She doesn't seem surprised to find me there, nor to see the patient sitting on the floor. To the nurse, she says calmly, "That's all, Marie. Everything's all right. I'll take care of it. Let's get her back in bed."

I make a move to help, but one look from the nurse stops me. The patient, back in bed, opens her mouth as if to cry out, then immediately closes it. The doctor draws the covers over her with hands that are confident but gentle, while murmuring, "Don't be afraid. I'm here. There's nothing to fear."

Again the patient opens her mouth but does not speak.

In the hall, I ask the doctor, "Why do you think she's afraid?"

"Because she knows."

"She knows what?"

"That she's going to cross the threshold."

"She told you that?"

"I know it without her telling me. It's my job to know."

We walk out to the garden. Night has fallen. Seated on the same bench as before, we look up at the stormy sky. It's going to rain.

"Why did you come back here? It's quite unusual for someone to visit a patient he doesn't know three times in a single day."

"Indeed. But there are moments when I have this curious, almost painful feeling that she isn't a stranger to me."

"You think you met her before?"

I look at the doctor in the shadowy light. Does she think I might once have had an affair with this woman? Might she be right? Anxiously, I search my memory. I haven't had many women. One-night stands, yes, quickly entered into and even more quickly, by mutual consent, forgotten. One night in Brussels, I was initiated into novel byways of love by a tourist who was several years older than I. Her name? She refused to tell me, saying only, "Just call me Désirée." Désirée vanished the next day. A journalist, in a hotel somewhere east of Suez, while we were making love, kept asking me about celebrities featured on page one in the newspapers. She left on assignment that same day. Which among them might have ended up in this hospital? None of them spoke Hungarian. So then, who is this old woman? What part might she have played in my life? Meanwhile, the doctor was evidently mulling over the same questions.

"The first time I saw you with her," she said, "I had a sense that you knew her."

"So did I."

"You have to admit it's bizarre."

"I still have that feeling."

"You'll have to search your memory."

"I am searching."

"Would you like me to help? I'm a psychiatrist, after all."

"I don't know where to begin. Her face is disfigured, her memory is gone, and she's oblivious to what's around her. How, therefore, am I to find the clues that will lead my thoughts to a known place?"

"Yet, from a strictly medical viewpoint, there's no indication of mental illness. No senility or Parkinson's. It was her body that was so injured. You must have been told about it."

"No, they just said it was an accident."

"Yes, an automobile accident."

Again I notice, as I did earlier in the day, that there is something poignant, something attractive, in the solemnity with which this woman expresses herself. Yes, if I were younger, I'd know what to say to her. Indeed, the next novel I sell to Georges Lebrun could be about the many challenges an old man faces; about all the ways he is doomed to failure. I would rage against his inevitable defeats: all those women he will no longer be able to seduce; all the voyages he will no longer undertake; all these projects that will fail or be abandoned. I'd recount his sterile dreams, the ways he's found wanting, his complexes—in a word, his impotence. The famous French novelist would know how to make it a best seller. But where would I find the time for it?

"And you?" the doctor asks me. "What are you afraid of?"

"Who says I'm afraid?"

"Again, it's my job to know such things."

"I'm not your patient."

"That doesn't keep me from noticing," she says, then adds after a moment's silence, "and wanting to help you."

The first raindrops fall, heralding the storm.

"I fear for the woman up there," I say.

"Is that all?"

"No. I'm also afraid of her."

"Although you don't even know her?"

"Maybe I knew her. And maybe she knows things about me that I myself don't know. Things about me or that concern me. That's what scares . . . but . . . that's not all."

"What else is there? Go ahead. You can trust me."

"I'm also afraid of you."

"Of me? Afraid of me? How can I be a menace to you?"

"You threaten my freedom."

She smiles, and I like her smile. "I take that as a compliment. Am I mistaken?"

"It's a compliment."

I take her hand; she does not withdraw it. I love the warmth that comes over me. At once I feel blessed.

"I want to ask something of you," she says suddenly.

"Just say the word."

"I'd like you to tell me another story."

I look at her in surprise. Odd request, a story, at this time, when an old woman nearby is about to meet her death.

"How do you know that I like stories?"

"You tell them so well, and your life is full of stories. Besides, your being here is part of a story, isn't it?"

"Would you prefer a beautiful story or a sad one?"

"Sad stories are the loveliest."

I feel like saying, The stories that happen to us are sad, but what's lovely about them? A woman—maybe it's Ilonka—is going to die up there; isn't her story enough for you? I close my eyes, as I always do when troubled by doubt, and once more I see my father leaning over my bed. I hear his grave

voice saying, "Happiness is waiting for you in your dreams."
He wants to put me to sleep, but I stay awake because I want
to know what happens next.

I owe my love of stories to my father. He used to say that
a man without a story is poorer than the poorest of men.
Ever since, when I meet anyone new, a foreigner, a madman,
I want to ask him to tell me a story. Somewhere, I remember a beggar answering me by saying, "Congratulations. Do
you know why God created us? So we could tell one another
stories." But suppose the beggar was wrong?

"Lili," I say, "someone should write the story of a man
who has no story. It has neither beginning nor end; it is neither beautiful nor ugly, neither sad nor joyful—it's just
empty. Empty of life? Inconceivable. Nothing ever happens?
Impossible. Since this man does exist, Death is waiting for
him, so he must have a story, even though it's of no impor-
tance. It doesn't matter whether or not he remembers it.
Even if he forgets it all, he'll have lived his life. But suppose
his story is that of a life forgotten, lost on the byways of
dreams void of hope? Oh well, maybe one day we'll know it.
But one day—when is that? That question is a story in itself.
It's neither new nor old. It's just a story."

Lili looks serious as she thinks over what she has just
heard. She's not satisfied. She still wants a story. But from
what well of memory shall I draw it? This story, did I hear it
from my father?

"This is what happened to Jeremy, an intelligent, sensible
boy, maybe a bit precocious. He was convinced he could
never break out of the silence that enveloped him inside and
out. He first realized this when, at the fair, he saw a woman,
young and sprightly, who was a member of a troupe of acrobats who flew through the air under the great tent like angels

defying the laws of gravity. The children clung to their parents, ecstatic and terrified. The adults cried out joyfully each time the trapeze artist, about to fall to earth, at the last second would catch the hand or foot of her partner, who appeared out of nowhere.

"Jeremy, in his excitement, remembered what he had read in a book of ancient wisdom: Man must always think of himself, morally and mentally, as an acrobat. If he doesn't pay attention, he's likely to fall to the ground. But in another volume, or another dream, Jeremy learned a different lesson drawn from the same acrobats: Remember that your life depends on others. If one of them is absentminded, it is you who will die.

"The acrobats stayed in town for a full week. They gave two shows a day. Jeremy went a second time, to their last performance. Again, the spectators cried out, but this time in horror. Whether due to an instant's loss of concentration or a stroke of fate, the young woman reached out too early or too late. She fell from very high up. A moment later, her slender body was writhing in agony down below.

"She didn't die right away. Nurses and doctors took her to a hospital. Jeremy was near the exit. He got a good look at her bloody face, and he heard her last words: 'We die alone.' "

I fall silent. The story is my father's, but the words are not. And now I clearly remember that his story ended differently. The young acrobat did not die.

"That's it," I say. "The end."

"That's not it." She looks at me stubbornly. "Perhaps it's over for my dying patient, but not for . . ." She pauses. I search her face for the words she dares not say. "You're not an acrobat," she resumes. "Nor am I."

I want to tell her that we're all more or less acrobats, each in our own way, but it's begun to rain. The doctor gets to her feet.

"Let's go in to the patient. Since she has spoken occasionally, perhaps she will be able to satisfy our curiosity. I told you: Here, for better or for worse, all things are possible."

A voice inside me says: Not everything is possible, even here.

SUPPOSE IT REALLY IS ILONKA?

The thought cuts me like a knife. Perhaps fate isn't blind after all. Perhaps it's capable of fantasy, even compassion. Don't all these chance encounters prove its good intentions, its determination to accomplish what cannot be imagined? Ilonka here, unknown and unknowable, in this hospital ward? It would be against all the odds. It's a long way to go, this exile's route from a Budapest apartment to a New York hospital. And yet, anything can happen. Even in the white immensity of the Siberian Gulag, couples who had been separated would glimpse each other when two trains halted; friends would meet while being transferred from one prison to another. Twenty, even fifty years after the most cruel of wars, friends and relatives who had survived Auschwitz or Treblinka found one another in Europe, in Israel, in America. Is the moment now propitious for the unfortunate victims of fate and the madness of man? On occasion, events lose their way, make no sense, contradict themselves. The great Israeli writer Samuel Joseph Agnon quotes a passage in the Sephardic Kabbalah. According to this passage, History sometimes goes insane: Then a day will last a month, a month a day or just an hour. . . . Is destiny toying with Ilonka? And has she found a way to triumph over madness?

The doctor is speaking; I'm listening with half an ear. Should I tell her what I've discovered? She wouldn't understand. Did I say *discovered*? To tell the truth, that was the wrong word to use. As I think it over, I realize that on my first visit this morning, I imagined I would see the beautiful singer who saved my life. Somewhere inside me I've kept on anticipating it. A small voice within me keeps badgering me: If fate has brought you here, to this land so far from your own, it's because it insists on reuniting you with the woman to whom you owe your life.

Ilonka, marvelous Ilonka. I owe her everything. I think of her more often than I do of my mother. Thinking of my mother would be too painful. Afraid of imagining her in that cattle car, then at Birkenau. Afraid of seeing her last moments. I prefer to remember Ilonka. I had assumed she was dead. Otherwise, why did she never answer my letters from Paris and New York? If it's really she, I'll ask her. She'll answer me with a smile or a nod. What matters is that she be able to see me and touch me and feel me. The rest will follow. She will get well. We'll spend our days and nights reminiscing.

Memories are flooding in.

JANUARY 1945. BUDAPEST LIBERATED AT LAST. THE siege is over. The guns are silent. The old capital city, once so proud of its bridges, its buildings, its boulevards, lies in ruins. Gone are the Nyilas, the collaborators, the militia. Few buildings are undamaged. Drunk with victory, Russian soldiers wander the deserted streets arm in arm, drinking and singing. Tomorrow, they may be corpses in the snow in Poland or Germany. Local people, especially the women, hide from them. Ilonka holds me close. "What's to become of us, my precious?" She's afraid, and I don't understand why. "But for us the war's over, isn't it?" I ask. She rocks me in her arms; her tenderness makes me want to cry. "The nightmare is over, but the war is not," she says. Her hair hangs down limply, she looks old and sick. "I'm not beautiful to look at," she tells me. "Isn't it true that I'm not beautiful? Aren't I ugly as sin?" I embrace her and protest. "You're beautiful, Ilonka. You're the most beautiful woman in the world." She explains that right now it's dangerous for a woman to be beautiful. The soldiers of the Red Army don't behave well with women; it's better to look old and ugly and repulsive. "You could never be repulsive," I tell her. "Not for you, my boy, but for them." "But they're our friends," I say. "They drove out the Germans and their collaborators. Jews no longer have to be afraid to say they're Jewish. Why are you afraid of these good Russian soldiers?" Ilonka tries to smile. She says, "But I'm not a Jew." "Don't be afraid," I whisper in her ear. "I'll protect you, you'll see."

Incredible but true: I did protect her. Yes, I, little Jewish boy that I was, protected the celebrated singer, the star whom Budapest's new all-powerful masters dreamed of. Yes, I saved Ilonka from humiliation and chagrin.

In my mind's eye I see us there. We go hand in hand to stand in line at a bakery. We find it hard to get around. It's a cold gray day; mud and dirty snow lie amid the ruins. Suddenly, a Russian soldier appears and grabs Ilonka by the arm. "Come, you!" he yells in her face. He keeps repeating those two words, all the Hungarian he knows. He's drunk. He stinks. Ilonka struggles. As for me, I cling to her, crying, "No, she's mine!" People in the line see what's happening, but they pretend not to notice. By chance, an officer emerges from a building and comes to our rescue. Cringing, the drunken soldier disappears. The officer hands me a piece of bread and scolds the onlookers in bad German. "Cowards, that's what you are! You see a boy defend a woman's honor and you do nothing! You disgust me!" And he takes us into the bakery. The people are hostile and resentful, but they dare not show it. As for me, I'm proud of myself. I protected Ilonka. I kept my promise.

I SEE US AGAIN, TWO OR THREE WEEKS LATER. We're in bed. It's still early. We slept badly. The room is freezing. I'm wearing three shirts under my pajamas, but my body is still shivering. Holding our blankets tightly, we listen to the wind whistling through the ruined rooftops and the charred branches of the leafless trees. Suddenly, we hear an unexpected sound: heavy footsteps mounting the stairs, or what's left of them. Pounding at the door. We hold our breath. If we don't answer, maybe they'll think no one is here, and they'll go away. But they pound harder, and now the door creaks open. Four men enter, three officers and a civilian. With them comes the wind from Siberia. And fear, a great wave of fear that keeps me from breathing or even thinking. I hide under the coat I'm using as an extra blanket. In vain, the cold still seeps into me. I try to push it away. Never have I shivered so, my entire body shaking. I keep my eyes closed but my ears open, my senses on the alert. I hear everything. I hear time as it goes by. Two Hungarian and one Russian officer accompany the civilian. They surround the bed. The civilian, who is tall and thin, speaks angrily. "We know who you are: Ilonka Andràsi, the nightclub singer. You collaborated with the enemy. You're under arrest. Come with us." Ilonka makes no protest. She hasn't told me so, but she was expecting to be apprehended and mistreated. As she is already dressed, she gets easily to her feet. All she does is point to me and say, "And the child, who is going to care for him?" The civilian turns to me. "Who are you?" Holding back my tears, I reply, "You're making a mistake. She's not a bad person. She did nothing wrong. She worked against the Germans and against the Nyilas." "Shut up, brat," says a short, stocky man, one of the Hungarian officers. "We didn't ask your advice about this scum who gave such pleasure to our country's assassins. We want to know who you are." "My name is Pé—no, it's Gamaliel. My name is Gamaliel Friedman. I'm a Jew, and it was Ilonka who saved me." The tall, thin one interrupts. "That's a lie! She went to bed with the fascists; she was working for them. As for you, you little bastard, you must be hers, so you're no Jew!" "Yes, I am, I'm a Jew, I'm telling you. My parents are Jews. And so am I." I feel as if I'm about to burst out sobbing, but I'm able to hold back my tears. The civilian and the two Hungarians talk among themselves in lowered voices. Ilonka has started weeping. I see disaster ahead. They're going to separate us. What will they do to her? And what's to become of me? Where and with whom can I wait for my parents to come back? I get ready to jump up from my bed and to implore them to take me with Ilonka. To prison, anyplace. I'll share her cell and her ordeal. I want whatever happens to her to happen to me. The Russian officer, meanwhile, has been observing me with interest. He comes over and says a few words to me in his language. "I don't understand Russian," I say. He asks, "How about German?" "I understand some German." "Good, we'll speak German. You say you're a Jew. Where are your parents?" I tell him I'm waiting for them. "They were deported, but they'll

come back." He switches languages. "Do you speak Yiddish?"
"Yes, some." Now he's paying close attention. "Since you're a
Jew, or claim you are, prove it to me. What do you know
about Judaism?" I must have looked puzzled, because he saw
I hadn't understood his question. He rephrased it. "What for
a Jew is the most important of prayers?" Frightened, I'm
about to say the Our Father, the prayer in which Ilonka had
so often drilled me. Luckily, I catch myself, though I don't
really know why the Russian is asking me, and I reply, "The
Shma Yisrael: 'Hear O Israel, the Lord our God, the Lord is
One.' " "Good, very good. And Rosh Hashana, what's that?"
"The New Year." "And Yom Kippur?" "The Day of Atone-
ment. We pray to God to write our names in the Book of
Life." "And this year, did you pray like a good boy?" Yes, I
prayed, I prayed often, but alone and in silence. Now I recall
for whom and for what I prayed. For my mother and my
father. I implored God to protect them, to let them return,
even if they were sick, as soon as possible. I feel one tear,
then another, burning as they trickle down my cheek. The
Russian officer leans over me and wipes my face with his
sleeve. He gives an order that neither the tall, thin man nor
the short, stocky one seems to like. At that, he straightens up
and repeats the order. That is enough to make the third Hungarian officer signal the others to obey the order and leave.
The Russian officer sits on the rumpled bed and asks me to
sit next to him. "I'm a Jew, from Kiev," he tells us. "I've killed
a lot of Germans, and I'll kill more, to make them pay for the
crimes they committed against our people." He stops, and
Ilonka takes the opportunity to say, in her hit-or-miss German, that she's sorry she has nothing to offer him. She begins
to explain why, but he interrupts. "I'll bring you food and
coal later on. But first tell me who you are and what you're

doing. . . ." So we tell him the whole story. My father, my mother. The fascist terror, the cruelty of the Nyilas. The roundups. The sleepless nights. Evenings at the cabaret. The sacrifices Ilonka made to keep me with her. Two hours go by, and still we have not finished. The Russian officer gets to his feet and says, "I have to go back to headquarters. I'll come by this afternoon with supplies. I'll post a soldier outside to guarantee your safety."

He keeps his word. He brings us bread, sugar, coal, oil, and two fur coats, all repossessed from opulent homes where a month ago the fascist bosses were living. Ilonka hugs and kisses me, then says in front of him, "Thank you, my child. You saved me." And I—who saved me? My father? My prayers?

CAPTAIN TOLYA—THAT WAS THE RUSSIAN OFFI-cer's name—became a regular visitor. Thanks to him, Ilonka's and Gamaliel's circumstances improved, to the point of seeming extravagant to them. Their humble apartment was now livable. It was warm, and they had enough to eat. Most important, they were safe. Armed with official papers, Ilonka no longer feared denunciation. She found work in a sort of cabaret where Russian officers and Hungarian Communists, united in their devotion to the Red Army, danced and sang and drank the night away. If now and then a soldier who had had one drink too many made advances, she had only to mention the officer's name to cool the man's ardor.

Tolya went only rarely to the cabaret. He preferred to spend evenings with Gamaliel. He taught him to play chess, and, more important, he set out to inculcate him with the virtues of the Communist ideal. He told him about Stalin, the greatest genius of the century, if not all time, the supreme guide, the exemplary teacher who understood all things, who knew it all and perhaps more, a man who might telephone a poet in the middle of the night for the sole purpose of discussing his work. "But you talk about him as if he were God," said Gamaliel, dismayed. "There is no God," Tolya replied curtly. Gamaliel was baffled. "How about my prayers? The prayers my father taught me, and you know them, since—" "Yes, I know them," Tolya conceded. "When I was a child, I learned many childish things. Then I grew up. You'll grow up, too." Gamaliel spoke no more of God, but at night, before going to sleep, he would think about his parents and their prayers.

Tolya was the first who spoke to Gamaliel of his parents' death. Until then, Ilonka and her young protégé still had hope. She ran from one government office to another, checking updated lists of survivors, interrogating members of the Jewish community, and always returned forlorn, empty-handed. But Tolya had access to better sources. He discovered when and how Gamaliel's father had died. He had been executed in Dachau days before its liberation. As for his mother, she probably died in Auschwitz the day of her arrival with so many others, like so many others. "Be strong, my young comrade," Tolya told Gamaliel. "I know, it isn't easy. Try to lean on me." And from that moment on, Gamaliel, brokenhearted, refrained from mentioning his parents.

A few months later, Tolya was sent back to Kiev, where he was discharged. "Don't worry," Gamaliel said to Ilonka. "He won't forget us; I'm sure of it." Ilonka did not show her concern. They could not foresee that their protector, a committed Communist but also a Jew, would be arrested and tortured during the anti-Jewish purges in Stalin's Soviet

Union. In 1948, Ilonka lost her job: Communism disapproved
of nightclubs. A cousin who was a seminary student came
by regularly to confide his own concerns: The Church was
suspect under communism. Sometimes the dinner conversation would turn to Gamaliel and his future. The seminary
student feared a revival of the old anti-Semitism, now mas-
querading as militant Stalinism, and he offered the boy an
easy, practical solution: conversion. Ilonka spoke out against
it. "He didn't convert to save his life during the occupation,
and you want him to convert now? He might as well sign up
for the Communist youth!" Ilonka proved to be right. Tolya's
idealistic account had made a deep impression on Gamaliel.
To believe in Stalin was to express gratitude to the Jewish
captain from Kiev, to whom they owed so much. If Tolya had
invited Gamaliel to come join him, he would have moved
heaven and earth to persuade Ilonka to accompany him. So,
proud of his red scarf, he became a sort of Party Pioneer.
Doing nothing by halves, he turned into a zealous Communist. Moscow was his Jerusalem, the Party his religion, Marx
his Bible. Meanwhile, he decided he would no longer hide
behind his Hungarian name, Péter. Henceforth, he would be
Gamaliel to everyone.

Came the day of disenchantment. The Jewish heroes of
the resistance movement were accused of Zionism and cos-
mopolitanism, dismissed from the Party, jailed, tried, and
sentenced. Gamaliel himself was too young to suffer their
fate. But some members of his unit knew about his past, and
that was enough to make him undesirable to the leaders and
contaminated in the eyes of his comrades.

Came the 1956 uprising. He was out in the streets, among
the young rebels throwing stones at the secret police and
their informers. Like everyone else, he was delirious with joy.

Budapest was ecstatically celebrating its victory over the oppressors. The civilized world was on the side of the people, backing their struggle; the march to freedom could not be stopped. But Ilonka, wiser and more farsighted than Gamaliel, was pessimistic.

"You put your trust in the world and its humanity," she said. "You rebels make me laugh. You forget the Soviet Union's territorial ambitions. Stalin may be dead, but Moscow will never leave. Any retreat would be a defeat. Just wait a while and you'll see the Russian tanks again. . . . The day of repression is coming; it's inevitable. Don't stay here any longer. Go to Vienna while the borders are still open, then take the first train to France."

"And you, Ilonka, will you come also?"

"Of course I will. I can't be separated from you. Tell me when you get to Paris. I'll join you there. I promise you we'll soon be together again, and, like you, I keep my promises. So, young man, do you agree?"

No, Gamaliel did not agree. The illusion of victory had gone to the rebels' heads. Even when the Soviet tanks appeared, he, like the other insurgents, refused to believe they intended to drown their uprising in blood. Gamaliel was arrested with a group of young rebels, but he succeeded in escaping on his way to jail. He did not go home, for fear of endangering Ilonka, but he was able to telephone.

"I can only talk a moment, Ilonka," he said. "There are still mobs of people on the roads, in the trains, at the borders. They say they're not checking too carefully, so it's easy to slip across. Leave right away; don't take anything. We'll meet in Vienna. Rendezvous at the French consulate."

Once he was in the Austrian capital, Gamaliel waited for her day after day outside the consulate. He had obtained his visa for France, and the consul's secretary, moved by his story, had promised to get one for Ilonka as soon as she arrived.

But Ilonka did not come. He tried to telephone Budapest, but the line was out. He was able to reach a friend, whom he asked to check on her. His friend called back the next day to say he had gone to Ilonka's and rung the doorbell; no one had answered. Still, Gamaliel did not give up hope. He waited another week; then the consul's secretary, taking pity on him, advised him to go on to Paris. Once there, he would send the secretary his address and she would give it to Ilonka as soon as she arrived. Heavyhearted, he took the night train with a group of other refugees. Along with leaving Austria, he was also leaving his childhood.

Ilonka did not keep her promise.

Gamaliel never saw her again.

ONE EVENING IN NEW YORK, GAMALIEL AND HIS
friends were having dinner in Eve's apartment. The conversation turned to despair. Each man evoked it in his own
manner.

For Diego, it was the day when, as a sergeant in the Foreign Legion, he came face-to-face with a former SS officer
guilty of massacres in Poland, the Ukraine, and France. Tall,
broad-shouldered, built like a bull, with a boxer's nose and
ears, he didn't care about the rumors concerning him and
would take on any man who challenged him. Diego had
sworn during the war in Spain that if he ever set eyes on a fascist he would make him regret the day he was born, but now
he realized he would not be able to live up to his oath. His
superior, when informed, coldly reminded him that the law
of the Legion was that any man who joined it left his past
behind.

"If I ever felt despair," Diego said, "it was because of that
man. Each time I saw him, I thought, If a bastard like that

can walk the earth freely, with complete impunity, then our world was poorly made and our victory in 'forty-five was but a pathetic charade."

Bolek reacted heatedly, as usual. "Injustice may inspire anger or rebellion, but must not create despair. Injustice has been part of our world since its beginning. The wolf is stronger than the lamb, and there's nothing we can do about it, except to pity the lamb and shoot the wolf. Despair is something else. That's when you no longer believe in anything.

"In the ghetto," he said, "I sometimes doubted not our eventual victory but our capacity to take part in it. One night, we were informed of the death of Asher Baumgarten, a poet and chronicler. We in the resistance movement used to tell him what was going on behind the walls, and he was to bear witness to our suffering and our struggle, for History's sake, for we were sure we were soon to die. What Emmanuel Ringelblum was doing in Warsaw, we wanted to do in our town, Davarowsk. We counted on Asher. We counted on his objectivity, his talent as a writer, his mission as the carrier of memory. On the day the Germans rounded up the last of the children, the ghetto was in mourning, feeling shame as well as pain. The next night, Asher killed himself. He asked us in his farewell letter to forgive him for giving up, but, he wrote, 'I saw the children; I witnessed their cries and their tears. And I no longer have the words to tell it. . . .' There it is. That was the most despairing moment of my life."

Gad told of a more recent time, the postwar period. "I had a rich and happy life as a child and as an adolescent. I lacked for nothing. I had my own car, a studio in Manhattan, a group of friends. My father was admired for his generosity, my mother for her hospitality. People may have envied us our happiness, but they said we deserved it. My parents loved each other. My brothers attended the yeshiva; my sisters were college students. Then misfortune befell us. My father lost his entire fortune overnight. Worse: He lost all his friends. He was alone and miserable. He couldn't understand. 'All those people who flattered me, who swore eternal gratitude, where are they? Why did they vanish?' he asked. He was alone one evening in his den, and, for the first time in his adult life, he began to weep. The door was half-open, and I saw him. Those tears filled me with despair. Not long after that, he called our family together and told us he had decided to take us all to Israel."

"I understand," Bolek said. "But I think sometimes it would be better not to understand."

"How about you, Gamaliel?" Diego asked.

Gamaliel hesitated. Should he summon up his memories, still so painful, of those last months of the war in Budapest? Or the days of waiting in Vienna?

"As for me, I despair only when I'm in love," he said, trying to lighten the mood.

No one laughed. So he spoke of his mother, of Ilonka, of Esther. He thought of them with joy, but then, at once, sadness came over him.

"You're really unlucky," Diego said. "All you have to do is love a woman for her to vanish from your life."

Yes, Gamaliel thought, I haven't had any luck. My good luck died with my mother, probably somewhere in Poland. But I was lucky with Ilonka, wasn't I? I wouldn't have survived without her. I wouldn't have known the day of liberation. I wouldn't have met Esther, or Eve, or Tolya, or any of my friends. Hadn't Ilonka been a second mother to me, doing for me what any mother would do for her son?

Thursday, late in the evening

Dear Father,

I'm sixteen years old and I'm fed up, understand? Fed
up with being your daughter, fed up with not being able
to have you as my father. I'm an orphan, deserted by both
my parents. Both of you rejected me. That's the truth,
and it's very sad. I wasn't pretty enough, or intelligent
enough—that's my tragedy. I could never hold either
of you.

I'm leaving, and I want you to know this: I'm going
away forever. You will never see me again. No one will ever
see me. I've had enough of living with the hatred I inherited
from you. I cannot, I will not go on living in this evil world
where childhood is defiled every morning and scorned every
evening. I mean my own childhood, you realize. You will
also realize that I hold you responsible for it. Why did you

abandon me when I was still a little girl? I needed a father. I needed you. You left me, left us. Worse still, you deserted us. Was it for another woman?

Mother was ill. Did you ever try to help her? She was suffering all the woes of this life. Did you ever try to relieve her pain? She was calling out for you, and you, you were living it up in nightclubs. So she gave way to depression. Does that come as a surprise to you? And her depression turned into despair. How could you not have realized it? At last she decided to die. And you, where were you? Who were you with when she lay dying?

You were a bad husband, but were you a good father? I thought so at first. So did Sophie. We were naïve; we were blind. You spoiled us; you gave us toys and candies. You would come to us at bedtime and kiss us good night. In the morning, while Mother was still sleeping, you would fix us bread and butter and a bowl of chocolate. You would ask about school and offer to help with our homework.

It was all an act. You were faking. It was vile. You deceived us. It took us a while to catch on. Then Mother explained it to us. You're a monster of evil. You hurt those who love you. Mother wanted to help you forget the horrors of your past and to enjoy peace and happiness. She loved you to distraction. She would have made any sacrifice for you. It was because of you that she distanced herself from her own parents. She hardly ever saw them. But you, you married her for her money, and to do her harm, to torment her. You never loved her. You were incapable of love then, and no doubt you still are. The women you love in your heart of hearts all belong to your past. They're all dead.

Sophie and I are alive. You resent us for being young and

living, and devoted to the memory of our mother. And for
wanting to enjoy the future that awaits us. I've had enough,
I tell you.

   That is why I am going to join Mother.

                                    Your daughter, Katya

Gamaliel then read the second letter, which he had
received three years later.

Dear Father,

   I'm nineteen and I'm writing you from my ashram. I owe
you that much. After all, for better and especially for worse,
I am your daughter. This letter will be my last sign of life.
Do not answer it.

   They must have informed you on the day it happened, or
a little later. I don't know just when. No doubt it was your
pal Bolek who, thanks to his connections, could give you
the news. You telephoned our grandparents; they refused
to accept the call. Grandmother forbade any commu-
nication with you. In short, three years ago, Katya tried to
commit suicide. Like Mother. But poor Katya was luckier;
the gods were kind to her. They were able to save her at the
last minute. She was taken first to a hospital, then to a
special private clinic. The family provides for her. She is
well cared for, still in therapy, and always angry. Angry at
me because I love her. Angry at the doctors, at the other
patients, at the sun for being too bright, at the night for
being too dark. Just angry at life. And angry most of all at
you, who gave her this life. She continues to hate you. She's
consumed with it. Why isn't there a cure for hatred? A pill,
an injection? I wonder if our neighbors did right to call the
ambulance.

You did us a lot of harm. You drove Mother to suicide, Katya to madness, and me to resignation.

Do you know what frightens me the most, even now? It's the knowledge that I am your daughter. I carry your seed. I have in me your destructive evil.

I do not say that you were never good to us, because you were. You never punished or struck us; we never lacked for presents. Were you being sincere when you kissed us, when you took us to play in the Luxembourg Gardens? If so, your sincerity was only superficial, artificial; you used it to conceal the dark forces inside you. Like Katya, I could sense those forces stirring, sometimes without reason or excuse, in the middle of a sentence or even a kiss. Thus I am at a loss to tell you the immediate, tangible reasons Katya and I parted from you. Ask me what we hold against you—what you did or said—and I could find nothing to tell you. It's a feeling we had. We weren't aware of it ourselves. It was Mother who opened our eyes. For her, it was something else. She gave you so much, and you, you made her life a hell she could escape only into death.

Here in this ashram, they teach us the basic principles necessary for self-fulfillment and for one's insertion into Creation. With their help, I seek to learn how I am responsible for the past, as well as the meaning of my future. Thus I consider myself responsible for what happened between us. Responsible for Mother's suicide, for Katya's sickness, and even for yours.

I am unable for the time being to put these thoughts into practice. I am seeking. Here they help me in my search.

Already I know that we may meet again, in another life, or another stage of this life. Then we will try to heal the damage we have done to each other.

*My wish for you is that you may find happiness with
whatever means you have. I pray to the gods that they not
cause you to make others suffer.*
This prayer is my way of bidding you farewell.
                              Your daughter that was, Sophie

For years, Gamaliel had been rereading these letters without being able to comprehend their meaning. They didn't
seem to be about him. Why was he so despised? He could
perhaps understand Colette's hatred, violent like that of all
depressives, but that of his twin daughters was utterly
beyond him. Never could he have imagined they could so
resent him. Had he not been a good father, caring about their
well-being, their enjoyment of life, their success? He had
long believed they loved him as he loved them. What mistakes had he made? Of course, their mother had done her
best to turn them against him. Then again, he sometimes
wondered if their resentment was not well-founded. If only
he could have talked to them, questioned them, explained
himself. . . . But, despite all his efforts and Bolek's unstint-
ing help, he was never able to make contact with them. All
doors were closed, all spontaneous impulses of the heart
barred. . . . And now? It was too late. His daughters might
even be dead. . . .

Gamaliel felt exhausted. Having scrutinized his past so
carefully, he could no longer look at it with enough detach-
ment to tell what was true and what wasn't. In any case, he
had bungled his life. Bad husband, bad father, bad lover: failure all along the line. Were his daughters' accusations justi-
fied? All his certainties were gone. No more light anywhere.
He deserved his isolation. Everything he had tried to build
had fallen apart. The little good he had done had resulted in

fiasco. Whose fault could it be other than his own? If he could start over, he would know how to avoid those pitfalls. But at his age, remorse replaced ambition. And anyone will tell you that if God Himself cannot undo what has been done, certainly man cannot. Then why this feeling of guilt? Go ask Kafka's Joseph K. If the whole world turns against you, you must have done something wrong. Don't try to buy your acquittal at someone else's expense. That would be too convenient.

Of that, Gamaliel was well aware.

SINCE HE'D LOST HIS DAUGHTERS, THERE WERE times that Gamaliel wanted, without knowing quite why, to howl in the sleeping streets of Manhattan or in the midst of an indifferent crowd. He needed to vent his anger and his pain with a cry so powerful, so devastating, that no one could stop it. Passersby did not so much as glance at him, and he came to doubt whether he had made a sound. Sometimes, when he was standing before a store window in broad daylight, or in a darkened movie house, he could not keep himself from weeping, from sobbing, as if in the clutches of some invisible torturer sent by Colette from beyond the grave. . . . Woe to the man who shouts in silence. Woe to the man whose suffering pursues him even into his dreams. He is punished because he insists on living in a world that rejects him, sentences him to anonymity, denies him happiness even when he feels close to the woman stretched out beside him, her head on the pillow. And yet sometimes Gamaliel would sing all night long when he was intoxicated by the memory of Esther or was lying beside Eve when she was half-asleep. From one mirage to another, and where, on what rock, will he founder? Does God howl because He is alone? No. And Mother, Gamaliel reflected, she who was so compassionate, she never howled. He never heard her raise her voice, and that was why he thought of her with still greater sorrow.

He often felt the urge to cry. It might come to him in the middle of a meal, just because he'd recalled his first love. Tears would come to his eyes. Just like that, over nothing. When he was with friends, or at the theater, he would see his daughters once again—the graceful Katya, proud of being the "elder" of the twins; the mischievous Sophie, who liked to settle herself in his lap with a determined air that seemed to say she intended to stay there forever—and he would be seized by an urgent need to tell the whole world how lonely and angry he was. He would remember Ilonka, her kindly caresses, the warmth of her chest, where he loved to lay his head, and he would have to restrain himself from cursing the universe and his own life. He would see his father's face, his worried brow, hear his hoarse voice, and see his mother's serious expression, then her smile, which could lighten the somber days of winter and turn terror into hope. Then burning tears would trickle down to his mouth—and at that moment, he could not comprehend how there could be any joy in living.

And yet . . .

A CALL FROM THE DOCTOR BROUGHT MATTERS TO a head: Zsuzsi Szabó's condition had suddenly worsened. Lili asked him to come at once. It was almost midnight.

One look at the patient was enough to tell Gamaliel that the end was near. She was in a deep coma, an oxygen mask over her face, her breathing shallow. There was no hope.

"Her heart is giving out," the doctor said. "She had an attack during the evening. Her body is worn out. You know that. In my opinion, there's nothing more we can do. I'm sorry for her." She looked down and added, "And also for you."

Gamaliel stood at the bedside. He gazed at the frail body lying still under the white sheet. "Did she say anything?" he asked.

"I don't believe so. I wasn't here. Another doctor was on duty."

"Could you find out?"

The doctor left. When she returned, she had nothing to add. "It was too late. She was already unconscious."

Thus Gamaliel would never know who this woman with the unrecognizable features and walled-off silence was. Was she Ilonka? Perhaps. After all, he had been told she spoke Hungarian. But that was not enough to identify her. The doctor had looked at her papers. The name seemed to be Magyar; she was said to be a widow, born in what was then the Austro-Hungarian Empire. That didn't mean anything. Right after the war, it had been easy to buy or trade identities. Her personal effects? A small bag stuffed with clothes and papers. Some cheap jewelry. Some odds and ends. No letters. A couple of candles. No address for next of kin or relatives in America.

"I was fond of her," the doctor said. Then she corrected herself immediately. "I used the past tense, but she's still alive. Excuse me. Matter of habit, I suppose."

After the doctor had told a nurse to stay at the patient's bedside—"Inform us of any change in her condition"—they went out in the garden.

"I, too," said Gamaliel, "I, too, feel a kind of affection for her, and I don't know why. I don't think I ever met her. I don't know who she is or where she came from. And certainly not why, if it hadn't been for your message, I should have come to see her. Except if . . ."

"If?"

"If she is Ilonka."

And he repeated what he had already told her about this marvelously compassionate woman who had occupied a unique place in his young heart. At a certain moment, Dr. Rosenkrantz took his hand. Gamaliel did not withdraw it, while remaining absorbed in his memories of Budapest. "Ilonka had a soul," he said.

"Can one have a soul?"

"She could, and I saw it as clearly as I see you now."

She squeezed his hand, and he uttered words he had not known were in his thoughts: "Do you know Budapest? Someday I'll take you there. I'll show you where I grew up, with Ilonka as my guide, then Tolya. Who knows? Maybe Ilonka is there waiting for us. . . ."

"Unless . . ."

"Yes. Unless that's Ilonka up there. We'll never know, will we?"

"Probably not. I believe it's too late," the doctor said.

Gamaliel was struck by the sadness in her voice, and by the sudden awakening of his own desire. He glanced at her. He was moved by her calm beauty in these moments when they were brought together by a life's ending. He turned and his gaze settled on her mouth. Her lips were sensual, generous, ready to open and give of themselves. A crazy idea flashed through his mind: Suppose Ilonka came here to die for the sole purpose of helping me to find the love of this woman and to welcome her into my life?

They remained silent for a long moment. Gamaliel expected her to take him back to the dying woman's bedside, but instead she led him to her office on the second floor. Its walls displayed the usual sorts of diplomas; books and journals filled the bookcases. She offered him cognac, which he declined, and hot coffee, which he accepted. They sat down on the sofa.

"Tell me more," said the doctor. "I like your way of telling about Ilonka's life."

"She was a special person," he said in a choked voice.

Once again, a familiar feeling, one he had often fended off, arose in him and took him in its grasp.

"And now say no more," the doctor ordered.

Gamaliel felt vaguely guilty. Should they be so close while

Ilonka lay dying upstairs? But it was highly unlikely that the unknown patient was Ilonka.

Fatigue and the need to forget overcame him. Suddenly, he felt at peace, and was not even surprised by it. He reflected, without bitterness for once, that the death of others reminds us of our own age, and that he himself was feeling old. But he'd been old for a long time. A Hebrew poet said of certain Jews that they are born old. And Gamaliel recalled the Jewish journalist who during the war cabled a dispatch about Auschwitz and then, when he looked in the mirror, saw that his hair had suddenly turned white. The story was also told of a young Talmudic Sage who became an old man overnight. It was true that there had been times in his tumultuous life when Gamaliel had felt momentarily rejuvenated, usually during amorous encounters. But more and more, he had the feeling that his life was over. Was this true now?

THE NURSE KNOCKED AT THE DOOR TO INFORM them that the end was near. They dashed up the stairs. The patient was softly sighing; the irregular rise and fall of her chest was barely perceptible. Gamaliel wondered if she was suffering. As if she could read his thoughts, the doctor said gently, "She's not in pain. We did everything so she could leave in peace."

She motioned to the nurse, who removed the patient's oxygen mask. Her breathing became erratic. Then it ceased.

Gamaliel bent over her and studied her faded features, hoping somehow to see the face of the unforgettable Ilonka. He had read somewhere that at the last minute death erases wrinkles and scars, that masks come apart and fall away. But not this time. The features of the nameless old Hungarian remained scarred by her suffering.

Gamaliel left a kiss on her forehead. He wanted to say something, but he could not find the words. Do the dead hear what we do not say to them? He was turning the question over in his mind when he felt the doctor's hand on his shoulder. She whispered to him, "Come. It's time."

Time to do what? he wondered. To live with her, separated from Ilonka? To wait for Death to return for him also? Who would come to mourn his passing? Not Katya or Sophie: All trace of them was lost forever in other worlds, other times. His friends would come, of course: Bolek, Yasha, Diego, Gad, Shalom. They would remember. Eve? She, too, perhaps, in her fashion, without letting on to Samaël. And the doctor—if, meanwhile, she had agreed to marry him? And Esther, whom he saw as a grandmother, playing with her thirteen grandchildren? It doesn't matter, he told himself. In the next world, the world said to be of Truth, other witnesses would be called to testify. But his novel, the *Book of Secrets,* which he had embarked on so long ago and had finally managed to organize, to structure—who would complete it? Who would recount what had happened in the disputation between the Blessed Madman, that incarnation of Rebbe Zusya, and Archbishop Báranyi? And who emerged the victor? Deep inside himself Gamaliel was coming to a melancholy realization. This novel with which he was to illustrate or even justify what he had truly intended to make of his life—this novel would never be completed. Well, what of it? People know that the son of Maimonides, Rabbi Abraham, wrote books that he never finished and that no one ever found. On the other hand, did not Henry James say that one should never claim fully to know the human heart? After all, even a failed destiny is still a destiny.

THE NEXT DAY, A FRIDAY, ONLY GAMALIEL AND Lili accompanied the old woman to the Jewish cemetery. If it is indeed Ilonka, he thought, she deserves a place among Jews. Since she had been declared a "deceased person of unknown religion," there was no rabbi present at the interment. But Gamaliel had thought to compose a prayer.

"Lord, receive this soul and comfort her, for perhaps she could not be comforted in this life. Grant her the peace that she surely did not know here below. Open to her the gates of love, which perhaps made her suffer too much. You know her. You who know each being who lives and all who die. Tell her that, without knowing who she was, we loved her and that, thanks to her, we shall love one another."

Suddenly, Gamaliel heard someone respond, "Amen." It was an old man, very tall and thin, dressed in black, leaning on a cane. He looked like a beggar. Gamaliel, thinking his memory was playing a trick on him, asked, "Did you know the deceased?" "No," the man replied, shaking his head. "Then what are you doing here?" "I'm searching," said the mysterious beggar of his childhood, whose voice had sounded familiar. A pale and holy fire glowed in eyes burdened with secrets. Gamaliel was about to ask him what he was seeking, but he held his tongue, as if he feared the man would answer, You. It's you I'm seeking. Perhaps he had come, as in the tale of the Besht and his disciple, only to find the end and the meaning of the story that was his own.

· · ·

THAT EVENING, IN THE DOCTOR'S APARTMENT, they prepared a light meal, but neither of them touched it. Resting on the bed, they exchanged memories and ideas in tones that were warm and intimate. Words of love came to them, words that were fresh and new, old and strange. Then Gamaliel started as an idea suddenly came to his mind.

"She had personal effects, didn't she? Where are they?"

"In the hospital office. They're kept in case a relative ever comes to claim them."

"Could I look at them?"

"I don't see why not, but it may not be necessary. I can tell you everything she left."

"What was in her bag?"

"Clothes, old newspapers, odds and ends. And two candles."

Gamaliel hardly dared breathe. Then he let out a cry so loud, it sounded like a howl.

"Two candles? You did say two candles? Are you sure of it?"

"Absolutely. I held them in my hands."

Gamaliel was stunned into silence. He saw himself with his mother in Ilonka's apartment in Budapest. It was late afternoon, almost dusk. His mother was preparing to light two candles. Ilonka asked worriedly, "Aren't you afraid they'll see us from the street? The Nyilas know your Jewish customs." "The curtains are drawn," his mother said. "They won't see anything. The Lord protects those who keep His laws, and a Jewish woman must light the Sabbath candles." Then, having lit the candles and blessed them, she added, "You know, I always carry the two candles with me. It was my father's wish. I remember him saying to me when I was still a child, 'Sabbath would be sad and lifeless without the light that you will give it.' Do you understand that, Ilonka?"

Gamaliel gazed at Lili, whose anxious expression suggested she feared what he might be about to reveal. He took her beautiful, pain-stricken face between his trembling hands and whispered very softly, as if he were confiding a secret, "I have a strange feeling. . . ."

He fell silent. As in a flash of light, he saw that all his life, through all his wanderings, in all the people he had encountered, it was his mother that he had been so desperately seeking. It was she who knew him best and she whose love was true. She could with a caress or a glance confer the happiness he sought. His mother gave him life and comfort. And Ilonka? She had done the same, but in a different way. His mother had left him too soon, taking with her the promise she had not been able to keep. Her tender, gentle touch, her bedtime stories, her smile, her tears—he had found their traces in other women; they, too, had vanished, their traces scattered on faces that came and went. And, he saw, he had never ceased wondering in his heart of hearts whether he would find her before he died.

The doctor was observing him worriedly. Gamaliel, in his turmoil, seemed abruptly to have rediscovered the energy to enter the Garden of Eden and strip the bark from the Tree of Knowledge. He had to, wanted to, but the words would not come—they stuck in his throat. Then the veil lifted. He felt lighter, at peace, almost serene.

"I have a strange feeling. . . . It's as though . . ."

He didn't explain. He coughed to hide his emotion.

"Save those candles. We will light them for our next Sabbath."

The doctor could only smile as she held back her tears.

Bathed in the bluish light of dawn, they felt in harmony. Outside, the seventh day of Creation announced its arrival, glorious in coppery light, ready to enfold the entire world with all its petty stories of love and remorse.

"And yet," Gamaliel murmured dreamily.

"Yes," Lili agreed. "And yet, we must go on, isn't that true?"

Gamaliel reflected before answering. Go on how? Speaking for fear of silence, loving for fear of solitude, or exile, or death; go on stumbling and recovering? Go on knocking on doors that open too soon or too late? Was that what life was about? A matter of trudging on the long, hard road, and acting as guides to those who follow us?

"Correction," Gamaliel said at last. " 'Go on' is not the right choice of words. I believe there are better ones."

"Have you found them?"

"Yes."

"What are they?"

"Begin again."

They were silent, watching and marveling at the sun as, after a moment's hesitation, it continued to rise, illuminating the houses of the rich and the poor, the valleys and the mountains, warming the wounded hearts of the uprooted.

A NOTE ON THE TYPE

THIS BOOK was set in Monotype Dante, a typeface designed by Giovanni Mardersteig (1892–1977). Conceived as a private type for the Officina Bodoni in Verona, Italy, Dante was originally cut only for hand composition by Charles Malin, the famous Parisian punch cutter, between 1946 and 1952. Its first use was in an edition of Boccaccio's *Trattatello in laude di Dante* that appeared in 1954. The Monotype Corporation's version of Dante followed in 1957. Although modeled on the Aldine type used for Pietro Cardinal Bembo's treatise *De Aetna* in 1495, Dante is a thoroughly modern interpretation of the venerable face.

Composed by Creative Graphics
Allentown, Pennsylvania
Printed and bound by R. R. Donnelley & Sons
Harrisonburg, Virginia
Designed by Virginia Tan